COUNTERFEIT
Conspiracies

Praise for the Bodies of Art Mystery Series

COUNTERFEIT CONSPIRACIES (#1)

"This fast-paced, action-filled whodunit was enjoyable and hard to put down...it was fun to watch the pieces come together in this well-written drama. I'm looking forward to the next book in this series."
– *Dru's Book Musings*

"Funny, fast paced and just a smidge of romance. What more could you ask for? Bring on the next one!"
– T. Sue Versteeg,
Author of *My Ex-Boyfriend's Wedding*

"A high-octane, fast-paced thrill ride of a mystery adventure that will definitely leave you anxious for the next installment."
– *Girl with Book Lungs*

"This fast-paced mystery had me reading far past my usual time for bed. I simply couldn't put it down because I was so drawn into the story. It's simply wonderful!" –
Dianne Harman,
Author of the Cedar Bay Cozy Mysteries

"The book takes you on car chases, shooting, great locations around the world all in the hopes of finding a missing friend and lost artifact. I read the book three times enjoying each time."
– *Book Him Danno*

"To save the day, Laurel takes you with her every step of the way on subways, planes, fast cars, and motorcycles all while being in danger. This book is truly a keeper, jump in a go for a ride!"
– *Destiny's Book Reviews*

"Incredible attention to detail. The author creates a world that you truly can get lost in. The book is also a fast-paced, fun read. I'm looking forward to reading book two."
Ier ebook

"An intricately woven tale with plenty of action and suspense. The story is crafted in such a way to keep readers guessing. The characters are well-written with smart and witty dialogue. An enjoyable read."

– *A Cozy Book Nook*

MARKED MASTERS (#2)

"Once again I have to hold on to my hat while we zip around Europe and land in lovely Florence where author Ritter Ames lures me in with her delightful vignette of Italian life seen through the eyes of an art expert."

– Maria Grazia Swan,
Author of the Lella York Mysteries

"Ames, with her great writing and brilliant story, has created a masterpiece of her own in *Marked Masters*. She leaves her readers doing their own research between the pages. Like Laurel, Ritter keeps the story with its rightful owner—the reader."

– *Crimespree Magazine*

"Boasting a great cast of characters, good conversations and the global background, this was a very enjoyable read and I look forward to the third book in this exciting series."

– *Dru's Book Musing*

"Well-plotted and will keep you guessing until the very end...The action is nonstop and you will find that you can't put this book down. Mystery readers will enjoy the chase and be pleased with the outcome. I can't wait to read the next in the delightful series. If you like your mystery filled with hunky spies, then you should be reading *Marked Masters*."

– Cheryl Green, *MyShelf Reviews*

COUNTERFEIT
Conspiracies

A BODIES OF ART MYSTERY

RITTER
AMES

HENERY PRESS

COUNTERFEIT CONSPIRACIES
A Bodies of Art Mystery
Part of the Henery Press Mystery Collection

Second Edition
Trade paperback edition | February 2016

Henery Press, LLC
www.henerypress.com

ISBN-13: 978-1-943390-45-8

Printed in the United States of

To all family and friends who have been there throughout the writing journey. Thank you, everyone.

ACKNOWLEDGMENTS

There are many people besides the author who play a part in getting stories like this one from epiphany to publication. The idea for this series teased my mind for some time, but didn't come together until a few years ago when Elizabeth Guy still published her wonderful monthly newsletter *The Verb*. Each issue of *The Verb* not only contained brilliant observations and information for writers, but also a flash fiction contest. My entry and subsequent win in the "Killer Thriller" contest not only gained me a bit of money and a signed copy of a Lee Child novel, but writing the contest entry and receiving a detailed critique by Elizabeth Guy helped cement the true picture of Laurel Beacham as the protagonist in the Bodies of Art Mystery Series. The win and Guy's insights allowed me to brainstorm the story arc and actually complete the first book. Which helped me complete the second and a third (so far).

I have to thank my brilliant editor Erin George, whose insights and suggestions made this book so much better than it originally was. She challenged me in all the right ways to make my characters shine even brighter on the page. Best of all, she was never too busy to answer any question, and never left any answer half-finished. Time from a supportive editor is an incredible gift, and I truly appreciate all of Erin's kind assistance.

I also need to thank one of my fellow Hen House authors, Gretchen Archer. You know what you did, Gretchen. Thanks again.

Finally, my readers play an incredible role in every book I write. No author can make a living at this business without fans. Mine are there every step of the way helping to keep me focused and enthused, and doing everything they can to help me promote my work. There's nothing like word of mouth sales—whether it's someone handing a friend a book, or writing a review on Amazon—to help authors and readers get together. To all my street team members, my Facebook friends and newsletter subscribers, and to anyone who reads my books but hasn't yet connected with me on social media—I couldn't do this without you. Thanks so much.

ONE

Clouds shrouded the moon. The Dobermans, Zeus and Apollo, snoozed by the rose bushes after devouring the tasty treat I had offered. Waves crashed in the distance and gave the crisp sea air a taste and smell of salt spray. The estate's showplace lawn ended a hundred yards away at a private beach.

Like my previous visit, I wore head-to-toe black. For this jaunt, however, I hadn't donned the ebony-beaded Vera Wang halter gown and Jimmy Choo stilettos I sported the last time. No, for the current foray, my Lycra garb more closely resembled Catwoman with my blonde hair hidden under a dark hood. Night vision goggles finished off the ensemble. The difference between arriving invited versus an incognito—and illegal—entrance. I pulled up my turtleneck to cover the lower part of my face and fitted night vision goggles over my eyes.

As I slipped through the mansion's side door, the left wall security pad flashed. I patted the ring of leather pouches attached to my belt and removed a cute little gizmo I'd picked up in Zurich that resembled a garage door opener. Only this handy gadget decoded electronic security systems, rendering them harmless. The tiny warning whine never had a chance to turn into a scream; my device made friends and invited us to enter.

I slipped down the rear hall and up the staircase my research had uncovered in a back issue of *Architectural Digest*. At the upper landing, infrared lasers protected the area from unwelcome visitors. I opened another pouch, withdrew a small, specially formulated aerosol can, and sprayed in a sweeping pattern. As the particles fell, laser lines were revealed in vivid detail. Seconds later, I'd picked the lock on the turret gallery door.

The last time I stood in the gallery the master of the house provided a guided tour and made a blatant pass beneath the gaze of a Dutch Master. My ability to deflect the Lothario took grace and diplomacy, plus restraint to curb the strong desire to disable his favorite body part. Still, the event had been worth the effort. A six-month quest was over, and I had found my Holy Grail of paintings.

"My father started this collection," the slimy billionaire had bragged. "He made purchases while stationed in Europe in the mid-1940s. I added to the works and specially constructed this temperature-controlled castle safe room."

On this return visit—my acquisition finale—I slid into the darkened gallery. The circular space, lit only by the minimal luminosity filtering through a half-dozen narrow arched windows, allowed my shadow to mix with those already in residence. Night vision goggles allowed the glorious set of Rembrandts and French Impressionists to glow alongside the beauty I came to liberate.

It was a vibrant seascape, circa 1821, and a breathtaking scene of energy and clear passion. A little known work by a well-respected artist, which had been cherished by the family of its previous owner before eventually falling into the hands of the billionaire's father. Gazing upon the work, I could almost hear the buoy bell ringing in the distance, but the room's current illumination left the scene too dark to see beyond the receding foamy water. I shivered as if the wind picked up; the painting was that powerful.

I heard a noise. A human-moving noise.

I had to hurry. I slipped a blade from my belt and ran it along the frame's edge.

The moment the canvas was free, I heard the master of the house bark, "What are you doing?"

I spun to find him standing behind me. Holding his gaze, I sheathed my knife and dug into another pouch, then threw a capped vial into the darkness between myself and potential capture. The glass broke, and when the chemicals inside hit the air, a dense smoke obscured all vision. But I had already calculated the distance to the nearest window, moved to it, and affixed a suction cup with a braided nylon line to the wall. The painting protected in one hand, my remaining gloved fist, now fitted with brass knuckles, shattered the narrow pane. I slid through the turret's slit window, taking a few shards of glass along for the ride. Then I rappelled down the rough stone wall to the manicured lawn.

"Zeus! Apollo! Robbery! Attack!" my impotent enemy screamed.

Next morning, the painting and I slipped into the back of Greg's shop for the new frame constructed per my specifications. A close facsimile to photos, and infinitely better than the garish gold number that restrained the seascape during its turret imprisonment, the burnished brass frame even evoked a nautical theme that conjured the look of a spyglass.

I changed into blue coveralls and left his shop with the newly framed painting wrapped in brown paper. Magnetic signs attached to my van implied a courier service, as did the faked breast pocket insignia on my uniform. The drive to Mrs. Lebowitz's tiny home was quick.

"Yes?" she said, answering the door. A Holocaust survivor, the only one in her family to make it out of Europe alive, she was a child when the Allies freed her from Auschwitz.

My brown-wrapped package once graced her grandmother's dining room. Before it was stolen by Nazis and purchased with fictionalized provenance by my adversary's father. One of my pro bono projects to not only return the art to its true owner, but to insure masterpieces such as this one did not get locked away from public sight.

"Mrs. Lebowitz, I have a very special delivery."

Eighteen hours and one chartered jet flight to Italy later, I was still running on adrenalin as I played the part of an art world socialite representing the New York based Beacham Foundation. Easy enough, since I'd perfected the role over the last five years, except that nothing was going right tonight.

"A quick and easy pickup," Max, my boss, had told me. "Everything is taken care of. Don't worry."

It was another black-tie affair with nothing more to go on than a name and small photo that Nico, my research wizard, had slipped me earlier with a flute of Dom Pérignon. Not a perfect method but it worked for us. As the foundation's leading art recover expert my life was pretty much a series of different hotel rooms every week. Tonight's event was one of a series of smaller jobs directing me to the person who held an art object I needed to return to the person or institution that had true ownership. Mrs. Lebowitz's job had been a rushed opportunity when I had little choice, since I'd not only learned the painting's location, but also information regarding a potential sale in the works. On the other hand, this evening's pickup at another glittery party was "my day job."

Despite Max's assurances, things began tanking with a flourish before I'd even arrived. First, I'd received a bogus text with driving instructions that sent me in the wrong direction. Once I'd found the correct location, I went in search of my objective in the early meet-and-greet stages of the party. Our contact in the photo was nowhere to be found, despite my best efforts in searching this extensive *castillo*. Finally, and probably the most disturbing after all that had gone wrong, I'd noticed one of the attendees seemed a bit too interested in me. I'd dodged him once in the entry, again in the ballroom. And here *he* was again. Churning through the crowd like a heat-seeking missile. A Rhett Butler wannabe in Armani. There was a canniness to the way he looked at me that said I was an assignment instead of a prospective assignation.

I tried to figure which camp he fit into, but got nada. With so many players in the art game, it was hard to keep everyone straight, both above and below ground. But a new American would have stayed in my memory, especially a tall male one with a deep Southern accent. Was it simple egoism, or did he work for someone plotting against me? My money lay on the latter. Especially after the diverting text.

He blocked my way. "How 'bout we take a late night stroll outside? A lil birdie tol' me the air on this Italian bay is soft as warm satin slidin' over your skin."

Disregarding my first impulse, which would have left him with a broken nose, I kept my breathing and temper at even levels. I needed to find out what his game really was—but not now.

"Why don't you ask that lil ol' birdie to join you?" Did the bogus text come from Mr. Wonderful, here? The man who had paid me too much attention to me all evening? My palms were damp as I ran them down my black sheath, ostensibly to smooth the material around my hips, but actually to dry my sweating palms.

"I'm afraid that lil birdie has moved on to bigger and better things." One of his strides halved the distance between us. "You know, honey, while gentlemanly manners forbid I refer to a lady by anything other than beautiful, I must say you're looking very pale at this moment, even for a *natural* blonde, Miss..."

Miss None of Your Business! But I wasn't fooled. I saw the intelligence behind those teal eyes. He knew I was Laurel Beacham. Hell, he probably knew my middle name was Iris and I'd streaked through the Cornell library freshman year. I didn't know how he knew—just that he did. I also knew anger had replaced any paleness on my face with a bright blush.

"I'm sorry, I don't feel well," I lied, turning before he could stop me. I strode quickly down a hall, relieved when a discreet lavatory door offered refuge.

I took a couple of deep breaths, regaining my composure. Though, as I looked around the lavatory, that composure quickly died.

A mosaic-tile wall separated the toilet from the lavish dressing salon. A pair of wingtips peeked from behind the wall at an awkward angle. I hurried around the wall and stopped short.

There was no mistaking him. Propped on the john was the man from the photo who I was supposed to meet. Half of his handlebar moustache was jaggedly slashed and discarded on the floor, while blood from a gash at his throat spilled down his round belly and onto the cushioned turquoise seat.

Even as nausea hit, my mind ticked over the possibilities. From the look of things, he had been dead only a few minutes. No blood trail, so he'd been killed where he sat.

I frisked him, careful not to touch skin as I explored bulges that could be the seventeenth-century snuffbox I'd been sent to recover, but the search proved fruitless. Something wasn't right. The snuffbox, though a valuable art object, didn't warrant taking the man's life. I needed to get somewhere safe and call Max, let him handle what had obviously become a complicated job. That's why he made the big bucks. Too many slipups already, and I needed to move quickly before I lost my nerve. The subliminal message all night seemed to intentionally keep me one step behind the objective. Leaving me to wonder what might have happened if I had gotten my hands on the snuffbox.

Straightening, I went to the sink and washed my hands. Twice. This party was definitely over. Time to find Nico and get both of us out of there.

Black ties and dazzling dresses swirled around the ballroom to kaleidoscopic effect. Still touched by shock, I marveled a moment at what crystal chandeliers did for precious gems and designer signatures. The international cast comprising the guest list had once made this job interesting, but now they just hindered my progress. I prayed Nico hadn't slid off with one of the real hired help for an assignation—his *modus operandi* when his phase of the work was completed. I couldn't face another systematic exploration of the Italianate estate's gold leaf, fine tapestries and Carrera marble.

I took a long cleansing breath, reminded my nerves to stay in check, and spotted Nico's dark curly head. Sans tray, he sported a tuxedo jacket obviously cached for ulterior purposes and stood chatting up an Yves Saint Laurent model known to the rags as a poseur. Nico didn't care. He had other uses in mind for her physical talents.

"The lights are very bright in here," I remarked, joining the couple.

Nico's eyes narrowed at what my words signaled. "Now?"

"Yes, they hurt my eyes."

Miss Poseur giggled. "*Essayez de lunettes de soleil.*"

Sunglasses in a ballroom. She was a bright one. Nico gave a resigned shrug and moved away.

A circulating waiter offered champagne. I grabbed a flute to better blend into the relaxed crowd.

My arm jerked, hit from behind, and I watched, helpless, as the narrow glass arced in mid-air, then shattered on the marble floor. Icy shards narrowly missed the exposed heel of a delicately shod duchess. A waiter dashed toward us to pick up the sharp pieces. I could not believe this evening.

"I'm so sorry…" I started to tell the duchess. But my words dropped off as whoever had bumped my arm suddenly had a hand at my waist. I froze, the hair on the back of my neck rising as I turned to face him. Mr. Rhett Wannabe. *Again.*

The duchess gave me a cool smile. Her dismissive gaze skipped over my shoulder and softened, her features donning a flirtatious mask at the man behind me. He leaned in and murmured apologies into her ear, causing her to giggle like a schoolgirl.

I didn't know which made me madder, his inescapable grip or the way this "Southern gentleman" both restrained *and* ignored me.

"Do you mind?" I spoke to Teal Eyes between clenched teeth. Creating a scene was out of the question. This job demanded a low-key persona.

But he still ignored me, continuing to converse in perfectly accented Parisian French.

With a gay laugh, the duchess raised a sparkling hand to pat his cheek and turned away, never acknowledging I was even in the ballroom. My inner child felt extremely slighted.

Before I could twist free, his other hand vised on my right arm and steered me toward the two-story glass doors that led to an elegant stone balcony.

"Let's go out on the terrace." Teal Eyes lifted a jet eyebrow in a Clark Gable gesture. "The lights against the dark sea should be lovely. Don't you think?"

"Does it really matter what I think?"

"Glad you agree."

Nico was a step behind us. I gave him a slight shake of my head. While my Southern Charmer was clearly not what he seemed, if I ran now, too many questions would remain unanswered. Who was he? Who did he work for? Had he killed my contact? I knew I needed to get out of there before the dead man in the lavatory was found, but I didn't know how worried I should be about Mr. Teal Eyes. And this might be my best chance to get a little background on the man. It was becoming clear he was on someone's payroll. No one in my business made himself this obvious without a reason.

Nico stood back while I obediently followed Southern Charm's lead. Strains of Isham Jones's and Gus Kahn's "It Had to Be You," my late grandfather's favorite song, wafted overhead, continuing a pattern of music for the evening as varied as the guest list. Only minutes before, the crowd had been doing its best Mick Jagger impersonations to a pounding interpretation of "Honky Tonk Woman."

Any other time I would have been enjoying the cosmopolitan crowd gathered to raise money for the latest Italian restoration effort. International wheeler-dealers, like my late grandfather, appreciated the historic value of the old artists. Contributing a portion of the night's "winnings" was a small price to pay for the honor of seeing family names on appropriate plaques.

Of course, the loss of said family fortune by a father who bet on anything that moved meant I had to work for a living. Something that raised eyebrows in "our crowd." Hence, getting my name on the guest list meant more than just wrangling an invitation.

The terrace was void of other patrons as we approached. Better for the inquisition I had in mind, but also easier to end up like my unfortunate contact. Not for the first time that night, I cursed the fact that my Giorgio couture was not designed to conceal a .38.

"Is this dogged persistence the line you usually take? The only way you can get a lady to yourself?" I opened.

"A lady would have been much more diplomatic when she rejected my advances." He took me near the edge of the terrace, and as far as possible from any eavesdropping guests. Nothing like great wealth to bring out the nosiness in people.

"So you recognized the rejections for what they were, but kept advancing," I responded.

"All I did was strike up a conversation."

"And ask me to dance, and offer me drinks, and shanghai me out into the Italian night with some line that probably came out of a bad romance novel."

I jerked out of his grip and moved toward the rock wall that separated the balcony floor from a sudden trip to the beach far below us. I paced as I continued. "Besides, where did you pick up that pitiful drawl? It never really worked for Gable, and you don't have the charisma to pull it off."

He stepped closer, stopping a few feet short of the rock barrier. He grabbed my right wrist with his left hand. I continued moving, deliberately taking a couple of steps too many. The pointed heel of my shoe accidently landed in the middle of his Italian loafer. Hard.

I heard a quiet oath as he dropped my wrist and swung his right arm. My stiffened forearm thwarted the potential blow, and I shot a leg out, aiming for his knee.

My foot never made contact. Reflexes better honed than mine reacted even faster. He flipped my foot heavenward and I overbalanced, falling backward onto my...

Well, let's just say the stone floor proved every bit as uncomfortable as it looked.

He then had the nerve to reach out a hand to help me up. Knocking it aside, I scrambled to my feet, but couldn't keep from rubbing my injured anatomy. Adding salt to the wound, he didn't even bother rubbing the foot I knew must be throbbing.

His drawl was replaced by a clipped English accent when he spoke again. "So the little lioness knows how to fight. I wonder what else she knows."

"Oh, I took self-defense courses with the rest of the ladies in my neighborhood," I said, smiling at the explanation I'd so often used. "Let's forget about me and talk about you. I notice you have a penchant for accents. First, Rhett Butler, then Maurice Chevalier, and now the Prince of Wales. What's next? Vladimir Putin? Look, I'm tired. Why don't you just tell me what you want, why you've been dogging me all night, and maybe, just maybe, I'll let you walk away without taking exception."

"I've been wondering the same thing about you," he said, only addressing the first part of my question. "You work a room quite nicely. In fact, the first time I saw such orchestrated movements was at a little soiree in Monaco about six months ago. Of course, the woman there was a graceful redhead, but..."

I kept my features a poker-faced mask as I waited for him to go on.

He took a deep breath and leaned against the railing. "Then three months ago, I was at a party on a yacht anchored off Crete when I noticed a sleek brunette laughing up at a man, obviously her lover, as they drank bubbly in the moonlight. Everyone has certain movements they make over and again. A living fingerprint if you will. Your gestures are unmistakable, like the way your teeth worry your bottom lip, removing your lipstick."

Startled, my teeth released my errant lip. Damn. He was right.

He chuckled then raised his right hand. "Yes, I would swear in a court of law that the redhead at the baccarat table and the brunette with her lover were the same long-limbed blonde I'm staring at right now."

I knew that yacht party. It was the last time I'd been with Simon Babbage, my mentor and the head of European operations for the Beacham Foundation. The last time we'd been a couple. The event hadn't gone well for us. Simon and I spent that weekend tiptoeing around facts we both recognized, the affair had run its course.

We'd been playing a part with each other as much as with the rest of the crowd. Everyone was there to appease a philanthropist who suddenly became too busy to fund foundation projects. It was also when a Dutch Master slipped out of circulation and into "the other realm." I'd always wondered if Simon and I could have stopped the theft if we hadn't been preoccupied with our own concerns.

I didn't remember Teal Eyes as a member of the party, but I decided to brazen it out. "You must be mistaken. I know I've never seen you before or I would have..."

"What? Run the other way? Grab me with both hands? Search and seize me?"

I looked at my watch. Where the hell was Nico? When I motioned him to stay behind I didn't think I had to remind him to watch in case I needed rescue. Who the hell was this guy?

"Who the hell are you?" I voiced my thoughts aloud.

He pulled a cheroot from the inside pocket of his jacket and lit a gold Dunhill lighter. "They call me Bond. James Bond."

It took everything I had to keep from slapping him. "Look, your fairy tale was flattering. Obviously I'm the girl of your dreams, but I've never been near Monaco, nor has my hair ever been red. Maybe you should have your eyes checked. Or see a therapist. I'll pardon your behavior on the grounds that you thought you recognized me. In the meantime, I'd like to salvage the rest of this night. If you'll excuse me..."

There was a sudden shift in atmosphere between us. I had about three seconds of "civil" left before he sprang into whatever action he'd followed me here for. I got two steps from the open French doors before his viselike grip had my elbow again.

"Excuse me, if I may interrupt?" An unexpected voice came out of one of the terrace's dark corners.

Relief flooded through me when I recognized the indeterminate accent of our host. As the suave billionaire approached, someone fired a roman candle from the beach, briefly illuminating the man's gentle curiosity with exquisite pyrotechnics. The aging playboy directed an apologetic smile in my direction, then turned to Teal Eyes.

"Claudio is looking for you, my friend. The game is about to start, and we've been unable to find several of those who reserved seats. Will you go at once, or shall I inform them you've been delayed?"

"I'll be there shortly, Giovanni." My captor's southern drawl was firmly back in place, and his tone remained even. However, the momentary tightening of his hand on my arm told me here was a man who hated to be questioned or have his plans altered. He dropped my arm and smoothed down his jacket, limping slightly as he reentered the ballroom.

Alone at last, I headed straight for the wall and removed my stilettos before my feet hit the sand. Nico was on his own. I declared myself officially off duty.

TWO

I phoned Nico as soon as I was safely down the beach. He grabbed the car and picked me up along the road to town. Max blustered when I phoned, but he quickly understood the situation and promised to handle the details, like contacting the authorities and notifying the interested parties that the snuffbox had disappeared.

"You're heading for Genoa, right?" I asked when Nico stopped to let me out at my hotel.

"Yes. I need to meet someone, then I head back to London."

"Be careful."

"You as well."

He waited until I was inside before he pulled away from the curb. I went upstairs to grab my luggage and head for the Malpensa Airport.

Two cabs, a plane flight, and one Tube ride later put me at Heathrow on my way toward a promised vacation that began the next morning. A week in a lovely B and B on Lake Tahoe. One whole week of soft pillows, fluffy duvets, and the crisp, clean mountain air I remembered from childhood visits. Even white sun and millionaire beaches pall after the steady diet I'd been on. I wanted the mountains. I wanted to feel the seasons change. I wanted my first break in four years.

The Pretenders' "Back on the Chain Gang" echoed from my red Prada purse and my heart sank. I debated not answering. I cursed myself for even having turned the phone on when we landed.

It had to be a new assignment. Everything else I'd worked on lately had been completed on time as promised. Except, of course, the last job, but the circumstances had left me no option but to abort. I squeezed the cellular, wishing the stranglehold would stop the signal.

The phone stopped ringing. For some psychotic reason I felt equally glad and fearful.

I didn't want a new assignment. I wanted the quiet vacation I'd been promised. I wanted to start writing a novel, even a silly trashy novel—anything that would be created and completed without second- or third-party suggestions or directives. A solitary luxury I had yet to experience. It had been four years since my last vacation.

The ringtone resumed its impatient eighties rock scream.

No one had to tell me I was good at my job. There was no one better. But I didn't care anymore. This was like one more cancelled birthday party because Daddy was drunk again. I didn't want to hear it.

With suppressed fury, I stabbed at the faceplate of the "smart" phone. If it's so smart, why did it accept this call?

"What?"

I wasn't surprised when Max's voice bellowed incoherently through the speaker.

"Calm down, Max." I held the thing out in front of me and screamed to be heard over his tirade. "I can't possibly understand a word you're saying until you bring the volume down several hundred decibels."

"Where the hell have you been?" he screamed, loudly enough that the woman standing next to me jumped. "Damn it, Laurel. You have an obligation to this organization. I should not have to listen to forty-nine rings before your phone is answered." My boss had a tendency toward hyperbole, and could chew up workers faster than George Foreman did justice to a plate of ribs.

Having survived a half-dozen years in the trenches carrying Max on my back, I knew giving excuses would do little more than fuel his volcano of self-righteous anger. But I also had no intention of becoming someone's idea of a virgin sacrifice, either—not that I even met the chief qualification.

"I'm in the middle of Heathrow. And, I might note, every person within a three-foot radius of me can hear you yelling."

This did the trick. The man valued privacy above all other things. "Laurel...ah, well...sorry...I ah..."

"You have a job, right?" Might as well cut to the chase.

"Yes, exactly. A pickup. You have two days to retrieve the object. I've already had the instructions sent to your email."

"I'm on vacation."

"But Laurel, I need you for this assignment—"

"There has to be someone else who can handle it."

I knew he was shaking his head even before I heard the answer. "No, this pickup has to be done by you. I can't trust anyone else with it."

"Why? What is it?" His histrionics didn't convince me; I'd heard it all before. But until I knew the specifics I couldn't suggest an alternative courier.

"Sixth-century jeweled sword and scabbard."

The man knew I despised handling items of war. No matter the age, I could always feel the tremors of the poor victims. And it never failed. The more bejeweled the hilt, the more blood known to have been wiped from the blade.

"No, Max—"

"Laurel, I know how you feel, but this time it's di—"

"I'm not carrying any more weapons. I don't care how old and valuable they—"

"Laurel, it's believed to be Arthur's," Max shouted.

I narrowed my eyes at the phone. "Arthur who?"

"*The* Arthur."

"You're pulling my leg. You don't seriously mean..."

"Yes." Smug self-satisfaction colored the simple word, right over the technologically advanced wireless communication. "Our source has what is quite possibly the sword of King Arthur."

"C'mon, Max. King Arthur and that whole roundtable storyline is a legend. A nice one, I agree, affording the Brits a few more tourists each year. But nothing has ever been proven."

Even as I argued with good sense and logical words, I had to admit I was intrigued. Just about any piece from that relative time period would be quite a find.

"A well-preserved parchment, not yet validated but to all cursory appearances a document from around the sixth century, was discovered with the sword," Max explained. "Word is, it looks like it could be the real thing. Everything must be authenticated, but without the items that cannot be done."

"Where was it found?"

"In an iron box set below the cornerstone of what had been a minor ancient church. The area's been one of England's neglected ruins for centuries. A pair of local boys discovered it when they decided to dig a cave."

"How industrious."

They called my flight. I stood and grabbed the handle of my carry-on bag. Even as I walked toward my gate, however, something nagged at me, something I knew he was holding back. "How were we contacted?"

"Wyndham-Hall heard about it and passed on the information."

"Who did the negotiations?"

"Babbage. In fact, he's the one holding it now. You'll need

to contact him at the London office."

"Who else knows about this?" My question was met by dead silence, which gave me positive proof there was something nasty about this. The only times my boss goes quiet are when he's trying to keep something from me.

The airline attendant looked at my first-class boarding pass and blue passport, then waved me through. I prodded harder. "Out with it, Max."

"We, uh, understand information about the piece has been leaked to Moran."

Damn. That man could steal your eyelashes without your noticing it.

"And someone else, Laurel," Max said, a strange note in his voice. "Someone new. I don't have all the particulars yet, but a man of around thirty was asking after the boys and their treasure."

"But you don't have a name?"

"Not even a good description. You can see now why you are best for the job."

"Yes." Why fight the inevitable? "I'm still entitled to a week's vacation."

Now that Moran was a risk, my role was inevitable. No one had a better success rate at foiling his plans than I. Mine may not have been a perfect record, but it led the rest of the field. Max should have saved time and started the conversation with the egotistical mastermind's name. I pivoted and began working my way back to the terminal, squeezing through the oncoming tide of passengers.

"What about that ski trip you took?" he countered.

"Get it right, Max." I broke free of the crowd and smiled at the puzzled look the boarding attendant gave me as I reappeared. I'd get online later to rebook my flight. "My adventure in Switzerland was while I was on the trail of that Van

Eyck painting, pursuing the defunct count who fancied himself the next ski champion of the world. I lost seven pounds, at least a yard of skin, and couldn't walk normally for a week after the so-called vacation."

"We'll talk about it later, Laurel. Right now, time is of the essence."

"We'll talk about it now. My plane hasn't left yet, and I can still get onboard."

A hissing sound erupted from a nearby cappuccino machine as a similar sound came through the phone. "Okay, okay. If you bring the piece in safely you can take a full week's vacation."

Easier than I'd expected. Then I smelled the trap. "Before the end of this month, Max. Not next year." I should have pushed for more, I was the one being inconvenienced after all, but I knew Max's limits. Also, and more importantly, I wanted to best Moran again.

"You're good, Laurel." Max laughed mirthlessly. "Per your terms. Please check your email and contact me immediately with any questions."

A click and he was gone. I stepped into the coffee bar and ordered a caramel latte with lots of whipped cream.

While I'll admit I was intrigued by the possibility of this piece, it was an art recovery expert's dream after all, the thing that put me over the edge and off my flight was the mention of Moran. The man was a ruthless viper, nearly unstoppable in whatever quest he undertook. I'd recovered works of art he'd spirited away from a Brussels museum, returned crown jewels to a Scandinavian royal, and shut down a hit on the Louve and watched his henchmen rounded up and arrested. But no one had ever caught Moran. Could I beat him again? Maybe trap him this time? Did I have that kind of luck? Because luck would have to once more play a part. Talent wasn't enough. I'd been too close too often, and he still slipped every trap. And until I knew more about the other player Max referred to, I planned to not dwell on the possibilities. I just hoped I could spot the mystery man before he or Moran spotted me.

I keyed into my secured email account and the screen flashed confirmation of the incoming case instructions, along with several files containing diagrams and pictures. Files previously forwarded to the foundation by the original contact, Wyndham-Hall. If only there was an app to see the timeline for the next few days. I called Simon. Now I knew why he hadn't been assigned to make the pickup in Italy the previous evening.

"Hi, love. I got an email earlier saying you'd phone. Got everything safely stowed away until the items can be checked for authenticity," he answered.

As he talked, I could hear the scratch his razor made over his tough beard. I knew the sound intimately. What Max and company didn't know was that Simon and I had shared an eight-month attempt at a transatlantic affair. The last time we'd spoken by phone was when it ended, both of us agreeing the delicious, illicit trysts took more time and energy than either of us could spare from work. It had been the best decision at the time, but hearing his voice now, even through the peripheral noise of the terminal, brought back a swarm of memories.

"You'll have to make it to the city without a welcoming party," Simon continued. "I have an informant meeting me this morning, and I don't know how long that'll take."

Water ran then stopped. Through a mental eye, I could see Simon shaking the razor before returning it to the antique, bone-colored shaving cup I knew stood on the basin. "Who's my competition?"

Simon gave an easy laugh. "Believe me, Laurel, this one-eyed, smelly Welshman is no competition. I'd much rather be wrapping my arms around you. But the rogue claims he's privy to information guaranteed to 'interest' me about a piece."

"About the...latest?" The barista started the coffee grinder. I could barely hear over the unholy roar.

"Right." Simon's answer seemed a whisper. "Laurel, this connection—"

"Yeah, this is no good for a private conversation." I shouted into the microphone. "Meet you at the office?"

"That would be perfect. I'll try to be there by two."

I sighed. Luckily I had my small carry-on, but the rest of my things were on their way to Lake Tahoe. I needed to email Max to have someone pick up my luggage. I'd spend the time until my meeting with Simon scouting out a hotel room and shopping for whatever I needed. What really cheesed me was that my best lock picks were onboard the Tahoe flight, riding around in the cargo bay in my luggage. Useless to me there, but they would have never made it through security so I checked them. Now I had to find a set of replacements.

Before putting the phone back into its pocket, I called a particular boutique hotel. One I had stayed in before and whose personnel had proven their discretion admirably. They had room for me. I headed for the taxi stand.

THREE

Milan will always be my favorite place to shop, but London stays in my top three. Until I could meet Simon at two, I spent the interim buying all the necessities I needed. With shopping essentials completed, credit cards depleted, and the holes in my wardrobe refilled for this job, I jumped in a black cab and headed for Simon's office. The morning and last night's adventure stole more out of me than I'd thought, but at least the shopping gave me the tools necessary to handle any new challenge that reared its ugly head. I rested my head against the high-backed seat and closed my eyes. Just a quick catnap to refresh my mind.

But it did little to refresh. Instead, I dreamed in some cryptic mélange, the images pushing me like a Fellini film treatment around Lake Tahoe, all the while carrying a huge silver sword. Footsteps charged through the underbrush behind me, and a voice wove through the trees, whispering in a clipped, English accent. "How far can you run, Miss Lioness? Do you really think you can escape?"

I awoke when the cab stopped.

"Here ya go, miss," the cabbie said. "Delivered as promised. And I'll drop these packages back off at your hotel. Would you like me to return and retrieve you?"

The dream left me feeling off-balance. A ridiculous manifestation of my subconscious.

The cabbie wore a black cap, which he had knocked back showing the queer look on his face by the time I finally answered. I smiled and hoped he didn't think I needed a keeper. "My friend will get me back. Thanks so much for your help."

I handed the driver a good portion of my emergency stash of British pounds. He doffed his cap, and I turned to look out the cab door at the building. A quaint example of early nineteenth-century English architecture, it reflected the conservative nature of the old-fashioned trust company that owned it. Simon's office was tucked away in one corner, off the main side of the building.

After getting out of the taxi, I set off on a brisk pace around to his private entrance. A concrete and stone wall chased along the sidewalk at shin level, with four-foot iron bars dancing along the top. I stopped at a brass nameplate engraved with the words *Beacham Ltd., London.* A couple of careful steps down and I was eye-to-eye with the brightly polished, lion's head door knocker that always made me think of Dickens's *A Christmas Carol.*

I reached for the brass knob. Locked.

Simon's little rendezvous must've lasted longer than expected. But surely Martha should be there. Simon's secretary felt it her sworn duty never to miss even an hour of a proper day's work.

I still had my key, but it took a few minutes of searching to find it in the oversized purse. As I slid it into the brass lock and gave a twist, I was surprised to hear the deadbolt give way from the inside. I pulled the key away just as the door opened.

"What do you want?"

Planted in front of me was a woman about my age wearing a blue power suit and a pair of large eyeglasses. She was taller and broader than I was and effectively blocked any view of the office. I had the feeling that was the idea.

Her long legs screamed athlete, as did the way she held her shoulders. But the glasses appeared to be fakes; heavy horn-rimmed frames with clear lenses. Interesting. She wasn't a cheap thug, either. Expensive salon streaks added fire to the thick, red hair she had caught up in a huge bun at the nape of her neck. I had no problem envisioning it down her back, flowing in vibrant curls. This wasn't tiny, blue-haired Martha. "I'm here to see Simon."

One shoulder twitched. The move was nearly invisible, but I was on guard for any tells. I still couldn't quite trace her accent, but it was definitely Continental, probably a hybrid. "Mr. Babbage is on holiday. You'll have to make an appointment."

Excuse me?

"Where did he go?" I was careful not to reveal anything.

"Scotland."

"Oh, Scotland's lovely this time of year," I extemporized. "Have you been there?"

"Yes." Wariness creeped into her eyes, behind their glass windows.

"I'm sure Simon will have a wonderful time. Especially if he took golf clubs."

"Yes, he took them. Brought his bag to the office so he wouldn't forget. I watched him carry them out." Her words came briskly; a lie detector couldn't have been more accurate.

"When did he leave?"

"This morning. Early."

"And he'll be back when?"

"A fortnight."

I nodded and took a step away. An almost imperceptible shift in her posture showed relief. "I'll try back later then. Thanks so much for the information. Oh, by the way, what happened to his last secretary? I think her name was, maybe...Marsha?"

"That's right." A widening smile revealed her pleasure at so easily fooling me. "She found another job. Felt she needed a change."

Martha had worked for the Beacham Foundation for thirty years, the last twelve with Simon. If she wanted a change now, so did the Queen. "How interesting. Do you happen to know where she went?"

"Some bank, I think."

I smiled and renewed my thanks. The redhead waited until I reached the gate before finally closing the door and slamming the bolt back into place.

Okay, so I knew the Amazon was lying and Martha was missing—possibly Simon as well. I focused on my breathing and kept my stride casual as I walked away, in case she was peeking around a curtain.

I could call the New York office on the intruder, but there was little they could do from there except notify the police. Which would not bode well for anyone should Simon just be held up with his Welshman. Until I knew what I was dealing with, better to keep things close to the vest.

And figuring out what I was dealing with meant figuring out what this imposter was doing in Simon's office.

"Took his golf clubs," I muttered, biting the corner of my lip as I frowned. Simon hated golf, thought it was the biggest time-waster known to the corporate world.

Entering the trust company's main lobby, I eventually turned down a hallway and entered a service area. A skip down a ramp led to another hallway—and a janitor's closet. I took a quick look around before slipping inside. Under the third shelf on the back wall was a small knob that felt like a knot in the wood. I pressed the spot, then quickly stepped back as the row of shelves swung outward to reveal a locked door. Martha had never been too keen on Simon and me *fraternizing*, so to smooth ruffled feathers he had given me the key to his back door. Or, as he put it, his escape hatch.

Keeping my fingers crossed, I inserted a small silver key in the lock and turned, hoping the end of our affair had not also signaled a visit by the locksmith. The key turned easily, and the door slid open, revealing Simon's private washroom.

I peeked through the crack in the door that led to his office. My fears were confirmed. The Amazon was ransacking Simon's office, working with an abandon that bordered on hysteria. Whatever she was looking for, she hadn't found it yet.

I moved back to the janitor's closet, pulled the door nearly closed, and reached for my cell phone. Looked like all the hours I'd spent absorbing the atmosphere while Simon devoured fish and chips would be put to good use.

After a number of rings, I finally heard a breathless, "Hello—I mean, Beacham, Ltd."

Assuming my best working-class London accent, I said, "Yeah, we got yer package by mistake."

"What?"

"A package, dearie," I enunciated the words slowly. "As in the post. Ya know, from the parcel service. Came in with the new menus. The bloody printer finally got the bloomin' things right."

"We have a package from the printer?"

"Nah, I got the printer's stuff. Yer's is from someone else."

"Look, I don't know anything about—"

She sounded ready to hang up. Time to send the hook out a little farther.

"I thought yer might be wantin' it, seein' it's marked urgent an' all."

"Urgent?" She was biting. I prepared to reel her in.

"Tha's right, dearie. Oh my, there's som'thin' else written

here as well. Let me see. Why it looks like it starts wi' an A. I'm afraid I can't see very well without me specs...let me...well, I ain't real sure, but it might be sayin' 'author.'"

The redhead nearly screamed. "What's inside?"

"Well, I could look if ya want me to, dearie, but—"

"No!" This time she did scream. Then in a calmer tone, she said, "I mean, that's okay. I wouldn't want to get into trouble with Mr. Babbage. He might want to open it himself. Could you bring it here, to the office?"

"Sorry, ducks." I was grinning so big my cheeks hurt. "Gotta make more chips for the late lunch crowd, I do. Yer gonna hafta come yerself."

A sigh escaped. "Where are you?"

"Jus' go out yer door and head five blocks east, then take a right. Sign in our window says 'Jenny's Chips.' That's me mum, God rest her blessed soul. Can't miss us."

"Who do I ask for once I'm inside?"

"Sheesh, didn't I just say? Jenny, a'course. Named for her I was. An' ya best 'urry. Once a line starts formin' you'll need to wait yer turn like ever'one else."

I broke the connection and clapped a hand over my mouth to keep from laughing out loud. When I stepped back into the washroom, I heard the Amazon hustling out of Simon's office, but I didn't move until I heard the key turn in the outside lock.

There wouldn't be much time. With legs as long as hers the redhead could cover the distance pretty quickly. I'd wanted to make it farther, but that might have meant a taxi ride, and my ruse would have been discovered much quicker. Given all the variables, I could only hope for a good fifteen minutes before she figured out she'd been scammed and returned to the office. I mentally adjusted the time estimate down five minutes, just to be safe.

My Prada went into a corner of the washroom for

safekeeping, and to aid in an unimpeded search. I locked the door connecting this office with the front one, then looked around. The place was a mess. Books lay strewn across the floor, pages rifled for God knows what. Paper in the wastebasket burned to scraps and ashes. Files scattered drunkenly on and off the disaster that used to be Simon's desk. Shredded paper embellished every surface like a macabre party decoration. Credit card receipts were mixed with paperwork on a Picasso. Bills of sale, bills of lading, and bills of office expenses, all crumpled and torn.

At some point, frustration apparently led to a bottle of Perrier getting thrown at the paneled wall, thin water streaks marking silent witness to the office chaos.

Strangely, Simon's pride and joy, a three-hundred-gallon saltwater aquarium had not yet been touched by the vandalism which dominated the room, its pristine condition a sad mockery to the rest. I don't believe in precognition, but even I had to admit that something fishy was going on.

First, a look at the desk calendar. The leather case didn't take long to spot beside the tipped-over rubber plant, but the pages had been rifled and ripped. All I found was a partial page for the day. Simon scribbled in a meeting for twenty-one-hundred hours, with the name Jones marked beside the time, and a GPS location with DOCKLANDS added. I pocketed the scrap, making a mental note to give the numbers to Nico for a translation I could actually understand.

There was no sign of a note on the morning meeting Simon mentioned over the phone. I couldn't find the previous day's calendar page either, so I could only hope the evening event was a follow-up to the original meet of the day.

A quick search revealed no laptop. Nothing to do but check the front office. I unlocked the door and moved quickly through the receiving area, finding the computer propped against the wall by the door, ready for the final getaway.

I grabbed the laptop and moved it to Martha's now spotless desk. Even the pictures of her nieces and nephews were gone. The drawers revealed little except a dog-eared copy of *Pride and Prejudice* and a few phone bills. I scooped up everything and stuffed it into my jacket pocket.

Back in Simon's office, I balanced the laptop and relocked the door, just as I heard noise coming from outside. In front of Simon's desk stood two sturdy visitor's chairs, the upholstery ripped open with a knife but the frames still intact. I grabbed one, wedging the back of it firmly under the door handle.

The outer door opened, and I was treated to sounds of fury from an angry Amazon when she discovered the laptop wasn't where she'd left it. The doorknob rattled and a key was stabbed into the lock, but the chair held everything tight.

Ignore her. Concentrate. The lighted tank filled my vision. Three hundred gallons of salt water perfection that only occurred through human design. The Amazon was looking for something here, and I needed to find it. But what?

The fish were beautiful, shiny rainbows, swimming in and around the huge chunk of pink coral that had cost Simon the earth. I remembered shuddering at the amount he'd spent the day it arrived, but he smiled and said the price was well worth it, before he quickly changed the subject.

Of course.

But how...?

The other chair might work, but the follow-through would be awkward and the effort could take more than one throw. The door started vibrating on its hinges, and I took another frantic look around. The chair would have to do.

A loud jarring sound made the door and wall tremble. The Amazon apparently decided to throw herself against the barrier.

As I moved toward the desk, my foot hit something heavy. I

retrieved the object at my feet. The ugly paperweight Simon's mother bought him last year for Christmas. The laptop went onto a high shelf near the escape hatch, and I hurled the heavy lead crystal at the tank with every ounce of strength I had.

Glass hit glass. For a second nothing happened. I crouched behind the desk and wondered what to try next. Then I heard a sound like a gunshot. The Amazon quit pounding. There was one second of silence, then a great cracking noise, like a thousand breaking glasses. The peace of the room was breached, and splintered glass and salty water swooshed onto the floor.

I raced over, trying not to notice the fish, floundering and helpless. It took a second to find the coral, but it was right there, near what was left of the tank, under a large, jagged-edged piece of glass. The twin pieces, naturally dissected right down the middle, came apart as I pulled. I could see how together they had formed the perfect cavern for fitting the waterproofed, saltwater-protected envelope that now lay in my other hand. An envelope holding one precious thumb drive.

The ramming resumed. I noticed a crack form down the middle of the door. Clutching my treasure, I grabbed the laptop and flew through the washroom door. The same moment, one of the chair legs splintered. I slammed the back door. Shelves once again in place, the locking mechanism snapped home, and I felt immense but momentary satisfaction. Even through the thickness, I recognized the sound of another mighty crack as the washroom door gave way. I smiled, wondering if the Amazon had enjoyed Jenny's Fish and Chips, and how long it would take her to find out how I'd escaped.

The thumb drive was returned to the coral and went into the pocket with Martha's books and the bills. I wanted to give it as much protection as I could. Getting Simon's laptop into my purse proved a bit more difficult, but determination won out. When I heard a gunshot on the other side of the wall, my smile widened. Guess the woman was tired of messing about with locked doors. Definitely time to get moving.

A service door led from the hallway to a sheltered exit, where I skirted a delivery lorry. With another backward glance to assure myself there was no fire-topped fury behind me, I blended in with the noontime masses. I needed somewhere to land for a few minutes and regroup. The crowd herded me toward a busy fish and chips shop in the opposite direction from the fictitious Jenny's. A perfect place to hide.

The shop was full of hungry diners. At the counter, still panting, I pointed at something on the overhead menu, caring little about what I ordered but simply trying to rid my memory of those other fish. The gorgeous wonders dying on Simon's floor.

"I so love a good fish, don't you? With chips on the side, naturally. My idea of heaven."

I froze. The sound of his voice fueled my already spiked anxiety. I prayed I was imagining things. Surely, he wasn't really there.

My hopes were dashed when the counterman brought my order and my imaginary friend swiped a chip.

"I must say, you're looking well, my lovely lioness. A bit more windblown than the last time I saw you, but the casual look suits you. Still blonde, I see."

And he was now fully British.

FOUR

I looked at him through narrowed eyes. "Who are you?" I made a grab for my things.

He ignored the attempt, holding my Prada bag high above our heads. Then he looked up. "What is this? Are you training for the Olympics or do attractive women always carry so much in their handbags?" Without waiting for an answer, he pulled a business card out of an inside pocket of his jacket and flipped it to me.

The sound of hot oil and lunchtime crowds sizzled behind us, but we might as well have been alone in the place. As with our last encounter, I knew that he knew I would go to any lengths necessary to keep from creating a scene. Time to reconnoiter.

"Jack Hawkes." I read, holding the card carefully between two fingers. Then with the thumb of my other hand, I rubbed the embossed shield that rose from the face of the card. "What's the design?"

"A family thing."

A quick visual sweep of the room to check escape routes resigned me to the fact nothing appeared promising. When I looked back at him, his grin was even broader.

Extending the card back, I said, "Just gives a name and phone number. Doesn't tell me anything."

He ignored the card. "Tells you more than you've told me. Care to introduce yourself? What do your parents call you?"

I smiled ruefully. "When they were alive, they called me Kitten."

Jack, or whatever his real name was, didn't let my sarcasm faze him. "I would have put money on Princess."

"You'll understand, then, when I assume you are affectionately referred to as Bozo." I patted his cheek, first softly then a bit sharper to distract him as I stuck a tiny audio transmitter to the back of his lapel.

"There's no need to be rude—"

"I'm not the one who keeps inveigling myself into places where I'm not invited."

With a shrug and a swift glance around the room, he said, "This appears to be a public place. I don't see invitations on any of the tables, and no one is at the door turning people away."

"You followed me here." I slammed the card down. He had the nerve to shush me.

"Enough," he warned, his voice barely above a whisper. "No need for explosions." He placed my bag on the counter, but kept it out of easy reach. He took my right hand in his left with a loose grip that could easily change to something stronger, and it did in about a second. He pulled me closer. "Come on," he coaxed. "I noticed you on the street and remembered you from Italy. Noticed you were traveling alone in a foreign city and wanted to offer some company. Just call me the British welcome wagon."

I slid my left hand into my jacket pocket and fingered the new lock pick case I'd purchased earlier. A quick flick of the zipper and my fingers were blindly reaching for a sharp tool. His eyes caught the flash of silver, but I knew he hadn't time to react. An instant later, the hand he had been using to grip mine was in the throes of stabbing, bruising pain.

"Never get between a woman and her purse."

He cursed, leapt to his feet, and grabbed a napkin to cover his injury. Free, I recovered the Prada he'd taken hostage. If he expected an apology, he was doomed for disappointment. But he moved between me and the door, so I shouldered my bag and tried to push past him. "Get out of my way and stay out of my life."

His right hand shot out, catching my arm. I'd about decided to play the helpless female routine and scream my way out when he picked up his card from the counter and slipped it into my Prada, stuck open because of the damned laptop. "Keep the card. You might need to get in touch with me sometime."

I jerked my arm free and forced a deep breath into my lungs. "Don't count on it." I spoke between clenched teeth, raised my head high, and strode out the door.

I skipped around the corner, using the old mirror trick to see if he followed me. At the same time, I blindly dug around in the dark depths of my purse for the iPod-sized receiver that allowed me to hear what was going on in Mr. Hawkes's little world. The ear bud didn't offer much for several minutes, beyond the sound of eating and crowd noise. Why wasn't he following me? This was getting weird.

After two minutes he hadn't exited the eatery, and I was getting a lot of funny stares from passersby. Still not satisfied, I used every trick I knew to not only keep an eye on whether I had a tail, but lose him if that was indeed the case. He never materialized again, and the only sounds I heard in the ear bud once he left the restaurant were his footsteps and surrounding city noise. Though, somehow, that didn't make me feel relieved. The boor was too good at popping up whenever I least expected. And, oddly enough, it happened every time I was in escape mode.

This definitely required some prolonged thinking. I wished

I had Simon to share a game of brainstorm badminton. I hoped for a call soon and sent him another text. Having heard nothing was slightly alarming, but not altogether out of the ordinary if he'd had to go dark to remain under the radar. The fact was, if the Amazon had gotten to Simon, she would have known where to find the thumb drive.

I just hoped she didn't have friends.

In the meantime, I had places to go and things to do. All without any backup.

I took a circuitous route to my hotel, even catching a number fifteen bus at the last instant, but kept feeling like I was being watched. In a game where I had to trust my instincts, my brain stewed busily over the fact that no evidence of being followed matched my paranoia.

At the hotel, I nodded to the doorman then headed for the front desk. No one had asked for me, and I received no message from Simon. I spent another seven or eight minutes pretending to read UK magazines in the lobby, and taking the opportunity to text Nico the GPS location from Simon's calendar, all while making good use of shadows to keep an eye on the front door. But I never saw Teal Eyes.

My instincts told me I was still missing something. I jumped into an empty lift, and at the same moment heard a phone ringing through the ear bud. Hawkes was calling someone.

"Cecil, it's Jack. We have complications."

"I don't like complications." The oily voice came clearly through the receiver.

"Didn't expect you would, but they're complications just the same."

"Tell me."

"Look, this line isn't secure, and privacy is sporadic, so I'll keep my report brief. Our bird has flown his coop. I can't go

into details right now. I don't have many. But I have located someone else who appears to be searching the same bushes we are."

"Do you have a name?"

"Not yet, but I intend to soon. She's the blonde I worried about at the party in Italy."

"The one where the snuffbox—"

"We need to keep specifics out of this conversation. It's too easy to catch a cellular signal." So refreshing to hear the worry in his voice.

"Can you handle her?"

I wondered if he looked at his bleeding hand when he answered.

"I'll give it my best shot. I planted a card on her and I know where she's staying."

He bugged me while I was bugging him? How utterly annoying. I remembered the raised coat of arms on his card, and his last ditch effort to get it into my purse. It had to have a GPS in it since I hadn't said anything on my route back to let him track me via audio.

"I'll go in sometime today and look around." Well, if he thought he was going to search my room, I needed to plan a little surprise for the creep.

"When?"

He sighed. *"Whenever she doesn't appear to be going anywhere I need to follow. You know, Cecil, it certainly would be nice to have some backup once in a while."*

"Jack, you're the best I've got. You wouldn't be satisfied with anyone I sent to help you. Besides, I don't have the personnel to spare at the moment. Too many projects."

Cheap bastard, I thought, just like Max. I almost laughed when I heard, *"You're one cheap bastard, Cecil. I'll do my best, but no promises. You have anything for me?"*

"Actually, no. I thought I had some information. I received a fax a few minutes ago about Babbage. Came in from Agent Crinoline. But since you told me yourself he's likely in Moran's care, it's old news now."

I sucked in a breath. Did Hawkes know where Simon was or was he guessing? Had he followed him, too? I prayed his information was incorrect even as a sinking feeling in my gut told me that was a long shot.

"How did Crinoline find out?"

"It was a pass-through from another agent. I can't really say where the information originated."

"Crinoline isn't in London?"

"No. New York, I believe."

"A pity. I really could use the help."

"I'll keep that in mind, dear boy. In the meantime, do the best you can and check in as often as possible."

"Right."

A few seconds later, I heard Jack mumble, *"When I have a minute to spare."*

The hotel room was the sanctuary I remembered: queen-sized bed with an ivory spread that blended well with the dark beige walls and teak furnishings. There was a table with two side chairs and a television hidden within an elegant armoire. Good lighting, quiet ambience, and a full bath instead of the abbreviated version I found too often in European hotels. All of my shopping bags were lined up atop and beneath the table by the window. I reminded myself to put the cabbie's number in my phone. It always paid to keep a list of excellent resources.

Hawkes, or whatever his name was, had gone quiet. I heard an *oof* and *excuse me*, but then nothing. I hoped the adhesive hadn't let go. Leather jackets are better than cloth, but one never knew when the bug could get knocked loose.

A quick bag count and brief exploration told me everything

had made it safely from cab to room. Before I did anything else, I slipped the picklocks into the top back corner of the closet's dark shelf, under the extra pillows the management kept there.

I loved shops that carefully wrapped each purchased item in precise, pristine tissue or taped boxes. I always felt like I was getting an extra birthday as I unwrapped them. The bags sat so pretty and inviting, bright colors and neutrals, stripes, patterns, and classic plains, that I wanted to dive in with relish. I was even beginning to forgive Max for taking away my vacation. Well, not completely. But I had to ignore the promise of pleasure and give myself over to work first.

I pulled Simon's laptop from my Prada and hoped the battery was fully charged, since I'd neglected to grab the power cord. Luck was shining on me, and I soon had a happy little window asking me for a password.

While we were dating I learned Simon had a penchant for password puns that tied to his name, but still had to try several before SIMONEYES worked.

Suddenly, I heard, *"Yes, I'm looking for a friend of mine."*

"And your friend's name, sir." The second voice sounded like that of the hotel concierge.

"Laurel Beacham."

Damn his eyes. I was right. He did know who I was. This was getting worrisome.

"I can call and announce you, sir."

I heard paper rustling. Hawkes said, *"I'm really just looking for her room number. Want to surprise her. This is for your trouble."*

"I'm sorry, but that is against the hotel's policy. If you would like to leave a message."

Bravo, I thought. I definitely needed to tip the guy.

"No, thanks. I really want to surprise her. I'll just catch her later."

Sure he would.

"Do you have a bar?" Hawkes asked.

"A small one down that hall, sir."

"Thank you."

The coral came apart even easier the second time, and I slipped the thumb drive into a USB port as I continued listening to alternating sounds of movement and silence.

The directory for the external drive showed only three files, the largest labeled MORAN, a tiny one named ARTHUR, and another file full of photos. I clicked the icon for the biggest file, and it loaded up Simon's encryption program to access the data. A few seconds later, the company's word processing program popped up, the screen filled with text in a small, funky font. I slipped off my shoes and settled in for a good read.

In the meantime, I heard Hawkes try to rope the bartender into a conversation, but since I hadn't talked to that hotel employee I knew he would get no information there. I pulled the ear bud out and slipped it into the same jacket pocket that held the receiver.

What I found on the tiny drive was much more interesting. I basically had a laundry list of crimes-against-art-and-the-world that could be attributed to, or at least strongly pointed toward, Devin Moran. Most I already knew, however I hadn't heard about the foiled attempt by Moran-financed forces to appropriate items from Sotheby's before the Princess Di auction, nor the regarded fake Egyptian vases and statuary that now resided at the British Museum.

"Of course, it isn't preposterous to assume the items in the B.M. weren't already forgeries that were heisted years ago by some equally ingenious rat," I said, irritable since this was long a worry in the art world.

Near the end was a list of properties owned by Moran and his associates: a castle in Scotland and a manor house in the south of France; luxury apartments in Prague, Moscow, and St. Petersburg; beach property in California and on Martha's Vineyard; another place in France, this time a mountain chateau near Puy de Dôme; and finally, a palace in the English countryside and a Mayfair townhouse in London.

"Boy, crime really does pay."

I exited the file and clicked on ARTHUR. This file came up as a blank page. Now what?

Scanning the photo folder showed only numbers, no names, and the thumbnail view of the pages looked like a collection of places and art. I hoped there was a cross reference in the MORAN file, but if not the places could be the properties described in the file. Comparing the documented locations and descriptions with the photos might help narrow down the properties and give some ideas on where to look for Simon. A quick look at the tiny views of the art pieces seemed to correlate with the ones referenced in the file. However, there was no more time. I grabbed an internet connection and sent the files to Nico via our encryption service, then closed the directory. I'd give him the actual drive the next time I saw him, in case he needed it to improve his chances of finding oddities. I withdrew the thumb drive from its port and shut down the computer to save the battery.

"Don't panic," I muttered. At least the list of locations gave me some place to start searching for Simon, and Nico was a magician with cryptic information. While I didn't trust Hawkes or his informants, Simon wasn't in his ransacked office to meet me as promised, and hadn't called to set up a new meet.

I probably should have called Max right then and told him, but I wanted more information before I opened that can of worms. Max had been out of the field for so long he didn't function well unless I already had an idea of the direction I needed to take or the help I required. And he had a nasty habit of taking stories I told him for use as lunchtime conversation fodder with his peers. Simon's disappearance made everything more serious in my book, and the way last night's snuffbox contact had been snuffed out created an even more critical need for me to count noses and be absolutely sure of who was and was not a player in this fatal farce.

The room phone gave a hesitant ring, pulling me out of my musings.

"Hello."

"Is this Miss Beacham?"

"Yes."

"So sorry to bother you, miss. But we seem to be having a bit of a problem with your credit card. Could you come back down and bring it with you?"

I caught my lower lip between my teeth to keep from cursing out loud. It was time to pay the piper for the shopping spree—not that any of it was my fault. Except for the fact I kept maxing out my credit cards. But I wouldn't have if Max hadn't made me reverse directions after my bags were already loaded for Tahoe. Yes, I could have had them routed back to me and waited, but I'd been given a two-day window for this job. Besides, I thought the card number I'd surrendered to the hotel still had a credit cushion. Obviously not. Damn.

"I'll be right down."

Max had to get to work on this, there was no other way. He would scream at me about fiscal responsibility, but this wasn't *all* my fault. My place as a Beacham required I at least try to uphold the image my grandfather had so fiercely created and protected. I couldn't help it if my dad squandered everything away before he drank our family finances into oblivion.

I straightened my shoulders and drew a deep breath. If it took listening to another lecture, so be it. Max may have been mentored by my grandfather, and gained trust through his frugal habits, but regardless of how my boss gained the top slot, my grandfather left me the legacy of lessons learned to allow my entrance into all avenues of society. Without maintaining the image, I couldn't go where the foundation and my job needed me to go and get introduced to the people I needed to see.

"Still, if I could have gotten the deposit back for the Tahoe reservation that this little job made me give up, my gold card would've had some breathing space now," I muttered aloud. The buck may stop *here*, as old Harry T. used to say, but Max deserved a hefty share of the responsibility this time.

The room alarm clock said four p.m., which meant it was late morning in New York, and Max likely hadn't even had his first cup of espresso yet. Since he'd yelled at me earlier at Heathrow, he'd gone to bed well past his personal curfew. It made sense to call him ahead of going down, but I reasoned he'd be less likely to start a lengthy lecture series if I phoned him from the front desk and related everything as a business problem.

"It is that after all," I said, practicing my upcoming speech as I searched for my wallet. "Accounting still has to reimburse me for expenses incurred last week in Italy. If he would issue me a corporate card—"

No point in going on with that tack; there was no way he would. The high balances I carried on five bankcards gave him ample reason to resist giving me another to run up to the limit. I dragged my purse closer and rummaged, looking for the wallet that carried the one credit card I thought I could still use and my phone. In the process, the business card Jack Hawkes gave me surfaced again.

My first impulse was to crush it under my heel, but first impulses aren't always best. Little benefit in letting him in on my secret just yet. I tossed the card into the brass trash bin next to the table. No doubt he would feel silly following around a

British rubbish truck in the early morning. Then, feeling almost paranoid, I picked up the coral and returned the thumb drive to its secret center before putting the heavy sea beauty back in my jacket pocket. While a little unusual, it seemed like as good a hiding place as anywhere else I could come up with at the moment. I scooped up the key from the table beside my purse and slipped my wallet under one arm.

I stopped at the door. Should I pretend to pull Hawkes in, give him my financial state as a reason to call? Play the damsel in distress angle? His clothes always looked like he had a few bucks, even if he never wasted a dime on personality classes.

"Don't be ridiculous." I mentally slapped myself. It was too soon to try an extemporaneous approach. I opened the door and again hooked the ear bud above my left lobe.

At the front desk, I picked up the first audible signal since I'd started listening again. It was a scratching sound I couldn't readily identify.

"I realize there must be some mistake, Miss Beacham, but it appears we will need to access another of your credit cards." The front desk clerk presented the rejected authorization by my credit card company.

"Let me make a phone call to my corporate headquarters, and I think we can get this taken care of to everyone's satisfaction." I dialed Max. As the phone rang in my right ear, my left heard Hawkes opening a door.

"Laurel. What information do you have?" After calling me at the airport at a time that had been the middle of the night for him, he'd apparently been up ever since. Or Max was just crankier than usual. Time to be authoritative.

"There's a problem with my credit card, Max, and I need you to approve—"

I wanted to pull the phone away from my ear—he was that loud. Instead, I pushed it closer to my head and stepped farther from the front desk, hoping to muffle his aggrieved response.

"We can discuss everything later, after I've been refunded for Italy and I get a credit from the airlines and my rental company for Tahoe. In the meantime, you must get the particulars from this nice, helpful person..." I smiled at the clerk "...and send him the necessary corporate credit information to cover my hotel stay here in London."

"We need to talk about this—"

"And we will, Max, but not right now." I really wanted to reach into the phone and rip off the little toad's lips. He might be the head of the Beacham Foundation, but anyone would think every expenditure came out of his personal bank account, especially if I asked for the funds. I was never sure why Grandfather had groomed him for this position, or maybe Max was simply an autocrat around me because he'd known me since I was a child. I lowered my voice, turning away from the desk as I warned, "Right now, you need to come through or I will change this morning's ticket from a credit to a seat on the next flight to Tahoe. And I will be on it—since I have luggage already there and accommodations paid for in Nevada."

"Touché, Laurel. Let me speak with the hotel employee."

"One thing first. You did handle that delicate matter we discussed last night. Right?"

"The proper authorities have been contacted. Continue concentrating on the job at hand."

"Terrific."

As I handed over the phone, through the ear bud I heard, *"Who travels with their stuff in shopping bags instead of suitcases? Is this woman crazy?"*

The bastard was in my room. I clenched my teeth. I heard the bags rustling, but no noise of anything actually being unwrapped. Probably figured he couldn't search them without my noticing. Then I heard a slight metallic ringing and a growl. I figured he'd found his business card in the trash can, must have used it to home in on my room number. The man was definitely resourceful.

Next I heard the whirr of the computer booting up, followed by a curse that obviously signaled the password screen. I listened to keys click as he attempted to stumble upon the correct "open sesame." The desk clerk completed his conversation with Max and handed back my cell phone.

"Things are taken care of, Laurel," Max said.

"For the time being. I don't know when I'll be on the move again."

"So you do have information?"

Damn. I was so busy concentrating on the audio from my room I let myself fall right into that one. "Not really. I'm still waiting to see if I can connect with Simon. He wasn't at his office when I got there."

"That's what I've been hearing. A number of people in the office here have been trying to reach him. Any thoughts?"

"Not yet. He had a meeting earlier. It may have run longer than anticipated."

It was a half-truth, but until I knew more I didn't want to tip my hand and inadvertently put Simon in any more danger than he already might be. I trusted Max, but there was no telling whom *he* trusted, and whom he might speak to before I learned the extent of any risk.

I said my goodbyes and turned to stab the button to call the elevator. Hawkes had apparently given up on the computer and was moving around my room. After a few minutes, I heard the sound of material being cut. When I heard the distinctive clink of the decorative chains on my Prada, I knew my bag was his latest victim.

I officially hated him.

After a few more seconds, I heard, *"There."*

Finally the elevator arrived, but I had to wait while a German family of five departed. A businessman jumped on to join me at the last second and pushed the button for the third floor, so I had an additional stop before I could reach four. As the car rose, I heard the ear bud deliver the sound of a door open and close. The door to my room. Unless he was waiting to greet me when the car arrived, I'd missed my chance at catching him in the act.

The fourth floor lobby was empty. Just as well. The longer I could be the cat in our little game the better, I supposed. Still, I wished I knew who the man really was.

Everything looked as I'd left it, except for my purse. The designer bag had a new design feature, a small tear that had been camouflaged by rejoining the leather with a bit of adhesive. Using my fingertips, I discovered the dime-sized disk that now lived under the bottom lining. Irritation made me want to flush it down the toilet, but professionalism stopped me from making such a mistake. If Mr. Hawkes wanted to play follow-the-bouncing-disk, I would have to make sure he had a good enough journey to make his efforts worthwhile.

FIVE

Whether Simon was in trouble or in hiding, the last thing he needed was for me to lead Hawkes right to him. I needed time to make plans and lose my tail. The best way to do that was to get lost in a crowd and plant Hawkes's bug on some unsuspecting tourist. Luckily, the hotel lay near Buckingham Palace, offering me a perfect option. I packed a couple of outfit changes, a pair of stiletto heels and another of high boots, and a few toiletries into the two largest shopping bags. Besides a little black dress, I included a new all-black cat suit. Like most women, I know the virtues of the LBD, but in my line of work being able to blend with shadows is as critical as becoming part of the monochrome at cocktail parties. I swaddled the laptop between the layers and nestled it halfway down the pile. Once I added my picks and new gizmos into the customized pockets in my Prada, extracted the bug from Hawkes's handiwork and reclosed the slit, I was ready. I slung the new trench coat over one arm. This was London in fall, after all, and the garment afforded my best camouflage as I moved through the city. I hung the Do Not Disturb sign on the door and bid the suite a fond adieu.

The desk clerk had assured me following Max's intervention that the room was paid for as much as a week if necessary. Whether I came back or not, the rest of my things could stay in the room without worry. But worry remained my constant companion whenever I gave myself the opportunity.

My bags and I and made our way to the nearest tourist trap.

Buckingham guards had made their daily change hours ago, but the masses still happily filled the area. Young and old perched on the fountain, and laughing groups milled along the pavement, posing before the massive black-and-gold-topped iron gates, and generally squealing about finally arriving at the royal pilgrimage. I allowed myself to breathe a bit and take in my surroundings. A quick look didn't reveal Hawkes obviously about, but I knew he was too good for that anyway. My ear bud only offered road noise and footsteps. Yet, it was the same road noise I'd been hearing in my other ear, which proved he was close by, if invisible.

I sauntered a bit. Pulled out my phone and snapped a few shots. Helped an elderly couple decipher their map.

Finally, I spotted an ally. Gerald O'Toole. That wasn't his real name, but his old-moneyed, banking family preferred he use the nom de plume since he'd decided about a decade ago that grifting was his preferred occupation. He was the one who taught me how winning at poker required more talent at reading faces than reading cards. I used those same lessons beyond the green baize table every day and counted Gerald one of my best early mentors.

He and a partner regularly ran a scam at sites like Buckingham Palace, where Gerry dressed as a London bobby and his compatriot was a pickpocket. Gerald drifted through the crowd in "public service persona" warning people to keep their valuables safe. He always went on to explain how pickpockets were common in the area and sure to be mere meters away. Which, of course, caused every tourist to pat pockets holding wallets, cameras, or other valuables, and allowed Gerry's partner to collect the booty with minimal effort.

I never knew when I'd run into him, but it was always at this kind of tourist destination, and at that moment he was a most welcome sight. He sported a newly grown ginger mustache and goatee. I wiggled a finger toward his face. "Trying a different persona, handsome?"

"Thought it would be nice for the winter months," he said.

More likely he was trying to change his appearance because his clean shaven face had received too much attention lately.

"How've you been, love?" he added and enveloped me in a hug.

I held my purse tight to my body, then checked my pockets when we broke free.

"Ah, your actions wound me," he said.

That's when I noticed my missing phone. I held out my hand and waggled my fingers in a give-it-back motion. "You think that wounds you, I'll do far worse if you don't hand over my phone."

"Just a joke."

"I'll believe it this time, but don't push me, Gerry." I pulled the card with the bug from my jacket pocket and used my fingers to hide it from public view. "But you can redeem yourself. Someone is using this to track me."

"A stalker?"

I frowned. "Not sure yet, actually. Could use your help to find out."

"Anything for you, love."

Closing my fingers lightly, I found the bug fit perfectly in a loose fist. "I'm going to walk away. I need you to see if you can spot the guy following me. He's about your height and has a Cary Grant-Clark Gable look about him. At least he did the last time I saw him. Dark wool jacket."

"Old Hollywood?" Gerry waggled his eyebrows.

"Good point. Probably a disguise. Anyway, I'm going to wave goodbye and very visibly walk away. I need you to go in the opposite direction and see if anyone matching his description takes off after me. He'll likely stay back a bit. Probably using his phone to follow the signal on the tracking bug he doesn't know I've found."

"Gotcher. Same number as of old?"

"Yes. Text me if you notice anything I need to know."

His eyes drifted. I knew he'd spotted a mark, so wasn't surprised when he took a step back, waved, and said, "Good seeing you, love. Talk to you soon."

Luckily, he headed in the way I wanted him to go.

Two kids splashing in the fountain created a believable diversion. I had a brief word with their mother. They were from Florida. Then I spotted my best moving option and hurried off to tag behind a horde of nearly a dozen students moving toward the Tube.

"Are all of you on holiday?" I asked one of the teens. At the same time, while they were focused on my words, I slipped the bug into the closest girl's knapsack.

"Trekking across Europe for gap year," the tallest guy said, a redhead who reminded me of Prince Harry. "Got a friend getting us into a West End play tonight. So just hitting tourist sites in the meantime."

"Dude, we need to speed it up," a blond guy in front called out. "We gotta hit the subway before the day's prices go up."

"Oh, you do," I agreed and pushed my way through to the front. Rush hour prices on the Tube were quite the *gotcha* for the unaware. "Come on. I'll show you a shortcut to Victoria Station."

My phone buzzed with a message, and I looked to see that Gerry sent a picture of Jack. I sent a *Thx m8* reply. I kept up a fast pace as I darted through alleys, leading the team through bustling lanes.

Just in case Jack realized where we were going, and the group hadn't shielded me completely from sight, I nipped inside with them, using an excuse to help them find the right platform. They moved through the gate, and I slid into a shadowed corner to watch. It would have been faster to grab a ride there and hop off at South Kensington, but I didn't want to run any new risk of getting trapped in a subway car with Jack. Especially since I spotted him moments later as he made his way through the same turnstile the group just used.

I returned to the surface as soon as I could safely manage and called Gerry to thank him. I lengthened my stride toward Sloane Square, heading for the Victoria and Albert Museum. The V and A was a perfect place for me to hide until dark. I knew someone in the restoration department who could slip me into a hidey-hole, and keep my things safe while I did my targeted wander aimed at locating Simon.

"Anytime, love." Gerry said.

"You didn't happen to know him, did you?" I asked.

"Not really..." He hesitated. "But he did look familiar to me. Probably at some event I worked once."

Worked. Yeah, right.

"You'll let me know if you remember."

"Absolutely."

"Great, Ger, thanks. Got to go, but keep in touch. Okay?"

"Will do, Laurel. You watch yourself, too."

It felt a little lonely when Gerry disconnected. He wasn't the best person to have in my corner, but at least he was someone. I may be young, blonde, and too much of a spendthrift for my boss, but that didn't mean I wasn't a cautious and intelligent person. The dangers in my life were real. Simon, my contact for this case, was missing. The only clue I'd been able to locate that could possibly help find him was on a USB drive with corruption problems. And I was playing cat and mouse with Clark Gable.

I thought back to the day before, the first time we'd met. It was soon after I'd received a bogus message on my phone, right before I was scheduled to get into the *castillo*. New directions, so close to the truth I hadn't realized they didn't quite match closely enough, that led me down a rabbit trail. It took time I didn't have to recover and backtrack from the mistake, then more time roaming the sprawling estate to try to find the contact. Time someone obviously used to kill him. Was I misdirected to save me? Or to trap him? Could I have been the proposed victim instead? And had it been Hawkes who'd sent the message?

Now I seemed on a second fool's errand. On my own because my compatriot was missing, but instead of bogey emails and text messages I had a bogey Englishman-cum-Southerner on my tail. Max would be angry at me for withholding information, but involving him before I definitely knew something could further muddy the waters. Especially if Simon returned in the next few hours. Max had so little field experience, and spent so much time pretending he ruled a nation, he forgot how to be circumspect when necessary. Besides, Scotland Yard couldn't do much this early in the situation, even if my worst fears were realized.

Which led to the real muddy waters in my life; the dockside ones I believed held the possible opportunity of meeting with the "smelly Welshman" who may have been the last person to see Simon. I had to hope his evening meeting with Jones was either the same or a confederate to whomever Simon met that morning.

My earbud picked up sounds of a phone ringing. I'd meant to pull it from my ear, but now was glad I hadn't. Obvious my shadow had not been tricked into hopping onto the train with the students. I heard Hawkes speak first.

"Yeah, Cecil, what now?"

"We've learned there's a second meeting scheduled tonight."

"I already know that and the general location, but no specifics."

"I'll work on getting those and text you."

"Brilliant."

"Where are you now?"

I heard a horn honk and a quick intake of air.

"Trying to keep up with my quarry, but it isn't easy."

"After last night's fiasco you need to accomplish this goal today. Whatever measures you must take--"

"I know how to do my job and what it entails, Cecil. Talk to you later."

"I'll call—"

"No! When I have an update I'll contact you. Anything you have for me can come by email or text."

There was a quick signoff between the two, then no further calls or conversation. Pedestrian noises streamed into the earbud. Though I knew he had to be close by since we'd both just left the Tube station. I did a quick scan of my perimeter, then struck off at a strong pace toward the Victoria and Albert Museum. My next sanctuary possibility. It was just far enough that a Tube ride would have saved some time and effort, but I had both to spare as I waited for the Docklands meeting. Walking above ground also not only let me check for anyone following me, but kept me from getting trapped on a train with someone I wanted to avoid. Nevertheless, my Prada sat heavy on my shoulder. I contemplated ditching the bag before the meeting to give myself more options for maneuverability.

"It's so great to see you, Laurel. Have you a place yet to stay while you're here?" Cassie Dean asked. She had cut her blonde hair since coming to London, and also sported a couple of thin fuchsia streaks.

"You've found a new look. No one could mistake us for sisters anymore," I said.

She laughed. "We really used that to our advantage at Cornell. Too bad you had to go and graduate ahead of me. Have you been waiting long?"

I linked arms with her and moved away from the front desk. "No longer than usual, Cassie. I knew someone would finally find you among all the artifacts. Patience builds character I'm told."

"You already have plenty of character, Laurel. Guess my work is done."

"I take it you like it here?"

"I don't ever want to leave. I'm hoping I can get a full-time position soon," she said. "Now that I've completed my Master's it's the perfect opportunity to try for something like this. Keep your fingers crossed for me."

"Always do, Cass."

She had written to me months before about landing a summer job as a conservation intern, and her excitement hadn't waned. Always a positive person, the true tip-off to her happiness was noticing how the no-nonsense leather clogs on her feet never quite touched the floor. The beige smock protecting her clothes showed the evidence of wood dust and stain.

"Yes, I'm fine for lodgings," I answered her previous question.

"Well, I have a flat with a spare room, just off Portobello Road." Her face brightened when she mentioned the place. "You're always welcome."

"Those places can be a bit pricey for someone only receiving an internship stipend, Cassie," I said. "Can't help being both pleased for you and a bit jealous."

"The owner offered the flat on the condition I'd renovate

the woodwork," she explained. "That's my specialty: plaster work and restoring historic wood and furniture. I'm as thrilled to work on the mid-nineteenth-century flat as I am to be here at the Victoria and Albert."

"I can tell." I laughed. Her exuberance was contagious.

She frowned down at my shopping bags. "That looks like clothes."

A quick look around showed no one within earshot. "Cassie, I don't need a place to stay, per se, but I do need some help. Can you give me a tour? We need to talk without being overheard."

Cassie blinked, then smiled. Anyone watching her wouldn't have noticed the shift, but I caught the look in her eyes and knew she perfectly understood. "Let's start down this way."

We journeyed through Italian Renaissance casts and copies, made for the use of nineteenth century British art students to study and sketch. When a group of the twenty-first century variety approached, Cassie slipped into tour guide mode.

"The idea of this room lies in the lessons offered," she said, masking our true purpose for being there. "Making art accessible to all, and providing a means for every working man and woman to gain an appreciation and education in the world's art."

She continued to wax poetic from the founding in 1852 when the Victoria and Albert began as the national museum of design and art. Ten kilometers of galleries held every imaginable kind of art discipline from around the world and throughout the centuries. Even with all the wonderful artifacts I'd been involved in gaining—and losing—I couldn't help but feel giddy at what this museum offered. Where else could you see an Indian throne, the first freestanding bookshelf, the Heneage Jewel owned by Queen Elizabeth I, and a staggering wealth of ceramics, metalwork, textiles, paintings, photography, and musical instruments all under one huge roof. The marvels from the once vast British Empire long after the fabled sun had set.

The students moved on, and our discussion switched to more pressing topics.

"I need you to take these shopping bags for me and keep everything safe," I murmured. I reached into my pocket and removed the coral, pushing it down the side of one bag to hide in the depths. "There's a laptop buried beneath, and a USB drive inside that coral piece that I need you to see."

"Sounds interesting," she whispered. "Follow me. We'll find an empty office."

Down another hall, she switched on the light in a room a little smaller than a broom closet. One corner held several monitors that showed various entrances.

"Not deluxe accommodations, but serviceable for our needs," she said. "This is just a backup area, and the guard always breaks about this time each day."

I took in the gray walls, the subdued lighting, and the triple monitors.

"This is fine." I withdrew the laptop, powered up the computer and pulled apart the coral. Cassie gasped. I put a finger to my lips. Despite her assurances, I wasn't completely ready to feel safe. "I want you to know what you're protecting. It only seems fair."

Pictures glowed on the screen, and I flipped through the digital gallery. I pulled a scrap of paper from the Prada and jotted down my cell number. "I need you to look at these when you can, Cass, but keep the information to yourself. Email or text me regarding any item you spot that has a history. No matter how innocuous it might seem, I need to know. I'm grasping at straws here and looking for any connection."

"You want me to keep this drive and the computer?"

"If you can. I have something I must do tonight. If everything goes well I should be by to pick up the whole shebang before midnight. If not, I'll need to know it's somewhere safe until you can get it to the Beacham Foundation."

She nodded. That was what I loved about this girl. She always *got* what needed to be done. No hysterics, no histrionics. She scribbled on a Post-it and exchanged it for the phone number I held. "Here's my address and phone. Take the number twenty-three bus to Ladbroke Grove Station. Or from here you can take the Tube from South Kensington and change to the Hammersmith and City."

I thanked her and bundled everything back into its shopping bag.

In her normal, overly restorative mode, Cassie grabbed a tissue and cleaned the screens on the security monitors. "Always leave a place looking better than how you found it."

That made me smile, then gave me an idea. I pulled out my phone and scrolled to find the photo Gerry sent earlier. "One last thing. Have you ever seen this person before?"

She took the phone and stared for a moment at the screen. Then she pointed toward the middle monitor. "You mean that man?"

SIX

"How in the hell did he find me?" As frustrated as I was to see him again, I had to admire his tenacity just a little. Even if his ability to stalk me did push things over into creepy. Had he planted a backup bug I hadn't found yet?

"He probably pinged your phone. Triangulated the location," Cassie said. "He knows you're inside this building, or maybe just these few blocks, but he won't be able to determine *exactly* where you are."

"That sounds plausible, but doesn't solve my immediate problem." I already had the feeling last night he knew too much about me, and that was confirmed earlier in the fish and chips place. Now I had to assume he knew my cell phone number too. I rubbed my temple, trying to diminish the headache I felt coming. Between the stress of running and the feeling my privacy was being invaded, the day was getting to me. "I have to get away from here, and I need to be able to communicate. I obviously can't do either of those things with my cell."

"Here's a quick plan." Cassie pulled her phone from a pocket. "Mine may not have every bell and whistle yours sports, but it's no slacker. We'll trade. Key any numbers in you know you'll need."

She walked to the back wall and opened a small cabinet. "Leave your cell in here and make an escape. The phone will hold him to the building, and I'll keep him busy. Or at least keep eyes on him. Once the guard returns from break, your man won't be able to search for the phone in here, even if he does narrow down the area range. I'll pick it up before I leave this evening."

"I don't want him following you either."

"Never fear." Cassie flashed her best impish smile. "Whenever I'm carrying it, the phone stays off. I'll turn it on only to check your messages. I'll call you if anything is urgent."

The control freak in me worried about this plan, but it really did sound like a good option, except...

"He'll still know where you live, even if he has several floors to check out before he finds you."

"Public places will be the rule. Never call you or have the phone on in my flat. It will be like now—he'll know the general area, but he won't be able to pinpoint the spot or me."

"You'd make a good spy." I gave her a hug. "Thanks, Cassie."

"No sweat." She grinned and pulled open the office door. "See you later. Remember, bus twenty-three to Ladbroke—"

"Or the Hammersmith and City line," I finished. "I'll remember. You really are terrific, you know."

She gave me a wave goodbye and slipped out of the door. I tucked the earbud back into place. Immediate road noise. The bug was outside, but I could tell from the monitors he was in the building.

Damn. It must have fallen off his lapel.

After I stashed the receiver into a pocket, I scrolled through contact numbers on my phone and speedily keyed the necessary ones into Cassie's. It took longer than expected. Though that could have been because I felt panicked. I shoved the phone into the cabinet the moment the last entered number dinged, and slammed the door. Then I raced from the office before the guard came back.

I met the uniformed employee as I rounded a corner down the hall, and we shared a smile in passing. Hoping Cassie had eyes on Hawkes, I looked for a way out, back option preferable. I should have asked Cassie before she left. There had to be a rear exit, but I couldn't risk standing out to any employee by asking for directions to the nearest escape hatch. Sigh.

Finally, what logic-based brain molecules I possessed that were not already consumed by anxiety realized Cassie's restoration area would need nearby delivery access. The escape hatch I required. Next stop, stairs to the lower level.

I stopped a second after the last step. The other side had to be the two-story pit, the area Cassie called the conservation room that showcased the restoration team with their projects du jour, while visitors gawked from a catwalk above.

"Can I help you?"

I pulled open the heavy door that separated the stairs from the conservation room. A young man with paint and dust in his hair sat nearby, straddling a three-legged stool. His steady right hand held a paintbrush with only a couple of bristles. Though stopped in mid-action, he appeared to be painstakingly transferring dots of paint from a color-riddled palate to an Old Master on the easel before him.

"Um, looking for Cassie?" I extemporized, sweeping the area with an almost three-sixty look, as if trying to spot my friend. "I was supposed to walk with her to the freight door."

"Take a gander up, love."

He pointed the end of his brush at the catwalk, and I nearly swallowed my tongue. There was Cassie, biting a lip to keep from shouting at me, with Hawkes in plain sight, his back to me as they talked. My breath caught. His hands moved in the perpetual elegant style I already associated with him, but I had little doubt they wouldn't be so gentle if he caught me at that moment. I'd heard too much in my receiver before it fell free. He had his orders and I had mine, even if I was improvising on the fly. Instincts kicked in, and I shuffled back into the stairwell. My guide gaped. Hawkes turned. There wasn't time to hide behind the door

I jumped forward and grabbed the painter's arm, pulling him to his feet. Hawkes pivoted on the catwalk and ran back to the south hall. I dragged the painter toward a hallway on one of the long walls. "Where's the back door out of here?"

"But you said Cassie—"

Cassie screamed at me through the glass, and pointed toward the far wall. "Laurel, go that way!"

"Get out," I yelled up at her. "He'll be back when he doesn't catch me."

I pushed away from the painter and sprinted in the direction Cassie indicated.

While my stiletto collection still winged its way to Tahoe, the short-heeled leather travel boots I wore were not really made for marathons either. The slick soles, while comfortable for plane rides, created a great sliding experience on slab floors. When I found the exit door, my body crashed through more than actually shoving it open. After I picked myself up from the alley pavement, I was on the run again. I dodged through the nearest couple of businesses and out the opposite doors, desperate to find a taxi or Tube station. South Kensington Station was closer, but with feet pounding some distance behind me I decided Knightsbridge offered a better option. I wouldn't have to risk heading south toward my pursuer. I almost felt Hawkes's hot vulture breath on the back of my neck as I charged ahead.

I apologized to the first few people I banged into, soon quitting to save the time and oxygen. My hope was the same people would be upset enough to slow Hawkes down as they criticized my lack of manners.

The mental map in my head lost all reference points. I knew the underground station was close, but not close enough. I finally nabbed a cruising taxi.

"Drive!" I dove across the backseat, panting. I simply pointed toward the windshield when the cabbie tried to confirm my destination.

"North it is." He gave me a cheery salute with his cap and put the vehicle into gear, like it was every day a woman hid on the floorboard of his cab. Then again, maybe it was.

Keeping low, I sneaked peeks out the back glass, trying to catch a glimpse of Hawkes without giving up my position. He shot into view the second our cab pulled away from the curb. I watched his eyes categorize and dismiss all available options on the road, until the laser gaze landed on our vehicle. With a twist and fall, I flung my body back down to a prayerful position and minimized myself as low as the human rib cage allowed. He was close but couldn't have seen me. At least he couldn't have been sure...right?

Wrong. A stormy male face filled the window glass as the cabbie slowed in traffic.

"Drive! Fast!"

A break opened in the next lane and the cabbie floored the accelerator.

"The git after ya, is he?" The cabbie shifted into the next gear.

"Yeah, bad breakup." I shot up in the seat and watched Hawkes lope a few steps toward us, then give up the obviously fruitless endeavor. He raised a hand toward a couple of taxis. One stopped, and Hawkes pulled a cell phone from his pocket.

"Probably calling re-enforcements," I murmured, then felt a chill at the thought. He could be on us in a moment or give out our cab's number to some nameless foe I had no hope of recognizing. Time to take precautionary measures. I called Nico.

"It's Laurel," I shouted when he picked up. The background noise was deafening. "Is this a bad line?"

"I'm on a helicopter," he yelled back. "What's going on?"

"A lot. Any chance you're close to London or are you still in Genoa?"

"Within visuals of City Airport even as we speak. I can meet you in half an hour."

"Good. I'm heading for the Docklands to make a rendezvous appointment written on Simon's calendar. Lock down this phone number so you can find me by GPS."

"I thought you were on vacation."

"Long story."

"Where's your cell? Another long story?"

"A friend is minding it. Keep an eye on the GPS on my phone, too. I want the cavalry to be able to find my friend if someone tracks her instead of me."

"Roger that. Identify Docklands area now. Will be in contact again soon."

"*Roger that?* Enjoying the chopper experience, Nico?"

"You know me, boss. I'm a chameleon."

I rang off just as the cab entered a crossing and the light turned. The area behind us filled with traffic running interference across Hawkes's path. Before I could sigh in relief, however, the vehicles around us slowed to a crawl and flashing lights ahead promised a bottleneck.

I looked back. The taxi Hawkes rode in was not at the front. If I stayed low and between cars...

"Where's the nearest underground station from here?" I asked.

"Next block and one, then right. Can't miss it."

"Thank you." I tossed double the fare to the cabbie and cracked open the door. I scooted across the seat and moved low again, clutching my Prada tight to my chest as I exited the cab. A couple of red double-decker buses offered the best cover nearby, but I ran hunched over to minimize the risk of Hawkes spotting my maneuver.

The cabbie's directions were spot on. I turned the corner and struck off at a strong pace toward the Tube stop, my bag heavy on my shoulder.

I was reminded I needed to consider ditching the bag before the rendezvous at the docks. Better maneuverability could never be discounted. Female superiority, however, overrode all conflicting data, reminding me the Prada wasn't just my emergency touchstone but my bottomless bag of gizmos and gadgets. In the end, picks and perks won every time.

Now that the bug was truly off Hawkes's person, I had no current information. But with the buildings and the bottleneck of London traffic shielding me from his reconnaissance, I had a much clearer and hopefully safer path ahead. Within minutes, my Oyster pass in hand, I was through the turnstiles and heading for the crowded platform. The train was right on time.

I joined the masses joggling in the busy train car at the tail end of rush hour in the London Underground. The next crowd crush would come as the dinner and theatre crowd made their way toward an evening's entertainment. I planned to use both times to my advantage.

Everyone carried a daypack or backpack that weighed their shoulders down like mine. Signs everywhere told riders to report any unattended bags. I clamped a tighter hold on my precious designer carryall.

I felt my heart jump before even realizing I had noticed the men. A short guy with long hair and a taller man in a brown coat. It was pure instinct—the internal radar we all employed to warn when someone expressed more interest in us than we wished. I hadn't heard anything, but in an instant I realized they were there because of me. I was positive the pair watched me in that sideways "not looking" way. The only question was did they work with Hawkes or for someone else?

It took total control to keep from revealing that I'd spotted them. They were trying equally as hard to not appear to be watching me. I didn't even consider calling authorities, they would just deny it, and I couldn't point to anything overt they'd done to prove bad intentions. I only knew I was right to feel menaced.

I also knew when I got off the subway they would be inches behind me. Maybe even in step beside me.

The hairy one in the ugly plaid jacket had a bulge in his pocket. Back home in the States, I would have immediately thought "gun." Here in the U.K., I more readily expected something heavy to knock me unconscious, or worse, with one blow. The weasely one beside him in the brown duffle coat undoubtedly was the knife guy. He had that look about the eyes, a kind of wariness saying all bets went to him in a fight. He wouldn't play fair by any means, but would be the one who walked away in one piece.

And I was trapped in a sealed subway car with them.

SEVEN

The subway car sped through the tunnel as I reviewed every available option. Nothing. *Nada.* Zip. My only chance lay in trying to extemporize an escape at the station. This Jubilee Line ended at the London Docklands, the now pseudo-official term for the area in the southeastern part of the city, transformed from what was once the world's largest port to redevelopment comprised chiefly of condos and commercial real estate. My original plan, such as it was while concocted on the fly, meant jumping off right before the targeted stop and finding a place to lie low until I could keep the evening appointment. I hoped to finally locate Simon, too, or at least the Welshman who was mentioned in our phone call. If I couldn't find the person I truly wanted, talking to the last person I assumed met with him at least seemed a positive direction to pursue.

Unfortunately, I now had these other two thugs in tow. I couldn't let them get wind of my plan, or lack of one, and they weren't my preferred escorts either. I passed the Bermodsey stop, itching to jump off so I was in the Docklands area, but not near enough to tip off my potential abductors. I had time to spare so my plan was to go to Canary Wharf and let the crowds there offer more protection.

We approached Canada Water, the stop prior to my goal. Time to make a decision. If I jumped off here, the larger street population might allow better cover and then—

The mechanical voice came on. "Welcome to the Jubilee Line. Canary Wharf stop is currently closed for repairs. For our travelers wanting to depart, please chose the Canada Water stop, or stay on to the North Greenwich and connect with the DLR to loop back. We apologize for any inconvenience."

Damn. Close downs and diversions. Why here? Why now? This common occurrence was the only thing I didn't appreciate about the London subway system. The Tube not only laid claim to being the historic first of its kind, but many of the same tracks and stops from a hundred years ago still moved the masses today. Which meant stoppages and premature disembarking whenever and wherever a line was being upgraded to try to meet twenty-first-century requirements. I had no desire to change lines at North Greenwich. The above ground options offered many more opportunities to dodge my shadows.

Leaving me no option but to exit at Canada Water and run.

The crowd surged, readying itself to depart the car. I felt more than saw the two men separate and get on either side of me. I could smell them. Or possibly it was my own fear I detected. Adrenalin surged through my system, and my nerves quivered in anticipation.

The first move came right as the train ground to a halt. That moment when it feels like the car holds its breath before the doors open. In my peripheral vision, I saw a plaid arm come up, the respective hand holding a chloroform soaked pad.

I pretended to trip, fell against the innocent business suit standing a bit in front of me, and ground my heel into his black wing-tipped instep.

"Oh, I am so sorry."

Everyone separated a little to give the poor man room to do an irritated hop-limp and glare at me.

"What the bloody—"

"I truly am sorry." The doors *whooshed* open, and I

grabbed an arm of my dark-haired victim and took his briefcase, as another man, who appeared to be his bookend in a Savile Row suit, braced him on the other side and said, "Here, mate, let's get you moving a bit."

Weasel and Werewolf remained visible in my peripheral vision, and I caught an alarmed look pass between the pair. My instincts had saved me again. But my victim-cum-salvation suddenly turned uncooperative.

"I'm fine. Just give me my briefcase and I—"

"Please, let me pay for a cab. You can't walk the rest of the way." I wanted to panic. This guy was my safety net. Once I lost him, the dastardly duo had a clear shot at me.

"No bother, I just have to—"

"I'm getting a cab anyway. I can drop you."

"I'm fine."

As I wound up to try a new line of attack, his buddy said, "Got it. Ta," and punched a button on his Bluetooth. I realized he had been talking on the phone, not to us, so it surprised me when he turned his brown eyes my way and backed me on my crippled-acquaintance issue. "Ah, Jeremy, don't make her feel even guiltier. Let her take you home. You still have ten blocks."

"Oh, I can't let you walk ten long blocks. And look how gray the sky is. It could start raining on you partway." My peripheral vision caught a glimpse of my two shadows in a huddle, obviously formulating their next plan of attack. The Docklands weren't as wild and woolly as the area's history implied. Over the past couple of decades, developers called in markers to get public transport extended, and changed the footprint of the place to include Canary Wharf, a battalion of skyscrapers giving the old inner City business district a run for its title to financial dominance. A number of the old warehouses were saved and converted to flats. People made their way to work, play and live there, and I was grateful for all the bodies to hide me.

We stayed in the middle of the crowd and moved out into the meager sunshine. I took in the view. The docks survived the area rehab, but now chiefly functioned as marinas for water sport enthusiasts instead of larger crafts.

"The occasional ship does periodically make landfall here at the old docks," Jeremy's friend responded when I asked. "But most traffic moved downriver to the Surrey Commercial Docks."

My actual target after dark. I filed his information away as we steered poor Jeremy toward the taxi line.

"Address?" the cabbie asked when we piled in the back.

I turned to the guys.

"After you," Jeremy's friend responded.

Oh, wonderful. A glance at the skyline offered a save. "Canary Wharf. And you, Jeremy?"

He nodded, still glowering over his foot. I felt sorry for him at first, but I couldn't help but think this was reaching overly dramatic proportions.

"Ah, give the martyr bit a rest, mate," his friend chided. Then he told the cabbie, "That's where we're headed too."

The black cab merged into traffic, and I watched as we left Weasel and Werewolf behind on the pavement, both with cell phones at an ear. In one way, I felt kind of bad for their employer, as they really should have tried some method of pursuit. That feeling lasted for about a nanosecond.

Figured it was time to make idle chitchat, so I stuck out a friendly hand. "Hi, I'm Laurel."

Yes, I gave my real name. In my business, one never knew when a chance acquaintance, especially one in an expensive suit, would later become a business ally. And trying to explain away an unnecessary earlier pseudonym too often gets complicated.

"Dylan." The friend, a young Clooney lookalike with Bluetooth, shook my hand. "And you have, of course, already *connected* with our dear Jeremy."

"I really am sorry." I offered my most apologetic smile. It was the least I could do since I had injured him on purpose—even if it was an act of self-defense. *My hero.*

Jeremy grimaced at me.

Call me heartless, but enough was enough. It wasn't like I broke his foot. At least I hoped not.

I turned to the more congenial, and more attractive, Dylan, even if I do dislike the Bluetooth silhouette. I'm never sure if the person is talking to me or to the always-there receiver. Time for small talk. "This area has really changed. I'd be thinking about trading in my job in the City district and calling this place both home and work."

"That's our plan eventually," Dylan said. "We have some feelers out now. I work in the legal end of the financial spectrum and Jeremy's a trader. If you hear of any openings at this end, we're ready to give notice." He flashed a smile and Jeremy grunted, the perpetual frown still on his face.

"Could you pull in here, please?" Dylan addressed the cabbie.

The cab slowed and stopped at the curb. I craned my head, looking through all the windows as I pretended to search for an imaginary friend, while I actually searched for any sign of my two adversaries. "Guess I'm early."

Before my seatmates had a chance to move, I passed enough pound notes to the driver, opened my door, and stepped into the street. Then I quickly ran around the cab and onto the sidewalk, waving goodbye as I hurriedly departed.

"Laurel, wait."

Dylan came up behind me. "Since you have a bit of time, why not join me for a drink, coffee, anything. Pub's right there."

He pointed at a trendy place just down the block. I had to kill time somehow, so nodded and took the arm he offered.

The look inside the pub was contemporary, but the lighting

was the universal dim everyone looks for in a place to drink and relax. Dylan answered his Bluetooth again as we ordered our pints.

He said, "Yeah, right. Exactly. Absolutely. The pub. Yes," and ended the call quickly. So I forgave him and answered when his lovely brown eyes stared into my blue and he asked, "You like that table over there?"

It was far enough from the window that my pursuers wouldn't be able to see me very well in the dim light, but offered a direct line so I could keep watch over the perimeter. "Sure."

Except Dylan did the gentlemanly thing and pulled out the chair which kept my back to the view. He took the surveillance spot for himself. No graceful way out of the situation beyond looking pushy or paranoid. I did a little twist in the tall chair, and crossed my legs to the side, achieving a bit of sideline vision as I gave him my profile and asked. "How long have you lived here?"

"Long enough to feel the wrath of the old Docklands communities," he said, giving a lopsided grin that made him even more closely resemble a young George. I was betting it wasn't accidental.

"Why's that?"

"Same old story. Redevelopment made the area more attractive to commuters like Jeremy and me, and the spit and polish made the area's property values rise."

His words reminded me of a *Guardian* story I read several years ago chronicling how luxury executive flats in the Docklands went up alongside rundown public housing estates. Yet, as hard as it was for change to be accepted, it did bring some pluses. "Doesn't the Docklands have its own symphony orchestra now?"

"Yes, the Sinfonia. Based at St. Anne's Limehouse. Do you like the symphony?"

I liked vibrant and culturally interesting places and the same in my men. Dylan was looking to fit this bill, though I didn't have the scheduling means at the moment to make a date. As I reached for a card to give him, the strap slipped from the back of my chair and my purse crashed to the brick red cement floor. Contents scattered in all directions.

"Damn." I crab-walked to grab the most embarrassing contents the Prada revealed, as he slipped from his chair to help. When the last fleeing lipstick was wrangled back, I turned to him, to offer thanks once again, and saw Weasel outside one window, his back to me as he scanned the street scene. I was under the table in a flash, using my chair as a protective blind while I watched Weasel cup his hands to look in, then walk quickly away.

"That was the guy from the train, wasn't it?" Dylan asked, holding a hand to help me back to my feet.

I nodded, trying to figure out how best to work this situation. Dylan was obviously curious, but I wasn't even sure what was going on yet. Instead, I decided to spin a bit of a tale. It would make him remember me better, sure, but if I played my cards right it could bring out the chivalry I hoped lurked in his beautiful soul. Okay, I was making assumptions, but so far his actions matched his exterior.

"Here's the thing, Dylan." I leaned closer to him and dropped my voice to a whisper. "I'm at risk of getting busted. I'm in London to help the FBI fraud squad, the unit in America handling art theft. The CIA put them in contact with MI-6 and I was supposed to have a liaison officer, but the only contact that has been made with me is those two guys on the subway who tried to chloroform me as we departed."

"Which is why you stomped Jeremy."

"Yes." I grabbed his hand. "My only hope right then was to create a scene to push them away from me. My cover has been compromised, and those two hoods are trying to sabotage a meet I have set up with an informant tonight. I can only assume there's a mole in our operation, and I don't know for sure who I can trust."

The best lies were always ones built on a kernel of truth. The best covers followed the same blueprint. To succeed, I had to use that practice in spades. Playing the damsel-in-distress card around an obviously interested male never hurt either. I held my breath and hoped Dylan believed me.

Dylan scrunched his lovely forehead a moment in deep thought, then looked behind me and grinned. "Well, well, aren't you in luck. You need someone you can trust in MI-6..."

A hand with vise-strong fingers gripped my upper arm. I didn't even have to turn around.

"...and I can vouch for this guy," Dylan finished. "Glad you could make it, Jack."

The voice from behind me confirmed every fear.

"Dylan, good to see you, mate." Hawkes's grip tightened. "And thanks for keeping my friend company until I could get here."

EIGHT

We ringed the tall table. The crowd around us had no idea the blonde chewing her lower lip was being held captive, or revising and discarding escape plans. The cloudy sky grew darker, due to the prospect of rain as much as the end of the day. I noticed Hawkes had an umbrella, black and expensive looking. Quite the Dapper Dan, our Jack Hawkes. I could envision him giving the curved handle a sharp twist to extract a hidden sword. Then I looked closer and noticed a longer and stouter middle shaft than normal, and had a feeling my daydreams were all too true. Funny thing, I couldn't be sure whether I was frightened by the prospect or a little awed. Much like my ideas about the man.

Dylan finished his pint and Jack polished off mine. I sulked, I freely admit, and they pointedly ignored me. However, Jack did keep a tight grip on my forearm as he "debriefed" Dylan, so he obviously thought me a flight risk.

I pretended to scan the crowd, but knew it was a lost cause unless I wanted to start a public spectacle. Which I didn't. This place was filled with pretty much an after-work crowd, all suits and tailored wear, a few visible tattoos and some piercings, but a pretty tame group overall. Even light jazz played over the speakers. Not the sort of locale one can count on for a good distracting rumble to start when one needs it most.

As soon as my tablemates finished their information dump, Dylan gave me a wink and slapped my nemesis on the back like old pals. *Traitor.* I watched him work his way back through the pub and out the door, unfurling his own black umbrella along the way. Then I turned on Hawkes. "MI-6? I realize you gave your name as James Bond the first time we met, but *MI-6?*"

"How do you think I found you, since you put my favorite bug on that group of college kids? I was almost on the train to the West End before I overheard their conversation and figured it out."

"MI-6?"

"What do you think?"

"I think you'd better quit answering my question with a question."

"That was a question?"

"There you go again!" My voice rose in frustration, then I cringed when I felt every patron's eye move in my direction. Leaning in, I whispered, "You know it was. Now, how did you find me? I want to know."

Glasses clinked around us as the noise level rose and fell. I wished for more privacy, but there were no better options. When he stayed silent, I added sharpness to my tone but kept the volume low. "Well, are you going to tell me?"

He grinned. I was so close to slapping him it wasn't even funny. But I kept quiet, and leaned farther into his personal space, waiting him out. Then I caught the tell. His gaze flicked up toward the ceiling for just a second. I twisted in my chair and followed the trajectory. *Damn!*

"CCTV? You tracked me through CCTV? You cyber-stalked me!"

He shrugged. "No, I cyber-found you."

"Semantics." I hugged my Prada with my free hand. Hawkes's revelation made me rethink my options. No doubt I could scream and try to escape, but if he carried law enforcement connections, what would a scene truly gain? He'd probably get me locked up for my own protection, and I'd lose the trail of Arthur's missing sword forever. Instead I repeated my earlier question, "How did you find me? It's more than just telling the CCTV watchers to keep an eye out for a blonde."

"Just basic procedure," he said, much too casually for my comfort. When I arched an eyebrow, he continued, "I posted your picture in various systems, and you were flagged entering the underground. Cameras took over and followed you. I was alerted, and when I spotted Dylan on the same train I contacted him and asked that he remain nearby. You were always protected."

I flashed back to Weasel and Werewolf crowding me in the train, to their furtive movement when I knew I was a second away from me getting chloroformed. "Protected? I had to stomp on a guy's foot to create a diversion."

"Yes, Jeremy, poor sod. Dylan says he'll hold a grudge, but you were resourceful with those thugs." He grimaced. "I know from personal experience that you're quite adept at grinding heals into insteps."

"You survived our Italian adventure."

"Not without a few bruises. However, I like feisty women."

"Maybe I can introduce you to a few of my friends."

The toothy grin he flashed did nothing to lower my blood pressure. To one side of the bar a rousing version of "For He's a Jolly Good Fellow" entered the scene, along with a platter of cupcakes.

"Who are you, Hawkes, and what kind of clout do you have?" I asked. "Are you really MI-6 or is that just a line Dylan believes?"

He flashed me a smug look, then turned when the birthday crowd started yelling for a speech. I wished I could get Hawkes to talk, no speech necessary, but he didn't answer. To keep from punching him, I clasped my hands so tightly together they nearly fused. I knew the tactic. He was keeping me angry to tie up my brain.

After a couple of deep breaths, I tried another approach. "I need to use the ladies'."

"That isn't going to happen." Since my arm was still vised in his grip, I figured he was probably right. Unless I got a brainstorm or figured a way to break his hold. Or his hand. Hawkes looked at his phone and swiped a thumb across the screen. "I've proven I can track you either with or without a bug. And since I have too much to do to keep running after you, we need to work together. What do you know about Marker and Firth?"

"Is that a location?"

He stared at me, incredulous. "The two guys following you."

"You mean Weasel and Werewolf?"

He had to wipe tears from his eyes by the time he stopped laughing. "Oh, I bloody love that. Brilliant. Yes, Weasel and Werewolf."

"Never had the pleasure before today. Don't really want to meet up with them again."

"No, you really don't. Each a nasty piece of work. They're under Moran's thumb."

I sat up a bit straighter. "What do you know about Moran?"

Hawkes leaned closer. "You know as well as I do that Moran is ruthless, cunning, and his favorite target items are priceless bodies of art with historic cachet."

"Old news, Hawkes. Where is this going? I don't need to hear a Moran lecture. I've had too many unsatisfactory experiences with the man."

He twisted my empty glass. "You want another pint?"

"I wanted that one, but you drank it."

"I'll—"

"No, I'm good. Will you just continue with whatever you

want to say, please? What you *think* I should know."

Both glasses got shoved to the center of the table with his free hand, but the other never lost its grip on my arm.

"Like you, I've run into the character a few times more than I've wanted," he said. "And also, like you, the outcomes were frustrating. Moran has more marks in the win column than I, and I hazard to assume your experience is the same."

"I've had the upper hand in our encounters," I bragged.

"The Maiden's Head Buckle?"

"He corrupted my source—"

"The Van Gogh?"

"We learned—"

"Do you really want me to go on?"

I seethed inside but kept a smile on my face, unsure exactly who I was trying to fool, Jack or myself. Moran was the only crook who nearly always got the jump on me. There was more, but the fact Hawkes knew all of this was as frightening as it was embarrassing. I didn't know how, but I needed to learn more about this man, and soon. I said, "The last time I encountered Moran was in connection with the Danish Emerald Parure. I received the highest congratulations on the recovery, from the queen regent herself."

"You have to admit it was a bit of luck on your part." He raised an eyebrow. "Bit of being in the right place, overhearing the right conspirator, all at the—"

"I get it." My hand itched to reach into my purse, grab the telescopic baton that usually resided there, and break his knuckles. That would set me free in more ways than one. But the darn weapons were illegal in the U.K., so I couldn't easily replace mine when I went on my earlier shopping spree. The Prada sat in my lap, ready to make the leap with me at first opportunity, but circumstances dictated I use the situation to grab intel while I could. "You know all, you see all, and you hide in my closet every night. But you have to admit I'm damn good at my job, and I can grab an opportunity when one presents itself."

"Absolutely." He glanced at his watch. "You are precisely skilled in the necessary talents required to complement my own and allow us to gain our objective."

"Are you trying to recruit me?"

"Let's just say secure an alliance."

This was too much. Who did this guy think he was? Who did he think I was? Correction, he obviously knew everything about me, just as I'd deduced in Italy. I shook my head.

"Hear me out," he said, his voice still so low in tone I had to keep my head close to his to catch his words. "Don't say no until you listen to everything I have to say."

I hugged my purse tighter with my unencumbered hand. Running sounded so promising a few moments ago. Now I had to readjust my ideas, to orient to his apparent need for roping me in on his plans. Although the big question was, how much would he really tell me?

"Honesty. I demand honesty, Hawkes."

"Fair enough."

"What do you have to say, and why should I believe you?"

"You're headed to the docks tonight to try to make contact with Jones, correct?"

I hoped my face didn't show my shock, but this was much more than I'd expected. "How do you know that?"

"Babbage was scheduled to meet with him this morning, but if the meet didn't happen, the backup was at nine tonight."

"How do you know that?" I repeated.

His eyes softened. "Simon has a new girlfriend. I introduced them. She called me."

I kept my poker face. "Good for him. She's not a tall redhead by any chance?"

"No, Jane is a blonde about your height."

He was trying to shake me with the revelation, bring me into his corner. But with the emotional bullying I'd suffered from my "peers" once my father disgraced the family, I'd learned to run ice through my veins on command. Protective measures in place, my thoughts went back to the calendar page I'd spirited out of Simon's office. The one that should have noted both appointments Hawkes just mentioned, with the name of Jones heading both prospective times—but didn't.

Instead, the scrap provided a location noting the docks region running southeast of where we now huddled, and only alluded to the evening meeting.

I couldn't be sure if the missing piece corroborated Hawkes's story, or if he knew about the scrap and used the missing area to make his case. He hadn't mentioned the Amazon and didn't say anything about a redhead when I asked about Simon's new paramour. But I wasn't ready to be lulled into thinking any of this meant he didn't know about the Amazon. Or didn't want me to know she was working with him if that was actually the case. Those were just two possibilities—besides his not knowing anything about her at all, of course. I needed to tread carefully. Use him like he may be using me.

Cassie's phone buzzed. Nico's name appeared for a text alert. A swipe of my finger showed the street address for the evening's meeting. His translation skills came through once again.

"Something good? You're smiling," Jack said. "Rather smugly, I might add."

"I tend to smile when I get something I want." I slipped my phone into a pocket.

"Now, now, didn't your mother ever teach you to share?"

"Only with people who reciprocate."

"I've shared information."

"Gossip about Simon's new love and information you've gathered about me. I already know all of it, and unless his girlfriend is someone I need to meet, I don't really need to hear that either."

"You don't want to hear about Moran, you don't like how much I know about you, you aren't interested in Simon's private life, and you won't tell me what your phone said." Jack stroked an eyebrow with his index finger. "If I had to guess...I'd say your compatriot just gave you information about this evening's meeting. If the message had instead reported Babbage or the sword was found, you would have responded as more relieved than excited."

How did he do that? Like the way fake psychics know what to say by asking a few questions and reading a person's facial expressions. "How do I look now?"

"Pissed off." Jack grinned. "I must have guessed correctly."

Stepped right into it again.

Which left me wondering when Hawkes could have seen the noted information on the calendar if he wasn't telling the truth about the girlfriend or working with the Amazon. I wondered how insecure I would sound if I demanded more information.

"I'm surprised Simon told anyone about his business."

"His girlfriend, you mean? She was in the office and saw the calendar when she tried to make a date for them this evening."

"So they don't live together?"

"Not yet."

"But she does live in London?"

He grinned. "Would you like her address?"

"Don't mistake my interest. I am very happy for him. Just concerned."

"I knew that."

Arrrgggh. I made myself breathe naturally. Yes, I was an art recovery specialist, but I prided myself on my abilities to blend, bully, and break anyone until I got the item and info I needed. Something told me conventional tactics would not work with Mr. Teal Eyes here. Time to try another tack.

"You seem to have all my credentials, Hawkes—"

"Call me Jack."

"Jack." I pushed hair behind my ear, knowing the action was a tell for frustration and that he would accurately recognize it as such, but unable to help myself. "Look, I need some references. Got any names I can call?"

"Her majesty is in town. You could try Buckingham Palace. I understand you were by there earlier today."

"You're telling me you've worked for the queen?"

"She was most appreciative. Much like your experience with Margrethe II of Denmark."

"I would never presume to call her by her first name."

"Understood. Just because Lizzie brought me in for tea after I stopped the theft of the Cullinan Diamond—"

"The largest gem-quality diamond ever found—"

"And still in the crown jewels due to the efforts of Jack Hawkes."

"But I thought you were MI-6."

"I never said that. Dylan said I was MI-6," he said. "But I have to ask, why is the number distinction of Military Intelligence the thing you fixate on?"

I smiled. The man so underestimated me. I didn't want to give everything away, though, so I focused on his question. Or fixated, as the case may be. "Because of my own contacts with the FBI and the CIA in the course of my work, I know the recovery of any crown jewel within the U.K. environs would fall under the jurisdiction of MI-5."

"If the prospective theft was on British soil, yes. But not if it occurred while the royal family toured South Africa. Then it would definitely fall under the purview of MI-6."

I realized suddenly how long our gazes had locked, but try as I might, I couldn't look away. There was something about the man, a sexy strength, a confidence I rarely encountered. "The Cullinan Diamond?"

"Yes, the Cullinan Diamond."

"So your interest in the particular item we're pursuing is due to its jeweled hilt?" I asked, wishing I had taken that beer he'd offered to fetch. I wanted to ask why he thought Moran had Simon, but I didn't dare. Doing so would reveal that I'd overheard his phone conversation. "Who is your prospective buyer, or are you connected with a museum or foundation, too? Or are you sticking to the MI-6 story?"

"In this case, my interest in the sword has nothing to do with art or profit, but rather to preserve a British treasure."

"But the Arthurian legend...It's just that, right? A legend. No matter how romantic the tale and lovely the bedtime story."

He shook his head. "Until I can see it for myself, and either get it authenticated or unmasked as a fraud, all possibilities are on the table. Legends exist because enough proof isn't yet available to call them real. That's not to say this sword isn't counterfeit, but it could also be precisely the proof needed for the Camelot legend. Or an early link in a chain of evidence."

At that moment, another customer jostled into the back of Jack's chair, rocking our table and the empty glasses.

"Sorry, mate."

The guy was huge. No way would he have thought he could make it through the gap. His gaze met mine for only a second...and I knew. He was here to get me.

"Block him, Jack!" I shouted and pulled free in the excitement, then pushed away from the table. My boots rang on the tiles as I fled for the exit. As I hoped, I heard Jack holding him off. The fact they didn't both come after me together said they weren't working together. Slightly comforting, until I realized it could also mean Hawkes was pulling an even bigger con. A double bluff was always a risk if I let myself get sucked in by the wrong person.

I slammed into the silver bar across the door and hit the sidewalk, wishing I'd grabbed Jack's umbrella during my escape. Too late. I looked around for a cab, but none stood unengaged. I almost stole one at the corner, until I saw a woman with a cane making her way to the door the cabbie held open and waiting.

Only options seemed to be to hijack someone's car or find a place to hide. The alley behind the pub gaped open a few feet away. I was a split second from choosing the best dumpster when Jack raced out the back door and grabbed my arm. This was getting a bit tedious.

"You have any wheels nearby?" I asked.

In response, he jerked me toward the street and produced an ear-shattering, two-fingered whistle. A driver popped up in the seat of an off-duty cab at the curb. The vehicle glided up to us just as the bruiser from the pub roared out of the back door.

"Guess I should try hitting him a trifle harder next time."

I slid onto the backseat. "Damn it, Hawkes, get in here!"

He hit the door locks as the cabbie broke into the traffic pattern, and we left the muscle-bound creep in the dust. At almost the same instant, Jack's phone rang. As he answered, he trained a gaze on me so strong I felt an almost physical push from the unwavering hold his eyes had on mine. Neither of us blinked when he said, "Cecil, I bloody well lost her. Our best suspect is MIA because you're too bloody cheap to provide me adequate backup. Get your shit together or get out of the game, guv."

I'd worried about a double bluff, but didn't dream I'd see him pulling one on someone else. One that protected me. And with his boss no less. Put him in a new light.

When he punched the key to end the call, I finally spoke,

"Why? Why protect me and turn on your boss?"

"We have a mole somewhere in this setup. Possibly more than one. I am not ready to share what I know with anyone. Even Cecil. Maybe especially not Cecil."

The fact his words echoed my own thoughts about Max added to his credibility. As long as they weren't part of a larger con.

I realized he was missing his umbrella. "Where's your brolly? I was wishing I'd grabbed it as I left."

"Too bad you didn't. I cracked it over the git's head, and the umbrella was the only casualty. Bloke has got a skull like iron."

He slipped his phone into his pocket. I used the action to segue into a new avenue of pursuit. "You and your boss believe I'm your chief suspect, huh?"

"Just as I'm likely yours. But you're looking more innocent all the time."

"No one has said that about me in years."

"Undoubtedly."

"You either, I'll bet."

He offered a grunt in assent, adding, "I'll save my wagers for something a little more risky. When the payoffs are higher."

I wasn't sure how to interpret any of this in relation to our next move, so asked instead, "What do we do?"

His lips offered that slow, sexy smile he produced the first time we met, and he switched to the southern drawl. "Why, we go rogue, darlin'. Sooner the better, I always say."

NINE

"I'm confused. You seem to have all the answers, and unless you're omnipotent, you must have quite a few people working on your behalf. Yet you just told Cecil you need backup."

"One can always use more help in the field."

"But..."

"Yes?"

My eyes rolled for the second time in less than an hour. "Hawkes, you have to have your fair share of confederates."

"Ah, but they aren't Cecil-employed confederates."

"And that makes a difference?"

"Quite. To my bottom line at least, since my dosh pays for their help and the recruiting along the way. Much like you and the pickpocket at Buckingham."

"I don't pay him, Hawkes."

"Again, you've forgotten to call me Jack."

"No, I don't think I did. I tend to shy away from becoming familiar with people who don't listen when I talk."

"I listen. You simply don't reveal anything important until I ask directly. So, how do you recruit help?"

I shrugged. "Charm, family ties, turning a blind eye when a certain pickpocket goes after a mark who's acting rudely."

"That's your criteria, eh? Any particular range of etiquette faux pas considered beyond rudeness?"

"Sometimes. Sometimes it's enough to be able to pretend to hold the act over someone's head."

"Nothing I've found on you suggests you've dabbled in blackmail."

"No, but I'm an expert at using guilt to get my way."

"Keep a bit to bargain with. Good to know."

"I'm sure you've never felt guilty in your life, Jack."

"Thank you."

"For what?"

"Remembering to call me Jack."

The cabbie turned his head in profile and said, "Looks like we've lost the bloke. Have a particular locale in mind, or should I just keep driving?"

Smash. I looked at the glass fragments in my lap that had been my side window a moment before. "What—"

Jack shoved me to the floor boards as bullets pounded a five-second staccato against the back window. The cab shuddered to a stop. Brakes squealed around us, and the buildings made the screams sound like we were in an echo chamber. Something big slammed the rear bumper. Another round of bullets gave me a fix on direction. "Out the door. Your side. Now!"

Jack's moves were smooth. Door open and outside in one fluid motion, he crouched and held out a hand to hustle me from the vehicle. He yelled to the cabbie, "Call 999."

We dove under a nearby lorry and rolled to the other side. I dragged the poor Prada along the asphalt, then slipped the scarred metal-looped leather strap over my head and anchored the bag halfway under my arm.

More gunfire. This time coming from ahead of us. Jack slammed against me, pushing my body flat and covering my back and head. The pitch of the cries rose. Obviously, the crowds weren't scaring the shooter.

"Brazen bugger," Jack whispered, his lips close to my ear.

My head was turned, one cheek against the roadway. I couldn't see him; his skull pushed at the back of mine, the lorry's fat tire keeping us hidden from the gunfire. I could smell his cologne over the trace petroleum aromas, probably mixed with a lot of testosterone and pheromones, too. I knew he wouldn't let me up until we had a plan of sorts. "Who do you think it is?"

"No clue. You okay?"

"Fine. Can we make it to that alley between the shops?"

"And be like fish in a barrel?"

"Best idea I see. Unless you have another." I heard a high-performance motorcycle in the distance.

"No, I—"

The roar of an oncoming Kawasaki drowned his words, and I smelled rubber as the machine screeched to a stop mere inches from my nose.

"Here." I heard Nico's voice.

A helmet landed near my head at the same time the weight holding me to the pavement slid away. Jack quickly switched places with Nico. I pulled the helmet over my hair, swung the ragged-looking Prada to the side, and climbed on behind Jack. My arms circled his waist. He gunned the crotch rocket once and we took off. Another bullet zinged by our heads and hit a delivery lorry with a furniture store logo. I watched Nico duck around the truck then disappear in the alley.

Sirens wailed around us. Jack wove the motorcycle through the vehicle logjam, shimmying through tight spaces and pushing the throttle when an area opened up for a second. I kept my knees tight against the bike, my eyes constantly on a search for our enemy. Law enforcement would only hinder us at this point.

"We can't have the authorities catch us either," Jack shouted over his shoulder.

"Agreed." I patted his shoulder for emphasis. I wasn't sure when he and I started operating on the same wavelength, but at that moment I could truly say I was glad Jack Hawkes was on my team. My heart pounded. I got a tighter hold as he twisted the accelerator.

When we slowed for a moment, a forearm clad in brown canvas grabbed the arm I used to anchor the Prada. I thought it was a purse-snatcher until I got a better look.

"Weasel!" I warned Jack, and kicked out with my heel.

Jack whipped around, trying to see what was going on, and almost lost control of the bike. I had to handle this myself. "Eyes forward. Get us out of here."

The skinny hood latched onto my hand and almost unseated me. I could feel the motorcycle wobble under us, and Jack overcorrect to stay vertical. Weasel moved closer. When the big guy came in to get me in the bar, the two others must have stayed outside to maintain the perimeter and spread out. I hoped Weasel hadn't been the one with the gun.

I wrapped my right hand around Cassie's cell. The curve of my knuckles thickened as they embraced the phone's narrow edge. I willed the plastic to add more *oomph* to my next hard won effort. My fist crashed into his shoulder, driving hard. I gave the punch everything I had. It wasn't enough.

He grabbed my shoulders, trying to pull me toward him, off the bike, and away from escape.

He thinks he's winning. Can't let that happen.

I hauled back as far as his grip allowed, then head-butted Nico's helmet into his nose.

Weasel staggered back. Crimson floods erupted from his nose and lip. One look into his eyes showed how cloudy his brain was after the blow. I slammed another kick into his torso and almost fell completely off the bike in the emotional rush.

"Go!" I slapped Jack's shoulder twice for emphasis and

wiggled back into the bike seat.

"Hang on." He hit an opening, running the Kawasaki so fast I couldn't be sure if either wheel actually met the asphalt. Cool, damp air rushed at us, calming my stomach. Excess adrenalin raced through my veins, and I had to fight an urge to kick out at everyone who passed close to the bike. Toes curled in my boots, grip tightening like a grappling hook around Jack's waist. I forced myself to breathe slowly, ducking my head to stay safely hidden by his broad back and shoulders as I took the few seconds of respite.

I should have paid more attention when we'd run out of the pub. I knew the first two hoods hadn't left the area. We'd gotten away from Weasel this time, but it was sheer luck. Wonder how many more were ready to come at us.

Jack looped the machine every direction on the compass, using alleys and avenues with equal abandon. I hung on, but took the risk to text "Thx" to Nico so he would know we'd broken free. I needed to start thinking now about a Christmas gift. The guy was truly a lifesaver.

After another half-hour or so, the tires wobbled over a cobblestone lane beside a small bistro, and the Kawasaki finally quieted from its nonstop rumble.

"You want a coffee?" Jack asked. His voice muffled through the full-face helmet.

"I want scotch. A double." I couldn't see his smile, but heard his laugh, and followed him through the door.

The helmets went on the extra chairs beside us, and we scooted up to a round table. I shook out my hair, then finger-combed it back into place and hoped for the best. Jack wore his customary casual air, giving the appearance we were only out for an evening ride. I would have been annoyed except the jerk was growing on me.

He moved to the bar and placed our order. I took the

opportunity to send a more detailed message to Nico, asking him to see what he could learn about the Mayfair address for Moran that I found in Simon's file. The phone gave me the "message sent" signal just as Jack returned with a tray holding two coffees and fish and chips.

"Messaging the waiter from the Italian job?"

I laughed. "You make it sound like we're bank robbers. But yes, I did notify Nico we are safe and thanked him. I didn't realize you'd recognized him in the heat of the moment back there."

"I'm genius at face recognition."

"Good to know."

He added quite a lot of sugar to his coffee. I followed suit, knowing even a little shock is nothing to play around with, and I'd had more than my share of trauma for the day. As I sipped, he said, "That's why I knew I'd seen you before when we met again at the *castillo*."

"Well, you were right on one of your observations," I said, thinking back to the encounter on the balcony.

He raised an eyebrow. "Only one? Where am I wrong?"

"You seem to know everything down to my shoe size—"

"Nine, medium width."

I closed my eyes, searching for my center in a job that was rapidly going sideways. "Anyway, use your resources. You obviously have more than the average Joe." I wondered how extensive a dossier he had on me.

"I don't have a Nico."

"And you never will. He hates smartasses."

Jack laughed as he sprinkled malt vinegar and salt onto his food. I tossed my pickled onion his way. "You don't like these?" he asked, spearing the abomination with a wooden fork.

"Your research apparently didn't go deeply enough into my likes and dislikes. Slipping, Jack."

"I forgot to check sites like eHarmony and Match-dot-com. It won't happen again."

The fish sizzled in the container. I could have cooled it down with vinegar, like Jack did, but decided to go purist instead. Let him think I'm more Yank than worldly. "What sites can a guy with supposed MI-6 connections access?"

"Supposed MI-6 connections?"

"Are you finally admitting you're MI-6?"

"I'm not admitting anything. Just asking a question." He sipped his coffee. "Tell me about Nico. How did he know where to find us at that crucial moment?"

I hedged, "Nico knows everything. It's why I can always count on him."

"He appeared like magic. I'm guessing GPS, right?"

I wiggled Cassie's phone. What was the point of trying to deceive?

"Then you must have contacted him earlier and told him you'd switched with the girl at the Victoria and Albert."

"She told you we swapped?" When he cocked an eyebrow, I knew I'd slipped into another trap. I grabbed a piece of fish and took a bite, despite knowing it was still hotter than I liked, just to keep from saying any of the angry words I was thinking at the moment.

He pointed to my phone. "Did you give him follow-up instructions in that text message?" When I kept eating so I couldn't answer, he said, "This is all going to be so much harder if we don't work together."

The couple at the next table looked at us, and the woman kept giving us one of those peripheral looks, watching us even when she pretended not to. I swallowed hard, then quieted my tone and leaned closer to Hawkes. "Work together? How are we working together? You're following me via bug or video. My contacts are saving your ass. You keep telling me just enough about myself to try to keep me off-balance, and give me just enough about yourself to make me think you're a glorified con man. And only revealing facts about the case that I already know. Tell me, Jack, why would I want to 'work together' with you?"

Yes, I used air quotes to make my point. I didn't want any misunderstanding.

He just laughed.

"I guess I should have shown my gratitude by letting you drive the bike," he said, while extracting a chip from my container. I noticed he'd already devoured all of his.

"Are you actively trying to annoy me, or is it natural behavior?"

"Well, I did pay for them."

"Excuse me for not showing my gratitude." I shoved them across the table and rose, finishing my coffee as I headed for the door.

I wasn't actually mad, but I needed to unhinge him a bit. His brawn could be important in the near future, and I always operated on a paraphrased version of the old school advice, namely "Until you know who's a friend and who's a bastard, keep everyone in your sightlines." This man definitely fit the full spectrum of those parameters.

On cue, he followed me out the door and tried to grab the bike's handlebars. I slapped his hands away. "Mine."

"You think you can handle this much power between your legs?"

"Guess it's time to show you exactly what I *am* capable of handling, Hawkes. Get onboard if you're brave enough."

TEN

In the next half-hour or so, I proved to Jack exactly how comfortable I was with a growling throttle in my hand. Overcast western skies grew steadily darker as the last bit of sun hid in the gray. Pedestrians moved more quickly toward home and hearth, and vehicular traffic tightened with every cab and bus reaching max load. On the scarlet and gold Kawasaki, however, mobile opportunity was almost limitless, and I admit to showing off at several points. My intent was to push a few buttons as I challenged sound and space barriers.

Come on, Jack deserved a touch of fright by this point.

Now in the forward position, I had the advantage of choosing my scenery as we moved closer to the docklands destination. I've always loved the many views of the London skyline, and I picked directions that showcased the best. My favorite two high points in London were Tower Bridge and the lovely Swiss Re building. Brits refer to the latter as the Gherkin, but the building always reminded me more of a giant Fabergé egg.

The haphazard footprint of this capital city, regardless of the defined neighborhoods, is a quirky collection of villages. The landscape lends itself to sweeps and swaths of roadways, leading to lanes and loops. And a potential to throw off drivers and pedestrians alike. Dead ends become parks and throughways change to lanes with entirely different names. The engine rumbled as we oriented in a zigzag east-southeast pattern. Despite not possessing the photographic London memory honed by cab drivers, I knew enough of the city's tricks and traps, and paced our path accordingly. I opened the throttle when any straightway sprang up before us. Jack simply hung on for dear life.

The hour sat close enough to full dark for all headlights and street lamps to offer the fuzzy glow that came from early evening and drizzly weather conditions. The streets were a bit slick, but the tires gripped like tiger paws. We skidded a couple of times, but only when I truly wanted to do so. Another quick turn, and I heard Jack's cursing in my ear, despite the barrier of the helmets. I smiled and wedged the bike through a sliver of space so close our pant legs brushed either vehicle.

A couple more kamikaze moves, and I felt secure in believing we weren't followed. I worried about what was going on with Weasel and Werewolf, and hoped Nico finished up in Mayfair soon and got an update from law enforcement. I couldn't risk contacting Scotland Yard, since I'd have to admit I was there and didn't stay for questioning. Personal ethics are truly a bitch sometimes, and we had only a brief window to locate the rendezvous destination and find a place to hide in case our prey arrived.

I slowed the bike and pulled out the phone, using my thumb to flip to the text message Nico had sent earlier matching an address to the GPS coordinates on Simon's calendar. There it was, ahead and to the left. A cargo yard filled with shipping containers stacked two and three stories high. The high-beam security lights and twelve-foot cyclone fence delineated the address. I was happy to note the gate stood open. I didn't see anyone, but I assumed the gate would be locked if everyone was gone. A lighted security shack stood to one side, but no one came out as we pulled up and entered the enclosure.

"Is this it?" Jack's voice was muffled by the helmet. He climbed from the Kawasaki as the motor hushed.

I could only shrug. "Our best bet for now. Help me hide the bike."

He grabbed the handlebars and pushed to get the tires moving toward a sliver of dark between two containers. I scurried ahead to shift any debris. When the motorcycle was safely stowed and adequately hidden, we took a moment to absorb the ambience and reinforce our bearings. The area was rows and rows of steel boxes stacked on acres of concrete, with the sight broken up by wide spaces at the ends where heavy machinery could manuever. The air was tinged with the scent of diesel fuel and hydraulic oil.

Stark lighting trained down on the open area designated via row markings that tied to the GPS coordinates Nico cross-referenced. The letters of precise cursive I'd seen written in Simon's hand earlier that afternoon to denote this evening appointment were branded in my brain. We had little choice for hiding places. It was either stay in absolute dark or glow in the open areas and bright light. A thin alley to the left, created by cargo containers, looked optimum for hiding.

"You think we'll find Babbage here?" Jack whispered, placing a hand almost proprietarily at the small of my back as I threaded my way through a narrow corridor between the numbered freight towers. Something about the move made it feel more than simple courtesy, but playing one-up-man right then was counterproductive.

Instead, I whispered back, "Guess we'll see soon."

With Nico at the Mayfair address on the hunt for intel tagged to Moran, this opportunity was all mine—well, mine and Jack's. And quite possibly the last chance to find and rescue Simon Babbage. Yes, I was banking on the hunch that the cryptic note about tonight's docklands meet was a second rendezvous with the same contact Simon alluded to in our morning phone conversation. We had no real clue to the agenda, so the meet could be true or a wild goose chase. All magnified because I still had no idea whether Simon disappeared before or after the earlier appointment, and with or without the sword. But hopefully I would find out something soon. The lack of defined facts automatically made me nervous. I checked my watch.

"Fifteen minutes."

"Yep, and we're synchronized." Jack tapped his watch face with one finger. "Let's grab some dark."

I pointed to another metal alley that gave good visual coverage to the point, while also radiating its lack of light like a black hole. "Over there."

Jack entered the space ahead of me, and we didn't go far. The back exit was blocked by another freight container, and the other oversized containers balanced above us not only helped cut off lamp light, but reduced further emergency exits to zero. Jack stood behind me. "It really is black in here."

"Yeah, but gives us the best possible view."

"Do you think there's a connection between Babbage's contact and Moran?"

"Finding Simon safe or gaining new information about Moran are the only things I can concentrate on right now, and all I can work toward," I said. "Until I know where there is or is not a link, I have to assume one. Beyond those considerations, Werewolf and Weasel come out of nowhere too often. And since you tell me their loyalties lie with Moran, I have to presume they followed me to the docklands on his orders."

"But their following you could have nothing to do with this appointment. It could simply be Moran wanting you followed. To further his ability to possess the sword."

I understood his argument, but the logic irritated me just

the same. Besides, if it was a double bluff on their parts, the duo could actually be working for Hawkes. They could be following orders to stay suspicious and keep trying to grab me, even if he was around. I only had Jack's word that Moran employed them. And it was especially handy that his friend Dylan was on the same train. "My contacts said Simon had the sword. Simon has disappeared. Hence, the sword has disappeared. Moran is the person I was told to watch out for when I began this misguided job. His dynamic dunderheads have stayed too close to me for too much of this evening. And I now have you as my faithful sidekick."

"I'm no one's sidekick."

I heard a scuttle sound from behind us. *Great, rats.* To cover my fear of rodents, especially in such tight environs, I turned what little I could toward him. "Maybe you need to—" That's when I heard the first *whack,* and Jack crumpled at my feet. Then my world went blacker than even the pitch-dark corridor.

When I came to, I used Jack's prone body to push up and into a sitting position. I gave him a solid shake and received a grunt in reply. My eyes wouldn't focus at first, but when they finally did, I pulled out my phone and saw we'd been out for several minutes. Even in my shaky state my brain processed the fact that someone must have gotten there ahead of us and had been hiding in the dark of the same corridor. Likely for the same reason we'd picked the space—it had the best view.

Both palms felt like someone had taken steel wool to them. I must have slid, using my hands automatically as brakes when I passed out. The crown of my head felt wet and achy, but my probing fingers came back with the verification my hair and the growing knot on my skull were damp from rain, instead of sticky from blood. The evidence didn't make my head stop hurting, but it meant I could forgo an automatic trip to the trauma unit.

My shove had apparently triggered Jack's subconscious to awaken, and he moved and moaned a bit before his eyes opened.

"What happened?"

I shined a penlight toward the back of the space and saw a short wooden stick a couple of inches square. "Looks like we got clubbed."

Jack checked his pockets. "Nothing was taken."

My Prada was still as heavy as ever. "Nothing from me, either." Then I looked around us. "But we're closer to the entrance now. Do you think we were moved after we were hit, or could we have fallen this far?"

In the distance, the bebop of English emergency sirens sounded. As the high-low cacophony moved closer, Jack stood to gain a better look at the area we'd planned to keep under surveillance. "I'm thinking maybe we were moved so we would be better seen."

A man with unruly brown hair and a beard lay curled in a tight ball several meters away on the concrete. His skin looked unnaturally pale under the stark lighting.

"Jones!" I cried, hoping he would recognize the name. I ran forward and placed two fingers against his jugular. A slight pulse. Hopefully the sirens meant an ambulance, but we needed to be sure. "Jack, call for help."

The Welshman, if this was the Welshman, was freshly stabbed, and barely breathing. "Mr. Jones," I tried once more. I could hear Jack talking to a dispatcher as I memorized clues. The knife was a large blade, generic-handled model. I knew better than to touch the weapon but figured it had been wiped clean anyway.

The ground was damp everywhere from the drizzle. I pulled off my trench coat, folded the garment into a hefty square, and placed it under his head to make him more comfortable. It was only after I'd done so I realized I should have left the scene intact. Still, the movement alerted Jones a bit, and I saw his lips move.

"Jones. Can you hear me?" I bent closer to catch anything he might say. "Are you here to meet Simon Babbage?"

"Peee-deee...dum." The sound came a second before two uniformed coppers rounded the corner at a dead run.

Jack materialized beside me holding the Prada. I thanked him, surprised I hadn't noticed it missing, and irritated he'd probably searched the bag while he had the opportunity.

The lead detective took that moment to speak, and I could only nod when he said the inevitable. "We'll need statements from both of you."

And there it was. We may have dodged the authorities earlier after the bullets on the boulevard, but I harbored no hope of slipping away after getting caught at an obvious murder attempt. My being American didn't help the situation either.

A tall man in a dark suit arrived, and Jack left me to walk over and greet him. "DCI Lambert. Good to see you."

"Hawkes, it's been awhile."

Of course he knew Jack. I didn't know whether to be relived or further suspicious at that point, but Jack did get us processed and our statements taken in record time. Still, we were pushing the midnight curfew I'd promised Cassie.

The victim was whisked off by an ambulance, but not before he was identified as one Jestin Jones, well-known for his talents at trading money for information. No surprise, he was originally from Wales.

"Did the victim say anything before he lost consciousness, miss?" a young detective-sergeant asked, his pen poised over a worn pad. I looked toward Hawkes and saw he was yukking it up with his DCI buddy. Before I looked away, his gaze met mine and he winked. I felt my blood pressure rising again.

Cocky bastard. I took a moment to breathe and compose

myself before I answered the officer's question. "Sorry. This has been a lot to handle all at once." He murmured a comforting cliché, and I smiled, dragging out my next words to add emotional authenticity. "All he did was make a breathy sound as he exhaled once. Then he took a kind of ragged gasp and lay quiet."

"Yeah, the other bloke said it sounded like he was calling some guy dumb, or was only a garbled bit of sound," the DS said, as he scribbled on his pad. "Possibly Peter-something. Was that your take on the moment?"

"I really couldn't say," I hedged. I didn't know if Hawkes was playing things straight or trying to lead the police astray, but I needed to wrap this up before we got roped in any further. "The poor man...I wish we could have helped. If you don't need me anymore, officer—"

"You've helped all you can, miss. Me guv said I could let you go once I had contact details."

I provided him my cell phone number, trusting it would go to voicemail while Cassie had it, and a contact number at the Beacham Foundation. "But please try the cell first. I'll be on this side of the Atlantic for a bit longer, and I don't want my boss concerned if he hears there's been a violent incident. He's kind of a mother hen."

Actually, he was a different kind of mother, but I wanted Max to stay out of the loop as long as possible on all counts, not just this potential slaying. It was too early for an official missing person report anyway and getting too late to admit I knew Simon was missing otherwise. And any doubt I harbored earlier about a mole in the hierarchy of the field we call the Art World was now a thing of the past. I was certain.

I had to shut down idle chitchat wherever I could, and letting Max know anything at this point would blow any hope of doing so. Once a secret is told to one person, it is no longer secret. And in our current world of nearly instantaneous viral information leaks, I couldn't risk this kind of sensitive data becoming part of the new normal. "Thank you, detective-sergeant. I appreciate your discretion."

"Perfectly understandable, miss. And could you tell me how long before you're due to return to America?"

I took a second to consider how to answer. It wasn't my purpose to lie, but I needed to give myself wiggle room. "I have an open ticket. A bit of business has brought me to London. But I should have everything wrapped up in a few days."

"Please stay available to us, and let us know if you have any change in plans."

"I understand."

What I didn't add was the fact that the breathy sound Hawkes told him sounded like "Petey dumb" could easily be the poor man trying to say the French village of Puy de Dôme. Pronounced "pee-dee-dum," it was an idyllic area of France where—I had learned from Simon's computer files—Moran kept a mountaintop hideaway.

ELEVEN

One of the trauma guys checked out the knot on my head and prescribed rest and a couple of paracetamol. That's acetaminophen to us Yanks. The tech also produced some alcohol wipes to clean my scraped palms. Jack remained the silent martyr and kept his abrasions to himself.

He set off for the motorcycle, but I gave a shout out and tossed him the keys. "It's yours," I called, and headed for the main road.

"Where are you going?"

"To find a bathroom and a stiff drink. Not necessarily in that order. And I'm getting there by cab."

"But the bike?"

"Text me the location where you park it tonight, and I'll tell Nico where to find the thing and return it to its rightful owner."

He stood for a moment in obvious indecision, then changed direction and double-timed my way. He stood tall beside me as the cab stopped at my signal. "You're right. A cab is a better idea for both of us in the short term."

I shrugged. There went my chance to text Nico en route. I'd have to wait until safely ensconced in a ladies' room somewhere. Unless that didn't stop Jack from following me either. "Suit yourself."

Jack climbed in and slammed the door. He gave the cabbie an address for an upscale hotel he knew with a quiet bar, then turned to me. He didn't lean back in the seat like I had, but instead sat poised on the cushioned edge and leaned my way. Not quite in my personal space but near enough to prove how interested he was in my answer when he asked, "Did you understand anything Jones said?"

I ran a hand across the back of my neck, raising my damp hair to fluff it a bit and hoped it made me look human. Jack had been well within hearing distance when I spoke to the officer, so I knew he was hoping I had held back information. Which was precisely what I had done and intended to continue doing. I would admit to exactly what I heard, but I didn't have to tell him I thought I knew what the sounds actually meant. The look in Hawkes's eyes said the response he was truly looking for from me was confirmation. Or hoping for some.

Waiting is good for the soul.

"I really can't add anything to what you said in your statement," I replied. "With that kind of injury, rapid loss of blood and the general fright throughout, the guy probably had no clue what was he was saying. Just rambling."

Hawkes blew out a long breath and crashed against the backrest, staring straight through the windscreen for several minutes. I waited, appreciating the silence to collect my own ragged thoughts. No new epiphanies bloomed, just the same repeated questions and possible pursuits.

My heart panged then for Simon. Not that I wasn't already concerned, but because I missed being able to call him about anything, run past him whatever esoteric idea I came up with in the course of a job. I didn't have that kind of trust for Hawkes, though I was starting to see I may have painted him with the wrong brush in the beginning. Until he opened up more about himself, however, I needed to tread carefully. What he and Cecil discussed in their second conversation still worried me. Plus, the CCTV clout he obviously had still ticked me off.

"So who coshed us over the head? Any more bad guys pursuing you?" Jack finally broke the silence, his words said in a teasing sort of way, but I noticed the weight in his eyes. He was serious. And he was right.

"Yeah, it was a little too anonymous for Weasel or Werewolf. Maybe you have unknown bad guys after you. Who's to say I didn't get caught in your crossfire?" I couldn't help it. Even though I acknowledged his hypothesis was as valid as my own, bravado was my middle name. "More likely, however, we were both in the wrong place at the wrong time, and the lumps we received were because we came between Jones and his killer. We just arrived before the victim, and the killer hadn't enough time to get rid of us more permanently."

"Small favors."

I didn't have the energy to offer any sarcasm.

Our cab surged with traffic through the darkened streets, and the buildings on either side made me feel closed in and sleepy. I didn't know how much of the feeling was due to my possible concussion and how much was just growing exhaustion from not enough sleep and too many repeated attacks. When he shined his light in my eyes, the tech said my pupils looked good, but warned I should have someone around all night to wake me periodically. I longed to be in a nice warm bed. My head hurt and it seemed like years since I'd slept. Now I needed a keeper, too? I didn't plan to give Jack the honors. Nico was first choice, but I required a modicum of privacy to contact him, even by text, and side by side in a cab with Hawkes did not meet those requirements.

Nico hadn't contacted me since he left for Mayfair. We needed new information, but I needed my friend more, and my concern for his welfare grew by the minute. Getting another co-worker caught in Moran's web was something I couldn't risk. Okay, yes, assuming Jack was leveling with me—even when I had been eavesdropping on his phone conversations—I was assuming Simon had been spirited away by Moran. Possibly by Weasel and Werewolf before they followed the evil-monger's command to thwart me at every turn. Their actions all afternoon seemed focused on snatching me, or slowing me and Jack down with bullets, so what else could I think?

I had more information than before—and more people after me. That morning I'd thought Jack my only worry. Another concern: I was positive he heard the word Jones said, but he wouldn't share if he knew what I thought it all meant. Was he fishing to see how much I'd already learned?

We were only a few blocks from the hotel when he said, "I think I caught a glimpse of someone in the shadows watching what was going on when we found Jones. But I didn't see well enough to recognize the person as anything more than a shadow."

"So we have nothing."

"Perhaps." Jack shrugged. "However, I did get the medical tech to admit your contusion was more pronounced than mine. Meaning you were probably hit harder than I was. Any other person pose a threat to you?"

"Right now, Hawkes, you're my only threat." I didn't add that his head was probably thicker than mine, but the grin he shot my way said he knew I was thinking it.

"Your words cut me, Laurel."

"I don't see you bleeding." I shook my head. "No, I'm sorry. I just don't want to start seeing threats where none exist." My instincts told me to measure what he said against what could be his actual goal. I didn't have the luxury of keeping him at arm's length, but I didn't have to wholeheartedly believe him either. "Another dead guy. What is different about this job?"

"*Another* dead guy? How many have you discovered so far?"

Ugh! I hadn't found out if he knew about the guy on the toilet from last night. Italy seemed weeks away, even if it was barely twenty-six hours past. Sloppy, sloppy, sloppy. Now I had to figure out a way to do cleanup. "Figure of speech. You know, another day, another dead body."

Hawkes reached over and caught my chin, turning my face so he could look into my eyes. "I don't believe you, Laurel."

"What can I say? You need to be more trusting, Jack." I was assuming Max had followed through with the authorities as he promised. After all, my boss did order me to focus on this job and not to worry about the other. I was following orders.

The cab drew to the curb and Hawkes grabbed my elbow. He gave a fistful of pound notes to the cabbie, then hustled me out of the vehicle and into the hotel. Soft music played in the lobby, and the carpet felt thick under my boots. What I wouldn't have given for a firm bed and a long night's sleep. Instead, we headed for the bar. Jack hung his jacket on the back of his chair. I pulled the Prada into my lap.

Under the dim lights, we probably looked like just another hook-up, especially when Jack ordered us both a scotch, then grinned at me and leaned close. Except he showed too many teeth.

He raised an eyebrow. "What other body did you stumble over?"

"Really, I—"

"Laurel."

It was the tone of voice. At that moment, I knew something about the MI-6 story was true, because he employed the same tone my contacts at the CIA and FBI were trained to use whenever someone was holding back information. Despite my justification a few moments ago, a little trust was in order. I couldn't see I had much choice if I wanted to be able to slip away later to reach Nico.

"The *castillo*. Last night. I was there to make a pickup, but someone apparently wanted the object more."

Jack blew out a breath. "The Greek?"

I pulled up my Prada and waded through the contents until I found the picture Nico had provided so I could find my contact. "This guy."

He stared at the photo and nodded. "That's the Greek. He was found in a back alley this morning. Victim of a robbery. Throat slit. Milan authorities are investigating."

So Max did follow through, and Jack had an in with the Italian police.

"The robbery and the slit throat are right, but I found him bleeding in one of the bathrooms," I corrected him.

"Of the *castillo*?"

I nodded. "About nine o'clock. Just before you found me in the ballroom and hustled me onto the balcony."

"Ah, no wonder you were wary of my attentions."

"Well, you had been kind of a tick to my backside all night."

"I was told to follow you. My intention was to get a look at the snuffbox and examine it before the handoff. The authenticity of the object was in question, and at the same time, the true purpose of the snuffbox and the handoff shot up red flags. I was sent in to try to get confirmation either way. I've been following you since to get another chance at the object."

"Someone thinks the snuffbox was a fake?"

"A possibility."

"I never got it." I looked at the clock over the bar. Nearly one o'clock. "I jumped over the balcony wall after you were pulled away for the card game. Both Nico and I left empty-handed."

"We know that now. Doesn't mean I'm not still interested in keeping you alive. You're associated with the snuffbox, and we had word of a micro drive hidden inside that contains plans for a major art heist in the coming months, at some facility within her majesty's borders. We still need to learn if there even is a micro drive, and if so, where it is now. Frankly, given everything that has happened, it wouldn't surprise me to learn the entire operation was an impromptu way to get you safely tucked away in an Italian jail and out of the picture until you could prove your innocence."

"That sounds like overkill—pardon the expression. Have someone murdered just so I can't go after Simon and the sword? Me framed for the murder?"

"Or they framed you to keep you out of the thick of things."

"So, am I a target? Or just trouble for someone."

Jack grinned. "My money would be a little of both."

But while what he said sounded a bit confusing and more than a little disconcerting at first, the theory did make a kind of sense when I thought about it all. I gave him a brief rundown of what went wrong the previous evening, and kept me from meeting with my contact before the murder.

Once the recap was finished, I put an elbow on the table and leaned into my fist. Lack of sleep was really starting to catch up to me, but the kind of fuzziness of my brain made me interpret things in a new way. "Right now, what I see as the only connection between these two cases is you following me wherever I go. You were tasked last night to get a look inside the snuffbox, but had no interest in the item otherwise. And now you're after the sword for its historic application?"

"If it's authentic, yes. After a search of your belongings at the airport and in your hotel, you were given a pass—"

"What legal right did you have to search my things?"

"All airport baggage is subject to periodic searches. Those new security reg—"

"But you searched my hotel room."

He looked sheepish for a second, then shrugged. "You knew

about that, eh? Sorry, but I have a job to do."

I sat up straight. "Let's talk about your job."

"Let's not." He gave me a piercing look. "Instead, let's discuss who would have been capable of sending you on all those wrong paths last night."

"And who framed me for murder."

"It's only theory at this juncture," he said, reaching out a hand to cover mine. I thought he was trying to calm my fears, but the next thing he said dispelled that idea. "Though, given the disturbing communiqués we've all received in the past months—the red herrings if you will—it is a credible presumption. We really do need to figure this out, and you need to be aware of everything around you at all times."

That was a frightening scenario. "How does Moran tie into this?"

"Art is not the only thing used to build the man's economic empire. Selling information to perpetrate new art theft would bring a substantial sum."

"And how big is this micro drive?"

He took my right hand in his and captured the pinky. "About the size of this lovely fingernail."

"So you believe Moran is behind all of this?" I asked, pulling my hand free as I tried to get my head around the implications Jack presented. My question didn't even slow him down.

"The art theft itself is serious, Laurel. You've told me about the bogus messages you've received at the most inopportune times, and they mirror the type sent to me and others in the business. If this heist is a valid concern, it's most likely perpetrated by more than Moran's team of thieves. Now with Simon's disappearance linked to the sword the ante is upped substantially. Especially after the murder in Italy. Whether or not the micro drive was ever secreted in the snuffbox."

"So why are you constantly everywhere I am? You know I don't have either item."

"Yet you seem to be a lightning rod for activity on both pieces." He took my hand and held it loosely in his, looking directly into my eyes as he continued, "I don't know if there's a correlation between the two thefts. But you have to recognize that it's in both our best interests to work together until something is resolved."

"What I'm beginning to recognize is..." I pulled my hand free and counted off on my fingers. "Moran could have Simon, and the sword, and the snuffbox. My boss told me the current fear was that Moran is after the sword. Men associated with him have been after me, but we don't know if it's to slow me from gaining the sword, or because Moran is sick of me being a pain in his business. If he had a hand in the snuffbox debacle, he may have ordered the murder of the Greek, whether to frame me or not."

"Yes, sadly the Greek was expendable. That's the story I'm hearing from the field. Until we know the truth about the drive and the purported plans it held, we're only hypothesizing over the reason for the murder. Regardless, the action puts an even more frightening spin on things. A spin I have to stop."

I caught my breath, and made my face a mask. What had I gotten myself into? How badly did Jack really want that snuffbox?

He realized his mistake and placed a hand on my wrist, for once not hanging on so tightly I couldn't run. But I didn't try to flee. Not yet, anyway.

"No, I didn't kill him." His expression softened. Gotta hand it to the guy, it would have been very easy to believe him. "I was just there to see if the micro drive did indeed exist. And appropriate it for Her Majesty. Rudimentary information says Great Britain will be the projected site of the heist, but the effects will be felt across the entire European art community."

"Why a physical drive, no matter how teeny-tiny, when it's so easy to send encrypted files into the cloud?" I asked. "If someone wanted to share the plans, why saddle oneself with the limits of moving the info by physical drive?"

"Good question. Control, maybe?"

Maybe. Or maybe the whole thing was another round of storytelling BS I had to wade through just to keep on-track to find Simon and the sword. Like those damned story math problems, where you had all the extra information you didn't really need, but you had to read all of it then sort out only the information that led to the answer. Those stupid math problems made my head hurt, and whatever this job was turning into seemed to be equally frustrating.

I killed my scotch. "I need to freshen up a bit. Getting knocked out in an alley is hell on a hairstyle. Order me a Cuba libre without the rum, and I'll be right back."

"One Coke it is." He raised an eyebrow. "Can I trust you not to run off?"

"Jack, if there's one thing I've learned in the last twenty-four hours, it's that I need all the help I can get with this thing. Your latest revelation puts a finer point on everything I thought I knew and now believe. Besides, you've proven yourself by telling me about the plans, the drive and the snuffbox. And the scenario that kept me out of an Italian jail."

I pointed to a corner near the front entrance.

"The restroom is over there, to the right of the big flower bouquet. I've been to this hotel before. I'll barely be out of your sight."

His shoulders told the tale, as I watched his muscles visibly relax beneath his cotton shirt. He was as exhausted from all of this as I was. I counted on that.

"Be careful."

"I always am." Right then I planned to carefully save my skin. Jack now knew more than I'd intended to tell him. Worse, as I ran back over what he'd shared I realized he hadn't really reciprocated in kind. As usual. All his words did was substantiate what I already knew or surmised, and any new revelations seemed geared toward making me more frightened of being without him. Maybe someone had wanted to frame me last night, but things had only been an inconvenience until Jack came into my world. He knew everything about me, but repeatedly pushed the conversation into another direction anytime I tried to learn anything about him.

He headed to the bar to place the order, and I strode back through the lobby, veering to my right and the alcove holding the restrooms. As I stepped onto the hallway's patterned carpet, I glanced over my shoulder. I saw him turn to the bartender and take his eyes off me. Time to make my move.

Changing course, I quick-stepped out the glass entrance. There was a shout—well, more like a bellow—when he noticed my detour. Too late. The doorman finished helping a couple out of a cab and I jumped in. I watched the uniformed arm slam the door just as Hawkes barreled onto the sidewalk.

"Hurry please. Entrance to St. Pancras International Station," I told the cabbie. I hit the door locks as Jack reached for the handle on my side. "I need to get away from this man."

"Oy, miss, will do." The cabbie pulled into traffic. "Persistent bloke, that one."

"Yes, it's his trademark."

As we drove, I pulled out Cassie's phone. Nothing from Nico. To keep from stewing about his silence, I called Cassie.

"Laurel! Are you alright?"

I frowned. "Yes. I thought I'd have to leave a messa—"

"I've left the phone on ever since I saw the last news report," she said.

"What news?"

"A murder at the docklands. The reporter said a British man and blonde American woman were interviewed but had no details. I didn't know if you were in danger."

"No more than usual." I sighed. "Look, I know it's late—well, early morning, actually—but can you meet me at St. Pancras Station? I'm on my way there now." Suddenly I remembered the plethora of CCTV cameras working around every Tube station. "Oh, and do you have a hat or cap I can borrow? Maybe a pair of glasses, too?"

"What?"

"I'll explain later, I promise." The driver didn't need any additional entertainment at my expense, so explaining to Cassie how Jack tracked me earlier, and how I was subsequently trying to avoid anyone recognizing my digital image seemed a little chancy in the cab.

"I have a scarf. And my brother left his Chicago Cubs ball cap here when he visited last month."

"Good, bring both." I was ready to change clothes anyway, and a ball cap would be just the right topper for a casual traveler. It was all in the attitude. "And we probably need to trade back phones before I leave. It's not safe for you to keep carrying mine."

"But how safe is it for you?"

"I'll get a burner phone if necessary."

The idea seemed to satisfy her. "Okay. I'll bring all your stuff, and the borrowed stuff too. I went over the files that would open on the thumb drive. There were a couple of pieces I remembered hearing were recently stolen. And one picture of a Raphael icon is rumored to be counterfeit."

"Good information to know."

"I marked which pictures by saving them all in a separate file. The rest of the file dates on the drive cover the past six months. Nothing more recent than a fortnight ago, except for the new file I created today."

"Perfect. Thanks, Cassie."

Traffic snarled again, and I quietly cursed.

"What's wrong?" she asked.

"Just traffic. We're completely stopped at the moment, so I don't know how soon I'll get to St. Pancras, but please hurry and meet me there."

"Okay," she said. "Look for me in the coffee area we like. I'll be there as quickly as I can."

"Take a cab. Don't risk the Tube."

"But if traffic is still miserable, and I'm ending up in St. Pancras anyway—"

I closed my eyes and massaged my right temple. The headache was worsening. "Cassie, you'll have my bags and your purse. I don't want you on the subway when you're overburdened with stuff. Trust me on this. How about if we meet at the street entrance instead?"

She blew out a breath. "You sure you don't want to hide out here?"

"Going to your place might put you in jeopardy. I can't do that. But if you don't want to meet me—"

"No, I'm not afraid for me, Laurel. I'm concerned for you. What's your next move?"

I caught the cabbie watching in his rearview mirror. Obviously, ours was one of his more interesting eavesdropped conversations of the day. "I'll tell you at the station. Just hurry, but be safe."

"Okay. You, too."

I cut the call and turned my face to the window, willing the cabbie to ignore me. I already had too much to worry about, and I simply didn't have the energy to countermand someone else's interest in my current adventures.

The person I really wanted to talk to was Nico. If he was actually in Moran's Mayfair address, an audible alert from my text could tip off someone he was nearby. Not the most patient person in any situation, I really had to work to keep from punching out a message anyway. My goal was to get to St. Pancras and catch a night train to connect with one of the scheduled Chunnel runs. To do so, I needed the ability to get a ticket. Without contacting Max, of course.

If he'd understood the words Jones said with his last breath, Jack would know I'm likely on my way to France. Especially if he'd heard through the window glass when I gave my destination to the cabbie as St. Pancras. I had no time to waste if I wanted to beat him to Puy de Dôme and find Moran's place there.

The phone vibrated in my hand. It was like ESP.

"Nico. Where are you?"

"Hiding out in a Tesco."

Not my idea of a safe place, but crowded and easy to spot someone paying too much attention to you, I guessed. "Did you learn anything?" I hoped he wouldn't mention Moran's name out loud. I was starting to worry there were eyes and ears on us everywhere.

"Nothing on dear Simon. Did learn the house's owner has flown the coop."

Good. He obviously didn't want Moran's name brought out either.

He continued, "I could not find an exact destination, but I did find an Air France timetable still open on a desk tablet."

"They left a computer behind?"

"No, a real tablet. Old school. Paper. Sorry. Should have been more specific. It's just that I haven't seen a paper timetable in so long, it surprised me to see one open to today's flights."

"Anything marked?"

"A squiggle near a Paris flight. Couldn't read it, but no great surprise since Paris has always been tied to Moran's escape routes."

No, not a surprise at all. Especially since Paris was the most likely city for someone on plane or train to stop before ultimately arriving at the same place where I was currently headed. "Look, Nico, I'm on my way to St. Pancras International Station. Can you get online and book me on a Chunnel crossing for today? The earlier the better. Then I need transport to the Puy de Dôme region."

"From Paris? And do you want a car or train ticket there?"

I massaged my right temple. Train would be the easiest, since I had no idea where I was going, but a car offered its own special perks. Between the Chunnel train and a train to Puy, I had opportunities for catnaps a car didn't offer. The problem was I likely needed convenience over sleep. "Get me a car that will have no difficulty in the mountains."

"Got it. I'll check things out and email your codes and data."

"I don't have any room on my credit card, so—"

"Laurel, if you had been able to do the booking yourself, you wouldn't have asked me. I'll get the passage booked."

"Thanks, Nico. Oh, and the motorcycle was left at a murder scene."

"I know. I sent someone to check on it when the GPS said it sat idle for so long. I was concerned you needed help. Last I heard, my friend is waiting for proof of ownership from the rental company before Scotland Yard will let him leave the scene—with or without the bike."

"Sorry."

"I know. Not like you do any of these things on purpose."

"Hey!"

He laughed and hung up. That's when I realized he was teasing. Running on nerves was truly affecting my sense of humor. Between getting drizzled on, tossed around, and pretty much scared out of my mind throughout the day, my body was having difficulty staying at anything resembling the right temperature. I rubbed my arms, suddenly feeling how chilled I was, and wished I still had the trench coat I'd put under the Welshman's unconscious head. The day's events had already given the trench a pretty distressed look, despite its purchase only that morning. Ending as a pillow under the victim's head gave it the hero's ending it deserved.

A change of clothes would definitely include a jacket. I racked my mind, trying to remember if a jacket was part of my shopping bag stash. Yep, one leather jacket. I was covered.

Doubly important, a clothing change might slow down Jack, too. When I considered how angry he likely was with me right then, and his ease of using national security methods to track me, I needed to do everything possible to make identification more difficult. I turned off my phone. No sense making it any easier.

TWELVE

Cassie and I hurried to the toilet so I could make my quick change. In a train station in the middle of the night, we expected to find a homeless person or two camped in the stalls, but the facilities were surprisingly empty. As I pulled on a traveling ensemble of dark jeans and a tee, I spilled a bit of my day's news, mostly about tangling with Jack. The risk of porcelain echoes reminded me to speak quietly despite the privacy, but before I finished her blue eyes looked ready to pop.

"You mean there's even more?" she asked.

I pulled on the leather jacket and hugged my torso. Finally warm once again. "I'm here to give you your money's worth of entertainment."

I frowned when the mirrors showed how pale my face looked under the fluorescent glare.

"Or the script for a month's worth of nightmares." Her sigh said it all, but my words goaded her into finding the only blind spot for us to hide in the space as we added the cap and a pair of low prescription reading glasses. Finally, she offered me a gorgeous vintage Hermes orange swirl scarf.

"Oh, I can't." I stroked the silk when she held it my way. I saw the gold coins patterned into the fabric and knew it also showed gold chokers within the print. I couldn't in good conscience take something that beautiful and classic unless I had a chance of getting it returned in one piece.

She shook her head. "No arguments. Even if you don't use it right now, you may need it later for camouflage. I'd just feel better to know you had it at hand if need be."

"I'll find a kerchief or something else to use instead. I promise."

"Laurel—"

"Besides," I argued. "I need to blend in. This fabulous scarf screams money."

Her chin crumpled a bit, and I appreciated her desire to help at any cost. "Okay, no tears. If you really want me to carry it along."

Cassie brightened immediately. "Think of it as a responsibility to help you stay safe. So you can return it to me."

Why did everything have to get harder before it got easier? At least I hoped things would get easier. "Come on. Let's go find some caffeine." Then I reached out and gave her a quick hug. "And thank you."

We had already returned each other's cell phones, and as we merged again into the crowd I texted Nico regarding the change in phone number. We found the coffee bar, placed our order, and grabbed a table. Before long, I'd finished my double shot espresso and the tale of the day's adventures. The combination of alcoholic drinks I'd consumed that day, added to the caffeine in the coffee kept my paranoia slightly at bay, but made me feel I could run a Roger Bannister four-minute mile.

"Why don't you go to the police?" Cassie asked. "Your ex is missing and you can't get the sword you came for anyway. If I were on the run or kidnapped because of an art object, I'd want every possible law enforcement agency on the job. And didn't you say his secretary was missing, too?"

"The operative word there is *was*." I'd kept my voice low while telling the story, letting the sounds of the crowd and the grinders work as white noise to shield us, but I leaned a bit closer over the table to communicate the urgency and secrecy. "Nico texted me a while ago that Martha is at her sister's house in Newcastle. I spoke to her and, without giving her enough information to create alarm, beyond waking her in the middle of the night, of course, I learned Simon insisted she take a month-long sabbatical starting yesterday. Her sister is widowed and has health problems, so the offer wasn't out of line. However, I have to imagine now that he did so because of concern that things might heat up soon."

"Making the idea of going to the police sound even better." Cassie took my hand as she spoke. I gave it a squeeze in return.

If it were anyone but Simon, I would have agreed with her. Those huge trusting eyes showed worry, and her expression telegraphed something else too. Maybe hesitancy? Was she starting to not trust me?

I caught the inside of my lower lip between my teeth as I contemplated my next words. The crowd streamed around us, still heavy despite the late hour because of all the international connections St. Pancras offered. Everything looked benign, just uncomfortably busy. Yet, my vision probed every shadowy niche and double-checked every profile in an effort to try to spot any of the males playing a role in this little drama. Cassie wanted to be reassured no one else would be hurt. She knew about the docklands from watching the news, but I hadn't even told her about the guy in Italy yesterday. So much had happened in those intervening hours. Would learning everything make her better understand my position? Or increase her wariness because she thought I should go to the police?

And was I even right? Would it be so bad to countermand the order I knew Simon would give if he was able, and take the next Tube train to Scotland Yard?

"The first thing I learned in training for my job was that a priceless work of art can tempt people to do crazy and dangerous things," I said. My eyes felt gritty from fatigue and the station's over-conditioned air. "The crooks do dangerous and crazy things to steal priceless objects, and people like me do crazy and dangerous things to make sure priceless objects are available for the world to share. And if they are taken, we do crazy and dangerous things to recover them. That pattern is broken if everyone else in the world knows what we're doing at all times. We simply can't administer our jobs under those circumstances. There are times where we work with authorities, sure, but in those instances we too often find the press learns about the operation prematurely. Especially in cases like this one where we don't yet have a handle on the scope of the operation."

I pulled the coral cache from the shopping bag Cassie returned. "Simon used this item for a very particular purpose. If security hadn't been necessary, he undoubtedly would have loaded his files into an email for me and sent them along, or put them into the Beacham Foundation's cloud server and told me what to access. He didn't do either of those things. Yesterday, he sent away his secretary. He told me to meet him this afternoon at his office. He didn't tip off either of us, the most trusted women he worked with, about this flash drive. Instead, he put one person in a safe place and trusted the other, me, to find the hidden object I knew nothing about. Someone went through his office ahead of me, but I was the one who found Simon's secret. I have to believe he counted on that."

"If he knew something was up, why didn't he warn you?"

"I've been asking myself the exact same question ever since I learned he moved Martha. The only time I spoke with him was in the middle of Heathrow on an unsecured cell line. Between the crowds and the capabilities of electronic eavesdropping, that's not the best of conditions for sharing sensitive information. I assume he'd hoped to contact me later but didn't have the chance."

"And you've been dodging bad guys ever since."

"And one Amazon." I grinned. I couldn't help it. "I just wish I'd taken a picture of her. Jack knew who Weasel and Werewolf worked for, but he didn't recognize my description of the redhead. I imagine the Amazon is in Moran's employ as well, but it would be nice to be able to email her photo to one of my contacts at Interpol or the CIA and see if she's in someone's system already."

Cassie grinned. "Maybe you should start carrying a fingerprint kit with all those gizmos in your bag. Could come in handy."

"You peeked!" I laughed when Cassie sent a horrified look in response. I'd put all the really secret gizmos in the Prada. Good thing. She'd have never recovered. "It's okay. Never agree to hold someone else's stuff unless you know it's not going to get you a jail sentence."

She waggled a slim finger as she said, "I've seen some of the things you pull out when you think I'm not looking. I'm sure a few of those would definitely interest those detectives who talked to you tonight."

"Good thing they didn't ask to search my bag then, right?" I still worried Jack had done precisely that. But her comment jogged my memory about how chummy Hawkes was with the DCI. Why *weren't* we searched? It was a murder scene, after all. It had to be due to Jack's connections. I worried if I'd made the best decision. Well, decisions. I felt more in control on the run alone, but he obviously had friends in the right places. Friends who could help or hurt my chances at reaching my objective.

My phone suddenly danced along the tabletop. Nico's face appeared on the screen.

"Hitting send to transmit all your train information now,"

he said when I answered. "I'm providing some breathing room to your Visa card balance, so you have the ability to buy more than a matchbook once you get to France. I also topped off your Oyster card because it was dangerously low, and I don't want you getting trapped in the London underground system. You are prone to forgetting those types of details."

"Nico—"

"You are most welcome."

"That wasn't what I was going to say."

"We will say, for argument's sake, that it is. Returning to the task at hand, I was able to secure passage on a Eurostar going from London to Paris. There will be a couple of stops to board more passengers, but no need for you to leave the train. I reserved a car for the trip from Paris, and you can drive to the small hotel in the region where I have a room reserved for one night. I will pass on all the directions by email. Tomorrow night's stay is the best I can do, nothing more. There is an annual celebration in the region. If you need additional time in the area, you must find someone's couch, or the car, or a hayloft to crash for a bed. Good luck and keep your itinerary handy."

"No change in procedures, right? All paperwork is still handled in London?"

"Absolutely. You can just walk off the train in Paris."

"Thanks, Nico. I'd be lost without you."

"You may stay lost with me. Your itinerary is pretty full, but I had to do some fancy hacking to get you anywhere near Puy de Dôme. Very popular place at the moment."

"Probably why Moran is going there," I mused. "Get himself and every*thing* and every *person* he's stolen lost in the crowd. But I will get there tomorrow, right?"

"Right. Late afternoon or early evening. You need to catch the next train out of St. Pancras to start this little adventure. I plan to meet you on the train to Paris."

"You'll share this Chunnel ride with me?"

"I am going to try. Finding a way into Moran's compound is more difficult than I expected. I hope to brief you en route. Got a new toy I want to give you, too. Besides, I think you need a babysitter, and I need to head east. And I am *really* getting sick of helicopters."

"Poor baby." I laughed. I couldn't help it. Cassie gave me a questioning look, and I waved a hand to tell her I'd explain in a minute. "Okay. Who's paying for our little junket, by the way?"

Nico chuckled. "Found that Max's AMEX Black credit card had loads of room for a few extra expenses."

"Max has a Black card?" My fingers tightened around the phone. A Black! That sucker had no limit.

"When you are the cheapest man alive, credit card companies clamor for your business," Nico said, breaking my reverie.

The rat bastard. Max could have already reimbursed me for the outlay I'd lost prepaying the Tahoe vacation. Oh, I know what he would say—all those admonitions about mixing up personal and business money accounts. Like I wasn't having to do exactly that because he wouldn't let me have a corporate card. And now I learn he has his own personal Black?

"Nico, keep that account number handy."

THIRTEEN

It was surprising how many people were still up and moving through London by subway in the cusp of the morning. From homeless with their possessions stacked beside them, looking for a bit of shadow to sleep, to backpacking students who carried all their possessions in duffles and checked timetables to see if their train lines were still running at the late hour. Or, rather, in the early hours. I was surprised at the number of families with bags, obviously transferring at St. Pancras from other lines or coming from Heathrow, and still moving through the city via the underground rails. I watched one small tot rub his eyes and scrunch his nose in frustration, before turning to his mother for comfort.

I checked the departure screens for the train number scheduled to ultimately get me to Paris. Darkness filled the entrance wall that by day offered outside light from the floor-to-ceiling windows and glass doors. We walked through the undercroft. The piano player had already gone home for the day, but the coffee bar catered to the night owls.

"Remember the ski trip a few years ago?" I asked.

"Gosh that was awful." Cassie rolled her eyes. "Everyone had to get everything they needed on the train, but Eurostar doesn't do checked baggage. I never even thought about that when we made our plans."

"I'm sure our fellow passengers hadn't considered it either." Everyone on the train fought for overhead space, floor space, and every space in between. I vowed then if I ever took another European ski trip it would be via air, or I would ship my gear ahead of time. Claustrophobic memories aside, I always looked forward to seeing the Eurostar platform at St. Pancras. The station is a work of art on an architectural level, and I silently thanked Sir John Betjeman for doing his good public best that eventually meant the artistic landmark was saved for London and all future travelers. Eurostar's departure venue was a glorious mix of glass, steel and historical accouterments, a brilliant compilation of Victoriana and victorious twenty-first century that made the art historian in me want to sing every time I arrived on its doorstep.

We stood in the check-in area I found an attendant and a kiosk and gave my code to get a ticket. Passport at the ready whenever I needed, ticket in place, Prada strap in cross-body fashion, and a shopping bag in each hand, I was ready for boarding.

"Platform ten, according to the attendant." I raised one shopping bag to point. "This way."

Cassie grasped the handle of the bag in my left fist. "Let me carry this one."

"Okay, but the escalator isn't that far."

Cassie and I matched the pace of the rest of the crowd as we headed for the correct escalator and platform, fighting our desires to run and hide. We semi-attached ourselves to groups heading in the right direction to make our bodies appear less conspicuous to the probing cameras. I pulled the bill of the cap down a smidge closer to my brow.

We stopped at the bottom of the moving stairs. Enough passengers were already mingling that I felt comfortable saying goodbye to Cassie and getting her out of the station. If anyone was going to come after me now, I wanted her far away from a scuffle.

"Cassie, you've been a godsend tonight." I set the shopping bags on the ground and gave her a hug. "I could have never gotten here, with all my stuff, without you."

She shrugged, then craned her neck to review the waiting passengers. "I can't believe this many people travel in the middle of the night. At least there's safety in numbers." She stared straight into my eyes. "Be sure to get in the busiest car, and sit near a bunch of people."

"Yes, Mom," I said, striving for levity.

The edges of Cassie's lips turned downward. "This isn't funny, Laurel."

"I'm sorry." I brushed her shoulder with a hand. "I'll be careful, I promise. But your concern for me doesn't outweigh what I feel about your safety. I want you to head straight home. Right now. And text me when you get there. I may not have good phone coverage on the train, but even if I only have one bar I should be able to receive texts."

"Okay. Should we have code words?"

I would have made a joke about Austin Powers, but I could tell by the set of her jaw she needed me to keep things serious. "Not a bad idea. If you need help, call 999, of course, but text me the name of your first pet."

"Snowball. He was a bunny."

Of course he was.

"Snowball it is. And mine was a German shepherd named Bruno."

"Really? How old were you?"

I thought back to that wonderful dog, twice my size and as loveable as he was huge. He'd been trained as a guard dog, and my grandfather brought him into our household after a spate of kidnappings ran through the families in our financial circle. The pain I felt as a fourteen-year-old when we had to put Bruno down for arthritis was still too close to contemplate. Arthritis aggravated by a bullet he took once while pushing me out of harm's way. Even after all the intervening years, I could see the dark concern for me that showed in his eyes as he performed the act out of both love and duty. Grandfather hired a physical therapist trained to treat canines to get him back on his feet. It gave us a few extra years with him, but a few is never enough. "I was five when Grandfather brought him to me."

"A puppy?"

"No, full-grown. He went everywhere with me." My eyes focused on the near distance, and I could almost see Bruno standing guard, watching out for me still.

The squeal of a train pulling in above saved me. Passengers shuffled more quickly in anticipation of their own boarding.

"That's my cue, Cass," I said. "Gotta go. But I really do thank you for all your help today."

"No problem," she said, wringing her hands as she spoke. "I wish you could check your bags so you don't have to keep an eye on them too. Will shopping bags work? Maybe I should have packed everything into one of my suitcases."

"Nico has me in business class." I retrieved the second bag from her, after unwrapping the handle from her clinging fingers. We shared a goodbye hug. "I'll find a place to put them in the racks over my seat. No worries."

Another quick hug and we went our separate ways; me heading upward for the platform and Cassie, I hoped, grabbing a cab outside. I'm not normally leery of subways, but after being almost trapped by Weasel and Werewolf I wanted to make sure Cassie didn't suffer the same dilemma. She might not have a Jeremy nearby, whose foot she could trounce as a diversion.

By daylight, the St. Pancras platforms always made me feel like I was in a gorgeous giant birdcage with the sky pouring in through the never-ending skylights. By night, the fluorescents do their job, with the light reflecting back from the heavenly glass above.

Lit signs in English and French directed me to the area forming the queue for my train's business class. The timing could not have been closer. Within minutes, my Eurostar was shushing into view.

All bright and light, interior brown upholstery and brushed aluminum trim, I chose one of the comfortable reclining seats in the back corner and grabbed a complementary English paper. I took a window. Yes, I was boxing myself in. The aisle seat offered quick exit out of the door, but it also afforded anyone coming from either direction a clear shot at seeing me—and me of them. The business class car wasn't even half-full, so both shopping bags went into the seat beside me. Again, another barrier to my exit, but also a second visual stop before anyone looked at me. There was ample space above, but closing off access to the connecting seat not only meant I could keep an arm looped through the bag handles at all times, but dissuaded casual camaraderie from other passengers.

Doors closed and the speaker came on with instructions and information relayed in a lovely Parisian accent. Even the English words sounded beautiful. I pulled out lip balm and swabbed my lips to fight the drying air in the car. Right on time, the train eased out of St. Pancras and headed for Paris. Above ground now, we made our way past a couple of public estate complexes, and through miles of train cars waiting their turn for departure. Streetlights lit the area, but encroaching trees masked neighborhoods, giving most houses the allusion of privacy.

In a blink, I'd plugged my phone into one of the handy ports. Simon's laptop was tempting, just to see if I could get a heads-up on anything, but I was bleary eyed and didn't have the attention span at that point. Besides, Nico would do a much better job of unearthing its secrets than I. So the machine stayed safe and buried until I could pass it on. He said he was bringing a new toy. This way I'd be able to offer one in return.

I lowered the lens of my glasses to improve my vision and scan my fellow passengers. No one seemed especially keen on watching me, no quick movements when I glanced a different way. All seemed safe for the moment. I kept the cap pulled low and tried not to make eye contact. I wasn't just wary of others. This leg of the trip needed to be an opportunity to rest, not chitchat.

A rummage through my Prada unearthed a couple of luggage tags I used to close the bags at the handles and provide identification. From past experience, I knew Eurostar got snarky when you didn't have names on everything, and if my stuff ended up in overhead storage the bags definitely needed tagging. I've even used Beacham business cards before in a crunch, but didn't want to do so while attempting to dance through incognito this journey.

I worried over whether my picture would be flashed at security checkpoints. Until I knew how much clout Jack truly had, it was important to plan for the worst. At least I could pick my seat, which was one advantage to Eurostar's cattle car option.

By the time we cleared London's environs we were thundering along at just under one hundred ninety miles per hour. This little informational tidbit came via the nice French-accented attendant who wanted to know if I needed anything—I didn't. The train stopped at Ebbsfleet International to take on more passengers, but still no Nico. Again at Ashford, strangers boarded, but not my friend. I remembered both places from coverage during the London Olympics, since the sports venues were spaced so far apart. Surely Nico hadn't missed his own train after reading me the riot act about the itinerary.

The man in the aisle seat across had an app on his phone that told how fast we were going, and he continuously updated his seatmate on the current speed. I hoped the toy Nico promised was more interesting than that guy's. Finally, one of the blokes in the row ahead of him said, "Will you bloody well shut up about the train speed, mate?"

A man after my own heart.

My interested porter returned and offered to bring me a juice. I hadn't realized how thirsty I was until he mentioned it. The plan had called for breakfasting in Paris before grabbing up the rental car Nico promised for the next leg of the journey.

My personal Eurostar attendant returned with my juice and explained where the train's bar/buffet was in case he wasn't around when I needed something. I was pretty sure he was giving me special privileges, since I didn't have any breakfast service on this trip.

After a few more words of small talk, he glanced at my cap and touched his own. "From Chicago?" he asked in his lovely accented English.

"It's a friend's."

He smiled, nodded, then slipped out the back door. The paranoia in me rose again, wondering if he was reporting on the American blonde who wore her hair up in a Cubbies cap. Maybe I should have let someone sit beside me so I wouldn't stand out as a single traveler.

To tamp down the concern, I hit a few keystrokes to send a "Where are you?" alert to Nico's number. I hoped he'd answer soon. My nerves were stretched enough.

A second later, I got a text from Cassie saying she was safe in her flat. Well, I could strike off one worry at least.

We hit the Chunnel and rode underground in darkness for just under half an hour, but the cabin stayed bright and light. I dropped off asleep at some point and woke when the loudspeaker greeted us on arrival in Paris, first spoken in French, then English, and thanked us for traveling with Eurostar. The medical tech at the docks had warned me to have someone along to wake me throughout the night. Thank goodness I hadn't taken his advice, since what little sleep I had accomplished was well worth the risk.

For a second, I wondered where Jack was, and whether he had someone to wake him.

The multi-storied glass façade of the Gare du Nord was a welcome sight, and our train slid into one of Eurostar's upper story platforms. I waited until everyone else departed before moving into the little hallway that led to the exit. The platform was not as airy as St. Pancras but visitor-friendly just the same.

Signs noted taxis to my left and the Metro to my right. I stayed with the crowd, but kept distance between myself and others, while the cap rode low over my eyes. With stairs in my near future, I slipped off Cassie's reading glasses and put them in the Prada. No point in risking a broken neck. I walked with the shopping bags held loosely at each side in case I needed to move one way or the other in a hurry.

I was ready when a hand grasped my shoulder from behind.

FOURTEEN

Anger and adrenalin pumped through my body and instinct took over. I stuck out my foot, tightened the grip on my cargo and twirled, breaking my attacker's hold with the pivot and catching his mid-section with a roundhouse kick. The guy's backpack threw him off-center and helped complete his quick trip to the ground. Best of all, everything I carried stayed safely in the shopping bags. Not one item spilled. Even my Prada hardly swayed.

Then I got a good look at my attacker. His curly black hair. His angry dark eyes.

"Oops. Sorry, Nico." I crouched down and pulled him into a hug, supporting his shoulders as he doubled over and moaned. It's amazing how rage dissipates almost immediately when the person you've been looking for suddenly becomes the one you attacked. "I was beginning to really worry about you."

He smirked. "I can tell."

"Well, you did say you were going to make the trip with me. When you didn't show my angst increased." I shrugged and moved the shopping bags into one hand so I could help him back to his feet. "Besides, you should be grateful for small favors. I could have slammed you in the groin."

"Yes, all those small favors." He rolled his expressive eyes at me as I got him by the arm and hustled us toward the staircase.

Just like at St. Pancras, the Gare du Nord banishes shadows through use of skylights, in addition to all the wonderful window walls on the outside of the structure. From previous trips, I knew the rental car companies operated from the area located right below the Eurostar arrival zone.

"I assume picking up the rental car is our next destination," I said as my feet hit the next floor. "But I don't suppose we could squeeze breakfast in first. Food was in the itinerary after all."

"If you prefer train station food, that's entirely possible."

"It would give us the chance to exchange our gifts."

Nico stopped and turned toward me, raising both dark brows as he said, "I don't want another gift like the one you just gave me."

"Nah." I waved my hand. "My kicks come as a bonus."

He laughed and propelled me toward the bistro area. "Then by all means. Let us find some croissants and a café for each of us."

Ah, coffee. My drug of choice.

We soon had our own outside table in weak Parisian sunshine. We scooted the chairs close enough to gain privacy to talk, and we both ordered the same thing, *petit déjeuner français*. The croissant was flaky, the juice the best second *jus d'orange* of the day, and my cup of Americano hot and highly caffeinated. I reveled in my food. Horns sounded in the street and a stiffening breeze kept the morning crisp. Leaves fell with a sigh, people hurried by us, and I luxuriated in the ability to relax for just a moment.

"That hit the spot," I said. "Should hold me for a couple of hours."

Nico twisted to reach the backpack hanging on the other chair and looked inside for a few seconds. His hand came out with a flourish, and he grinned when he put something unexpected in my hand.

"Glasses?" Not even attractive ones at that. They kind of looked like safety glasses without a bottom rim. And there was a funky second window in the top of the right lens. I noticed the earpieces were wider than normal, as wide as the plastic rim across the top of the frames.

Nico opened the earpieces and slipped the glasses on my face. "Be impressed. These are prototypes. With a few modifications I added, of course. Have you heard of Google glasses?"

"Of course. But they aren't on sale anymore."

He grinned, leaning close to whisper, "You don't need their version. This pair I'm giving you does much more."

"What can they do besides make me look nerdy?"

"Allow me to demonstrate."

Step by step, Nico showed me the capabilities of the glasses. How I could unobtrusively shoot video while peering through the lenses. Why the tiny square in the upper right corner of the right lens was a secret weapon when I needed to know additional information. The way I could open stream what I was looking at, so Nico or anyone else could view it on their phones or a computer.

"Think about the implications for gathering evidence, and the ease of documenting it for later use," he waxed poetic. "With the modifications I've added, well, be prepared to be dazzled. When you need a heat or radiation detector, you are going to be glad you have Nico in your corner."

"I'm always glad you're in my corner. I just wish you could give me some snazzier looking glasses."

He threw up his hands, the Italian in him overrunning his emotions as he burst into a tirade. I couldn't understand half of what he said, it was a bit more colloquial than the social Italian I was used to using, but the gist was that I was ungrateful and should be happy people care enough to give me tools to help me.

I didn't punctuate his comment with the fact they still looked a little too nerdy to wear with any of my Vera Wang gowns.

"Give me the case and the glasses, Nico. I promise to use them anytime I need their special powers." I held out a hand. "But I can still use our patented method of my calling you and leaving the line open so you can hear what's going on if I feel I need backup, right? I don't have to just count on my Buzz Lightyear eyewear alone?"

Again with the Italian that I probably shouldn't have tried to translate, followed by, "Yes, you can still do the open line." He let out a really long sigh.

"Well, Christmas is early for you, too," I said, switching subjects and slipping the glasses into my Prada. From the nearest shopping bag, Simon's laptop appeared. The fake coral was the second item I grabbed.

Before I could tell him what I had, however, he pulled on the Prada and made another disparaging sound. "What is this? Did you drag this bag out the back of the Eurostar?"

"I'm afraid it's soon due for a hero's funeral. Maybe a Viking funeral, so we can set it ablaze to float out to sea." I rubbed the side of the Prada, much like one would a genie bottle. "The poor thing has truly done its duty in the last twelve hours. It faithfully bungeed along with me while we've been nearly abducted in the subway, kidnapped by the person I hurt to get me away from the abductors, chased several times while in taxis, shot at while in another cab, rescued by motorcycle after I hit the pavement during gunfire, and—"

"I get it. The purse should be retired with honors."

"Yes." I brushed the leather again. "But not today. It still has miles to go before it sleeps."

Nico gave me one of those glorious Gallic shrugs and pulled the laptop close. "Is this Simon's?"

"Got it in one guess." I opened the coral and slid the USB

drive his way. "And so is this. Has a few corrupted files on it, but it could be interesting. My friend Cassie copied what she could onto her personal computer. You remember, she works at the V and A. She's quietly researching the art objects you'll find in the photo array. What she recognized at first glance is detailed in a file she added to the drive."

"Looking for ringers or MIAs?"

"Both. Anything else she can come up with as well."

"Good idea."

"Have some more information that may be related." I went into detail on the tale Hawkes told me about the micro drive and the snuffbox, and the possibilities created when the courier was found dumped in an Italian alley.

Nico rubbed the thumb drive between his fingers like one would a comforting icon. I knew from past experience it was his way to engage his brain. I kept silent and waited. A sudden horn blast shook him out of his reverie.

"Have you told Max about any of this?"

"No."

"Does he know Simon is missing yet?"

"No."

"Does he know about Hawkes?"

"No."

He gave me a long look. "I understand your reasoning, but this is becoming quite a bit more than going in and scooping up some art object to take back to the foundation."

My cup had one more swallow of Americano tinting the bottom, and I took a second to drain that last drop. "You're probably right." I returned the cup to the table. "I recently had a variation of this discussion with Cassie. But I think you better understand why I hesitate. You know what happened in Italy, and what we're now concerned it means. You saw the bogus phone message that made me late for the rendezvous and likely would have been my undoing if Jack hadn't made my warning radar go up before and after I found the dead Greek. The talk about counterfeit art treasures tying to the snuffbox, something we had no need to believe is fake, is especially worrisome. And since the item came through Max's connections, it could be embarrassing as well."

"I will contact Max and see how things stand," Nico said. "If there is any hint the snuffbox was fake, he needs to double check all of his sources. If we try, it could mean stepping on some powerful toes."

"Good point," I said. And I liked the idea of him calling and giving the information first. Max would get angrier if I questioned his sources than if Nico asked.

A businessman at the next table handed another man his card, and that reminded me about Jack's bug. "Did you have a chance to work on the coat of arms I sent in the JPEG? I'd like to know if Hawkes is on the level about anything."

Nico blew out a long breath. "I've found he has pull in all the right places, or someone with power is backing him for some reason. I don't have any kind of full dossier yet, but..."

"Any criminal background?"

"The only thing I can confirm is his schooling. Rich prep school and Oxford. But I can't find money tied to his name. The lack of information alone is enough to let me know there's more to this than they want as common knowledge. I have a strong suspicion we're going to find a connection to some kind of counterintelligence when we do finally learn more."

I thought about what Jack had said about the queen, what I'd laughed at initially as hot air, and had to wonder. Aloud I said, "Keep on it, and let me know if you find anything disturbing. After comparing notes with Jack last night I can't know for sure these two jobs are connected, but he seems to think they are. While what he says made sense, I don't want to be lulled into a false sense of security or unnecessary fear. His hypothesis unnerved me a bit and felt like a ploy to get me to trust him. But when I asked for credentials he changed the subject again."

"So what about Simon. Do I tell Max when I talk to him?"

I shook my head. "We know what Simon would want me to do. It's been less than twenty-four hours. We need to keep quiet until we learn something." I stopped and held up a finger. "One more thing. Did you know he has a new girlfriend named Jane?"

Nico frowned. "You know I knew about the two of you, correct?"

"I would have been worried if you hadn't. Nothing gets past you."

"You have no idea," he said, then gave a shaky kind of laugh. I almost asked what he meant, but he spoke before I had the chance. "I will see what I can discover. Do you have a last name for this woman?"

I thought about Jack's smart-mouth remark when he thought I was interested in the information. "No, I didn't ask. Just Jane. She's a blonde."

He waved a hand. "No matter. I will find out what we need to know." When he finished, he stood and motioned for me to go with him. "We will go pick up the car. If we pass a store selling purses or luggage, we should go in and pick up something nice for you to use."

"What, you don't like my bag lady look?" I asked, holding the handles of the shopping bags to shoulder height.

"Paris is a good location to make a change to current styles. Milan would have better options, naturally, had we known. But we haven't time for the side trip back again."

I shrugged. "Well, since I have some extra room on my credit card now..."

"Then let us go." Nico swept an arm over his head and

pointed toward the rental car cubbies. He gave me a broad smile. "We have places to go, a volcano to climb, and bad guys to beat."

"Is it me, or does that sound slightly ominous?"

Nico laughed and pushed me toward the shops. "Go find a new purse and luggage. I'll go now and get the rental car to meet you out front. I have to leave you on your own at Puy, but I can be sure you get there."

"Thanks, Nico."

I watched his gorgeous dark curls disappear in the crowd, then turned to follow orders.

While renting a car is never a quick and easy experience, after a half hour of waiting out front for Nico I was sick of watching the Paris street life. I called Cassie, who didn't answer. I didn't have much to say, but Nico wasn't answering his cell and I needed a distraction. Antsy didn't describe the way I felt. I wanted to get to the Puy de Dôme region, and I wanted to get there sooner rather than later.

No way I wanted to use this downtime to process. There was still too much to do and too many unanswered questions to spend time checking in with my inner self. I glanced at my watch for the hundredth time. What the hell took this long to rent a damn car?

I walked outside again and set down my new Louis Vuitton duffle. Nico was right, the shopping bags had to go, and since Max was footing the bill, and the designer bag was available, I really had no choice but to buy. I patted my Prada. The purse stayed for now. Something told me it was my lucky charm. Call me superstitious, but this job had already gone sideways too many times to take any extra risks.

Clouds had moved in over the brief sunshine at breakfast, and the weather turned miserable. I shivered in misty rain. I watched the street, busy with early workers going about their business, not paying them much attention because my eyes returned again and again to an Aston Martin DB5 Silver Fox parked illegally at the curb. No street patrol in the world would give this baby a ticket, much less a tow job.

Bond's favorite car. I looked around almost expecting to see a 1960s-era Sean Connery heading my way, but secretly knowing I'd probably end up with Pierce Brosnan or Daniel Craig instead. Not that I thought Brosnan or Craig were slackers or anything, but Connery's slightly manufactured accent could wring a sexual response from a dead woman.

I walked to the car and ran my hand over the perfect paint job, greedily cataloguing every remarkable feature. All worldly concerns fell away as I indulged my addiction for the pleasures of heavy metal in the flesh, not over the airwaves. I swear I had goose bumps.

"Need a ride?"

I froze.

Of course. My favorite Southern Brit-Wit. Why was I not surprised? Lose concentration for a moment and a girl could be stabbed, shot or stalked. All thoughts of the car of my dreams faded into the mist. I slowly turned.

Wearing a pair of jeans and a thin leather jacket, he leaned against the building as though he'd been posing there for hours. I could see the job description in my mind. Male model wanted. Strong, silent type. Photo shoot, streets of Paris, early morning. Only black-haired men with a penchant for stalking blondes need apply. Ability to appear and disappear out of nowhere preferred.

Did the man have nothing better to do than torment me? How? Why?

"How the hell did you find me? Did you ping my phone again?"

He grinned and gave me a half-shrug.

"I'm waiting for someone," I said, and pulled out my phone as it rang.

"I sent him on his way."

"Excuse me? Nico would never leave without notifying me first." I gave him my back and answered the call. It was Nico.

"Go with him."

"Why?"

"I talked to Max. He already knows about Hawkes and says we need to work with him. Max also gave me a new assignment that takes me back to Italy, to follow up on the provenance of the snuffbox."

We ended the call, and I turned to go to the car rental area. Jack was by my side in an instant.

"Get away from me, Hawkes. I need to rent a car."

"Not happening. We have work to do, and there's no time like the present." He took my arm and circled me back toward the street, then clicked a fob and the car beeped an inviting entry.

"If I know your shoe size, I definitely know you're a car nut, this particular model being in your top five," he leaned over to whisper mockingly in my ear.

"It is my top five," I admitted. "What are you doing here, Jack?"

"We need to talk, and there's no time like the present. I'll see you get where you need to go. Trust me."

There's that word. Such a tiny word for such a tall task. "It would be quicker for you to take a train."

"Like you, I want to have my own car when I get to where we're going. It's not that much longer to drive yourself. I've taken care of everything."

"Including Nico." I'd long known to follow my instincts when any risk was involved. And risk was really getting to be the story of my life. My gut told me Nico was right, but it still bothered me Hawkes wouldn't just admit to me he was MI-5 or MI-6 if that was the truth. I was supposed to trust him, but he didn't trust me? "I need to call my boss."

"You already know what he's going to say." He opened the car door and the lovely smell of new car mingled with exhaust and freshly baked baguettes.

I couldn't wait to get inside, but— "I'm damp from standing out here. I can't bear the thought of messing up this beauty."

Jack's laugh indicated he understood my reluctance and made me like him just a teeny bit. "No worries. The seats are specially designed leather, able to manage one slightly wet American woman."

Gripping the Prada tightly, I slid into the decadent luxury of the well-designed interior and let myself indulge the fantasy. "Do I have to hold my duffle in my lap or will it go in the trunk?"

His smile couldn't get more Connery. He grabbed the bag's handles and said, "I'll find room for it in the boot."

As he stepped around the car my phone buzzed with a text from Nico. *Don't worry. I have electronic eyes and ears on you.*

I wasn't sure what he meant exactly, but putting my trust in Nico and his gizmos had become second nature to me. The thought that he'd probably bugged Hawkes made me smile. The phone went back in the Prada. Jack opened the driver side door, turned on the engine, and music floated from the speakers.

We hadn't been on the road for more than an hour, with a few more to go, when he turned off the emotionally intense, deeply romantic Rachmaninoff *Concerto No. 2.* I groaned in protest. It was getting to the best part.

"Sorry about that. There's something you need to know."

Immediately the comfort zone I'd been enjoying

disappeared, and every muscle in my body tensed. How I hated the word *need*. Its use never preceded anything good. *Laurel, you need to eat your peas. Laurel, you need to finish your homework. Laurel, you need to be a good girl* was my all-time favorite. How did being a good girl help anyone? Men are taught, "Nice guys finish last," and we're told, "You'd better be a good girl." The whole thing reeked of centuries of male manipulation to keep the little woman pregnant and barefoot.

The windshield wipers silently moved back and forth as I concentrated on the damp countryside. "What's up?"

"Someone messed up and information got twisted." His voice was grim.

I pushed forward on the seat and turned to him. "Jones said Puy de Dôme. I heard him and I know you did too. It ties to one of the properties Moran has."

He wisely ignored the rhetorical question. "Someone spread the wrong info deliberately. Or Jones was giving us bad information in his almost-dying state. It's being investigated, but we'll probably never know what happened."

Code for "someone high up deliberately put out the wrong word." What the hell was going on?

"Are you going to tell me or do we have to play twenty questions?" I slumped back in my seat and felt like I'd let the car down with my bad posture.

"Point taken, Ms. Beacham. Moran's place isn't at Puy de Dôme. It's located at Le Puy-en-Velay."

"Le Puy-en-Velay?" I struggled and spoke slowly, but of course I butchered the pronunciation. So who told Simon the info on Puy de Dôme that was in the digital file I opened? Or did someone besides Simon touch the file?

"It's a not so big town in the area of Massif Central."

He might as well have been speaking French. Massive Central? What was that? I wasn't going to ask. I pulled out my phone and typed Massif Central into Google. "So that's where we're headed?"

We were still going to the same region, I learned, an area filled with mountainous regions, thick forests, and even a volcano or two. The zone was the oldest geological part of France, located in the middle of the southern region. I'd already expected a four hour trip from Paris, but once I checked internet maps on the new location I learned our destination was a little more than an hour farther.

"Yes. There's more," Jack said. "Do you want it now or later?"

I seriously considered waiting till we were closer, to go back to the relaxing music instead. It was the 'one more thing scenario' where you know you're going to scream if one more item is added to your mile-long task list. Curiosity and the drive to solve led me to say, "Now."

"As you can imagine, the intel has been flying fast and furious in all directions. Two items have appeared again and again."

Another dramatic pause. Was he trying to drive me out of my mind?

"This girl hasn't got all day, Jack." Well, I did. But who dealt in actual reality anymore? "Spit it out."

"Le Puy-en-Valey has a cathedral—"

"I can't imagine a French town without one or two. Get to the point." I kept flipping my phone screen to get more detail ahead of his words.

Jack ignored me. "Contained in the Cathedral of Notre-Dame du Puy are the *Black Virgin* and within its *Chappelle des Reliques* is a painting called *The Seven Liberal Arts*. They've been indicated as containing possible clues pointing to whatever Moran is up to now and how to locate him in the short term."

"Did this come from the people with the good information

or the bad information?"

"From reliable information." He cocked an eyebrow at me as an obvious acknowledgment of my sarcasm, then returned his gaze to the road and said, "Those locations will lead us to a means of locating Moran's property, and he is known to be currently in the area."

And Moran led to Simon and Simon led to the sword and so on and so on.

"Did the information say how—?"

"No. The chat is scanty at best. No real address, but estates in that area tend to more often have a name rather than a street location, or in addition to the address. Either way, anyone local would know the place by its provincial ties, and we don't have that information. The connection to the cathedral is all we have to go on."

"I'm assuming no one can find Moran's name in any of the local title records."

"You assume correctly."

My mind tripped into gear. I was tired of squinting at the small print on the screen, and I didn't want to enlarge it and let Jack see what I was doing. From the Prada, I dug out my old-fashioned guidebook, its pages marked with notes and torn with use. I could always depend on it not to let me down, unlike most everything else in my life. Gadgets and the 'Net were great, but poring over a guidebook and reading recommendations and information from someone who had been there and noted exactly what I wanted to know in brief form, took me exactly where I wanted to go every time. Before I dropped the phone back in the bag, I also took the opportunity to text Nico a few extras I was going to need at the other end. Just because he farmed me out to Jack so he could start on his next adventure didn't mean he was off-duty as far as I was concerned.

If Jack said anything more, I didn't hear him as I studied

the book. I eventually noted Rachmaninoff had been switched to Rammstein, a heavy metal German band that fitted my mood perfectly. No time for romantic moodiness, it was back to business as usual. Before returning to my book, my head full of pictures of ancient pilgrimages and religious icons, I noted indifferently the rain had increased. I also wondered how the hell the historic items on the pages were connected to murder and the mythical sword of King Arthur.

FIFTEEN

The hotel in the Auvergne region of France was tiny, tucked away in a valley under the arm of one of the surrounding mountains, a charming place to lose oneself and let time drift away on a tide of croissants, plentiful farm butter and strong creamy coffee.

Morning had disappeared already in the Paris arrival and the drive to our target area. Now checked in and trying to get comfortable in our allotted space, I followed Jack and the concierge, Madame Sorya.

"But please, call me Rosie," she told us, beautifully rolling her r's.

Rosie was silver-haired and appeared as practical as her no nonsense straight woolen skirt and cardigan twinset, but she showed her true personality with the brilliant lapis lazuli around her throat and at her ears. She kept up a running dialogue as we climbed the winding stairs to a room, making a promise of bouillabaisse for dinner, one of the few words she said in her nasally French that I could truly understand the first time I heard it. She unlocked the door before handing Jack the key and stepped back, murmuring something about enjoying our stay, I think. No promises on that front until I saw how well the détente between Jack and I held.

Jack, sensing my silent simmer, politely pushed me into the room and closed the door. "This is a great place. Food and sleep, the perfect prescription for a lovely vacation."

"I should never have let you shanghai me at Gare du Nord."
I walked over to the window and took in the blue skies and
rolling mountainside. "Nico reserved a car for me. I should have
made sure I got it. Now you have control of the steering wheel
and my free will while we're here. Don't think I'm going to ever
get happy about a practice like that, Jack."

He slid the room key into the pocket I knew also held the
car key. "We're going to the same places. What's the harm?"

"The harm is you've taken control. Left to my own devices
I'd probably be at Le Puy by now. We need to push on. We've got
to find Moran."

"Left to your own devices, you wouldn't have known about
the intel correction," Jack reminded. "Don't get concerned—"

"Then give me the keys." I held out my hand.

"What?"

"Those little metal things in your pocket." I snapped my
fingers. "Let me be keeper of the keys, then I won't be
concerned."

"But I'm the driver of record. And it's an Aston Martin."

I scooped up my phone. "One phone call, and I can get
another rental delivered to this hotel."

It was a stalemate, and he knew it. I held up the phone, and
he shoved hands into both pockets of his jeans.

I blinked first and turned away, hurled my phone on the
bed, then tossed the rest of my gear onto the folded afghan at
the foot of the blue chenille bedcover.

He remained in the doorway, all Mr. Calm. "We've been
pushing hard for over twenty-four hours. We both need rest,
food and time to figure out exactly how we want to proceed."

"I got a good catnap on the Chunnel train," I said. "That's
what we pros do. We multi-task whenever an opportunity
presents itself."

We needed to go to neutral corners or I was afraid I would

explode, and anger achieved nothing unless I wanted to give him the chance to know more about me on a personal level. Nope, never good. He already knew too much.

Those teal eyes of his held a wealth of sincerity, earnestness and sheer determination as they stared into mine. He should have been on the stage.

He looked at his watch. "I'm afraid I have an errand I must make. I swear I will be back soon. It is a prior commitment, you understand? We will go together to Le Puy. You know when we talked we agreed two are better than one on this, since so many things have gone wrong."

Nice euphemism for murder in the plural.

"If two are better than one, why am I not going with you? Maybe you or I have become the next target. Isn't splitting up a way to make murdering one of us easier?"

Jack left his post near the door and approached me, putting his hands on my shoulders. The grip of his fingers felt strong, powerful and sure. "I don't think either of us is in danger at this moment. I doubt if anyone knows where we are or that we're even together. Except for Nico."

He sighed in such a heartfelt way I almost felt sorry for him. Schmuck.

In his 'trust me' voice, he continued, "I know you're used to doing things your own way, and you've been really successful. I, too, am used to working on my own, but I'm ready to attempt this temporary partnership. Will you at least try to trust me?"

I remained motionless and stared up at him. Something uneasy and strange was happening. If I didn't know better, I'd say that somewhere deep inside I wanted to trust him.

For my eighth birthday, my father had promised to take me to the zoo. He had shown up hours too late, and even at eight years old I'd recognized he'd been drinking. The last time I'd fully believed a man meant what he said.

I wasn't sure I was ready to break the trend now. I'd learned long ago to go my own way and make my own decisions. But I wasn't sure I wanted Jack to know that. Time to play along and let events take their own nosedives.

"I will try to trust you. It's difficult." I pulled away. Pushing my things to one side, I sat on the bed. "I agree food and sleep are important, but only for me? Where are you going and what's so vital?"

None of it was any of my business, I knew, but if one didn't ask one lost the only opportunity to find out.

"Geneva," he said. "It's a short distance from here. I have a prior commitment I must meet. I'll return in a few hours. We'll make Le Puy by ten tomorrow morning. I see no reason for us to get there earlier—"

"Tomorrow?" All thought of remaining calm flew away in an instant. "Because Nico booked me here, we're still more than an hour away from Le Puy and it's nearly noon. Even if we do take some time to rest and leave later this afternoon that could still put us there by early evening. I don't want to wait until tomorrow. When Max gave me this assignment, he said it had to be accomplished in two days. Yesterday was day one, and today is day two."

"And that assigned timetable was when you were supposed to meet Simon and do little more than play mule to get the sword back to the States. Things have changed, Laurel, and our plans must change as well."

I hadn't realized I'd risen and assumed the classic Wonder Woman pose, but I could feel the testosterone channeling through my veins. "I want this finished now, Hawkes. Have you forgotten Simon? We don't have time for surprise side trips. If you think your business is more important than a man's life, I think this temporary partnership is *permanently dissolved*."

His gaze remained calm and watchful. "I've forgotten

nothing, Laurel. I know you're worried about your friend, but I must insist we slow down and take time to think everything through. While I don't feel we're in any particular danger here, I don't want to rush into something until I'm sure. Until *we're* sure," he said, emphasizing the "we're" as though I had any power in this one-sided arrangement, "that we won't be adding to the final body count because we didn't practice caution."

No sense in digging a hole next to the ocean. It'll just fill up with more water.

I looked down at the floor and cleared my expression, deliberately relaxing my muscles of all anger before looking him dead in the eye. "Of course, what you're saying makes perfect sense. You're right, my emotional involvement with Simon is affecting my professional decisions. Thank you for the timely reminder."

I stretched out on the bed, closing my eyes. "I know you drove and did all the work, but you're right, I'm pooped—too tired even to shower. Hope things go well in Geneva. Maybe see you in time for dinner?"

Silence. The old-fashioned clock on the table next to me slowly clicked away the seconds as he stood there. Maybe I had acquiesced too soon, but what did it really matter? The result would still be the same. He would go to Geneva no matter what my argument, and I would be happily stranded at this "great place."

I kicked off my shoes, and their landing *clunk* sounded loud in the room.

His voice was soft when he said, "Don't wait too long to eat, Laurel. You're looking a little peaked. I should return in time for dinner. Why don't we plan for seven?"

"Whatever you say." I even managed to slur my words a little as I pulled the delicate afghan up and over my legs with my big toe.

The quiet latching of the door signaled his departure. I stayed still, waiting for his next move. His reasoning might have been sound, but I couldn't trust him when he changed plans so unilaterally. Although my body was cold and achy in the certain way that showed it needed rest, sleep offered no temptation. My mind raced at a hundred miles an hour. There was positively no way was I waiting until tomorrow to get to Le Puy.

What the hell was he doing in Geneva? Not that I would ever know. All I knew at the moment was I needed to get to Le Puy-en-Velay and check out the cathedral. I didn't know exactly what I was looking for, but that was the next stop in my travelogue for this job. Whatever was or was not happening between Jack and I didn't change the facts of this operation. It was time to regroup and regain a lead. I could sleep later.

I'd hoped for a text from Nico by now, but my phone remained message free. I pulled Hawkes's phone from my bra. Gerry might stink as a pickpocket, but his teaching skills were brilliant. With Jack's hands on my shoulders, and his mind focused on the speech he delivered so persuasively, there had been plenty of time for me to swipe his phone from his jacket pocket.

I scanned his message menu but the paranoid bastard apparently deleted his messages regularly. I texted Nico and reminded what I needed ASAP. He wouldn't appreciate the additional prodding, but I didn't have any extra time. Who knew when Jack might return, and I wanted to be gone long before then.

A search of our bags uncovered Jack's bugging paraphernalia, and for a moment I couldn't help appreciating his inventiveness. While despising his methods at the same time. Whatever his game, he played it too close to the chest. We were partners. Sure.

I grabbed my daypack, stuffed in the necessary items for a

few days, and stored the rest in the ancient wardrobe. I laid Jack's bugs on top to make sure they were the first things he saw upon his return. If there was a return.

I checked that the door was locked and took a quick shower, carrying everything important with me into the en suite. Though I was only booked in the room for the night, I left enough money to pay for at least a week in an envelope addressed to the concierge on the highly polished dresser, with a note to please hold my belongings for later pickup. Hopefully the extra cash would keep my stuff from being tossed.

Before I left, I looked around the room with its generous rose-colored recliner complete with quilt and a window view of the mountains, and knew at any other time I would have enjoyed staying here...shades of Lake Tahoe and the vacation I still deserved. A bit regretfully, I pulled the door closed and crept down the stairs. I stopped by the kitchen and asked for a portable lunch as though going for a long hike.

The cook and his helper provided me with a cup of the delicious coffee only the French could make, liberally dousing the black richness with the thick farm cream I denied myself when in the States. The helper handed me the wrapped sandwiches and fruit. Thanking them both, I then stuffed the sandwiches in my crowded pack to the accompaniment of tongue clicking, scolding and sighs.

"Even smashed it will taste good," I insisted. I did my best to ask for simple directions, and they reciprocated with a lot of hand gestures. I pushed in the two bottles of water, wedging them past the sandwiches and into rolled t-shirts. Between my rusty French, the men's broken English, and a lot of hand waving, I learned how to find the nearest town. I said my thanks and stepped through the back door, almost getting knocked down by a large, undeterminable breed of dog who rushed past me and set off a cacophony of banging pots and shouts.

The marked winding drive headed toward the quiet street. The flowerbeds were overgrown yet attractive with fading varieties of flowers. The grounds glowed with green life, and the surrounding vineyards burst with fall fruits. I knew from my guidebook the Massif Central area of Auvergne had four departments, and I was in the Haute-Loire. My objective was Brioude, a town large enough to get me to the next stop in my journey, with a bus route to Le Puy.

It was cool, and I was grateful for my jacket and jeans. The overcast sky matched my mood. I turned on my iPod and blasted my anxious mind with Nirvana, System of a Down, Pearl Jam and Sheryl Crow, and tried to focus on the task ahead. Road traffic was spotty. I caught a ride in a tiny Citroen, but had to be dropped off by the couple when their plans took them left and I needed to go right.

I'd walked about a mile and was turning the corner on the deserted road when I became aware of another sound growing in volume over my music. The sound of a motor. I removed the ear buds to see if I could get another ride.

The slight sound turned quickly into a loud roaring. Out of nowhere, a motorcycle hurtled my way. Not a little crotch-rocket, but a heavy, ugly-looking monster, traveling my direction and going way too fast.

I needed to get off the road. I ran into the grass, heading toward a fence. A fence meant people didn't it?

The bike kept coming. My pack felt like lead weight on my back, but I wasn't about to let it go. I shot a glimpse behind, and I saw the cycle leave the road and barrel toward me. The driver was helmeted and unrecognizable, a big thug of a man. Or a very large woman.

I couldn't see the brand of bike, just a nasty mechanized weapon coming straight for me.

SIXTEEN

I hit the linked fence, thankful it wasn't barbed wire, and leaped over. If he tried to breach the fence, would the thin wire stop him?

Over the deafening roar of the bike came a louder report, followed by a burning pain in my right arm. I kept running without bothering to look down. There was another shot, and a bullet passed close enough to my ear for me to hear its whistle. What the hell was I going to do?

I was being used for target practice with no way to fight back. Instinct reminded me to start weaving. Fear helped increase my speed. Several more bullets zipped by, but over the sound of those I suddenly heard a honking car.

The motorcycle revved loudly, but the shots stopped. A quick glance showed the cycle retreat in a flurry of dirt, grass and rock, barely making a fast sharp curve to head back the way it had come. I ceased running, fighting to get enough air in my lungs.

The honking stopped. An older man, wearing one of those textured hats with a small bill that looks like a Greek fisherman's cap, exited the car and called out in a strong baritone, "*Mademoiselle, êtes-vous blésée?*"

My legs gave way, and I landed right where I stood. My upper arm burned but I didn't want to look. Instead, I took several deep steadying breaths, trying to get some oxygen into my system and slow my heart rate. The crisis was over. If I just had enough strength to walk back. I survived thanks to the old guy now walking my way.

He stopped on his side of the fence and repeated the question. "I'm okay," I replied, my voice a bit shaky. I held up one finger. "Give me a minute, please."

He politely waited until I could get to my feet. I walked warily toward him. Adrenalin was still coursing through me, and I had a new sense of suspicion. I reminded myself it was his action that stopped the person from shooting at me, but after all the switches lately it could also be a ploy to get me into the car. I halted a few feet away from the fence. He began talking nonstop in French, and wearily I shook my head. "American. I only speak English, and very bad French."

He frowned and said, "I will take to you to hospital."

"I'm okay. I don't need a hospital."

A hospital in France would likely have the same requirements as one in the States when someone came in with an obvious gunshot wound. With England the last stamp on my passport, I didn't need my name and newest agenda to get back to Scotland Yard. Someone there would undoubtedly want me to come back for an interview given our little midnight adventure on the docks and this latest gunplay. Any good policeman would assume they were related.

"But you are bleeding, *mademoiselle*."

I knew I couldn't avoid looking any longer. The wound wasn't good, but it wasn't as bad as it felt either. The bullet grazed my skin, but for now I could hold off with stitches if I soon got it bandaged tightly. Another jacket ruined, too. There was a big tear and blood pretty much covered my sleeve. An additional rend on the side caused the material to dangle down past my knee.

The Frenchman pointed to my back. Twisting, I saw it was

torn as well. Probably from the fence. Thank goodness I'd worn leather. I returned my gaze to my arm, which continued to drip blood.

"Not just your arm." He pointed to my face. "There."

I touched the side of my face and found he was right. A narrow abrasion surfaced a little ways beneath my chin. No idea how I'd received that one.

"Please come with me, *mademoiselle*. My late wife, she would have had words to say to me if she saw me keeping you here, standing and talking rather than helping you. My name is Philippe Aubertine."

I figured if he was going to discuss his late wife with a total stranger, he couldn't be too bad. "I'm Laurel Beacham."

I didn't bother to lie. If he was a dangerous guy, he already knew who I was. If he was a good guy, what did it matter to him who I was? The reasoning seemed sound enough for me to head for the fence, and I didn't feel too steady on my feet anymore either. He held the top wire up and helped me through. When he tried to carry my pack we had a little tussle, but he finally understood I wouldn't let it go and assisted me up the verge to his car.

He muttered something under his breath about crazy cyclists. Before loading me into the front passenger seat, he politely insisted on checking my back for injury. I dropped my pack and stripped off the jacket, doing my best to keep my damaged arm from him. I didn't want to argue with him again about a hospital.

His survey apparently revealed no blood or rip on the shirt. He took a bag from his trunk and I shoved the ruined coat inside. A beautifully laundered handkerchief smelling of lavender was placed into my hands. I pushed it against my arm and worked at not wincing. He helped me onto the seat. I placed the pack and the bag at my feet. He carefully closed the door.

I swiped at my chin before reapplying the originally bright white, now red, linen to my arm. My grimace couldn't be held back this time at both ruining the lovely material and the pain of the wound. I did my best to mop up the blood. Although I had ruined his hankie, I didn't want to ruin his upholstery, too.

Using most of a water bottle and his handkerchief, I cleaned up better than expected. To avoid shock, I also forced myself to choke down one of the sandwiches, thinly sliced beef on thick hearty bread that would have normally made my mouth water. Although the food tasted like chalk in my mouth, I knew I needed the sugar and the calories. The adrenalin dissipation had begun. I offered the other sandwich to my rescuer, but he declined with a polite smile.

We arrived at the town of Brioude. He insisted I needed medical help. A short discussion ensued regarding his wants and mine. I made a veiled reference to the incident and made him think someone, probably an abusive boyfriend, was after me. I finally convinced him I was all right due to his help and his handkerchief. He insisted I keep the handkerchief, and I insisted I really needed to get out of town.

"I promise. I'll get medical attention in Le Puy," I said.

Finally, he agreed and pointed to where I could get bus transportation. I pushed euros his way, but he refused to accept anything for the ride or the handkerchief and tipped his hat to me as he drove away.

Not surprising, my hands still shook, but I needed to start moving. I'd wanted to be out of the car but felt slightly bereft, as though I had lost my safe place. I pushed away the feeling and stuffed the bag holding my ruined coat into a trash bin. At least it was still fairly early in the afternoon, and I wouldn't miss the warmth too much.

My jacket might not have made it, but I had, and so had my shirt, except for a small drop of blood in the ribbing around the collar. I dug in my pack and found a long-sleeved black tee to pull on over the short-sleeved one. If the wound started bleeding again, I hoped the black color would cover it up a bit.

I heard a lot of noise coming from the direction the man indicated. I turned the corner and found myself in the midst of a mass of people crowded around several buses and an ancient building I assumed was a depot of some kind. I saw no sign indicating the building's purpose, but swarms of people surrounded the place, along with all their packs, bags and duffles. This looked like my way out of the area. I was surprised so many people were heading in the same direction, but Nico had mentioned events in the area as the reason he could only find a place for one night. With a murderous motorcyclist after me, I had little desire to return. With luck I would find the sword and rescue Simon, and we would be on our way back to London by nightfall.

Readjusting my pack, I pushed my way through the throng to find a door. A lot of shouting and good-natured jostling filled the space. My ears picked up something about costumes and contests and what sounded like a retelling of what happened the previous year. It was a struggle to separate one conversation from the group. I definitely should have paid more attention in French class.

I maneuvered through the open doorway and fought through the noisy backpackers, trying to reach the service desk. I kept a sharp eye peeled for anyone who seemed out of place. As well as anyone who seemed out of place and with grab-happy hands.

By accident, I happened across a queue. I didn't recognize the line for what it was because there was little forward movement. I kept in place until we finally reached a desk of some sort, where an obviously suffering man sat, smoking a gitane while sorting, stamping, and counting euros.

Ten more minutes passed before I was able to maneuver my way back to what appeared to be the end of the queue. Within seconds, seven more people filed in behind me. This must be the right place.

Again, I cursed my interest in my biology lab partner the two semesters I took French. In fact, some might say a little knowledge was a dangerous commodity in a place known for its people's fierce national pride.

Fortunately, the guy in front of me took pity on my feeble attempts to communicate with the uncooperative person behind me, and interrupted my struggles at trying to be understood. He touched my arm and shouted over the din, "I speak English."

I found myself looking up into a pair of deep brown eyes. He was about a head taller than me, with a casual air that said young and carefree. His brown hair was pulled into a low ponytail, a style which tugged at the romantic in me. I read curiosity and admiration in his eyes, too. Good. I could use those to my advantage.

I took a deep breath and projected my voice to be heard over the noise. "Thank God. I fear two semesters of college French didn't prepare me for the real world. The only thing I really learned in class was I didn't have an ear for languages. A great disappointment to my grandfather's plans for my future."

He smiled. "I too have a disappointed grandfather who is very angry that I left him alone in our shop during this very busy time of the year. As he put it, 'to waste time playing children's games.'"

I returned his smile with interest, and his features relaxed into the face of a man who knows he has struck gold.

"I read about Le Puy-en-Velay in my guidebook." I pointed to the ancient and battered copy of *Let's Go, France* I held in my hand. Then I stretched the truth a bit. "And I decided to visit. But I somehow missed it was such a popular site." I motioned at the surging throng of humanity surrounding us. "What's going on here anyway?"

He laughed, showing off beautiful white teeth. "I'm afraid you managed to pick one of the busiest times of the year to visit Le Puy-en-Velay. It's the *Fêtes Renaissance du Roi de l'Oiseau*. The whole area celebrates."

At my puzzled look, he explained. "It literally means, the 'Renaissance Festival of the King of the Bird.' In the sixteenth century, it began as a competition to pick the best archer of the region. The celebration today has become a way to return to the past." He smiled. "And a reason to party and act the fool. I'm Rollie," he said, offering his hand and holding mine for a beat too long.

I finally pulled away to adjust my pack unnecessarily. I didn't particularly plan to mislead him, but his interest was exactly what I could use to help me quickly learn about Le Puy-en-Velay.

He went on to explain about the annual celebrations, the stores, the craft booths and entertainments associated with the Renaissance such as acrobats and dancing bears, and a horse riding competition called "King of the Bird."

Rollie stopped talking as we finally reached the ticket counter. He stepped aside and waited for me to deal with the attendant. I tried muddling through my terrible schoolgirl French to explain my need to purchase a ticket. The girl behind me sighed loudly and made what sounded like a rude remark about *stupide Anglaise* to her friends.

The ticket master apparently spoke only French, and rattled off a rapid spate of words that sounded like he was consigning me to the devil.

"I need a ticket to Le Puy-en-Velay," I repeated several times in English and attempted fractured French, "*J'ai a bi—*"

Rollie jumped to my rescue, and said, "*Mademoiselle

besoin d'acheter un billet pour Le Puy-en-Velay."

The clerk again shook his head and rattled off another series of words that apparently meant 'no way on earth,' and for emphasis shook his head again.

Rollie turned to me, disappointment evident in his dark eyes. "There are no more tickets for this bus. You will have to wait for the next one."

SEVENTEEN

Oh, no. No way. I was not going to wait around for another bus. "Didn't you just buy your ticket?" I asked Rollie.

"No. I purchased mine many weeks ago," he said.

"Rollie, I'm willing to buy a ticket from anyone to get on this bus. Would you ask around and see if someone wants to make some money by selling me their ticket and waiting for the next bus?"

"If it is that important to you, I will gladly offer you my ticket and I will wait."

I didn't want to buy his ticket. I wanted him with me to help get me where I needed without further mishap or misunderstanding. Gallant I didn't need. "Did I misunderstand? I was looking forward to riding on the bus with you."

His eyes smiled before his mouth did. "As was I. But—"

"I'm willing to pay extra to compensate anyone willing to wait for the next bus."

A sullen voice spoke from behind. "I will sell for three times the cost."

It was the bitch behind me, the one who had pretended she spoke little or no English.

She and Rollie argued over an inflated amount. The clerk waded into the fray, yelling and gesturing for us to move out of the line. The people directly around us caught onto the drama and threw out their opinions and proposals. I ignored everyone and concentrated on the task. The woman's extortion was outrageous, but I wanted to get to Le Puy now, not later. I was ready to pay what she wanted, but I didn't want to draw attention to the fact I was willing to go beyond her first offer.

"Three times," she said, stubbornly. "I will take nothing less."

Rollie's indignation rose in volume as her friends' voices died down, obviously recognizing she meant business. I pulled out a group of euros and quickly counted out the money before glancing at her again. "If you wish to count it, I want to see your ticket."

Grudgingly, she pulled the ticket from her pocket and held it out. Rollie looked it over and confirmed the authenticity. I counted the right amount and held it out to her. "So we have a deal? Your ticket for these euros?"

"Yes, yes, we have a deal." She thrust her ticket at Rollie.

The transaction completed, I held out my ticket to be stamped. With a flourish, the clerk did so, saying something about time and waving his arm for us to be on our way.

Before we pushed our way through the crowd, Rollie asked if I needed food. I shook my head and indicated my pack. Then he did something I noticed French men doing many times in my work and travels for the foundation. He nodded and held out his hand. I took it and he gracefully opened up a path through the throngs of people, exchanging pleasantries all around. There was much back-clapping and greetings. He had most definitely attended this festival before.

The bus had not started loading people, only bags people wanted stored below. There were several benches scattered around, all taken, and the sun hid behind a cloud. I rubbed my arms, chilly once more.

He noticed my shiver and smiled. "September." He

shrugged. "It begins the cooling. Some days like summer, but others warn us of the coming winter. I would offer you my jacket, but it is gone already into the bus." He pointed to the man loading duffle bags into the cargo hold. "I can offer you my arm, very innocently, *naturellement*." He grinned, and so did I.

"I accept the offer of your arm while we wait," I said. "But only to get warm." He feigned disappointment and wrapped his arm around me. Thankfully, his hand remained higher than my wound.

I moved into his body heat. Grateful for both the warmth and the opportunity to be seen as a couple, instead of an American woman traveling alone in a bus filled with mostly French people and going to what appeared to be a mostly French festival. My discreet surveillance did not reveal any possible enemies, but I kept vigilant.

"Have you attended this festival before?" I asked to keep the conversation going.

"*Oui*. Many people come throughout the year to Le Puy-en-Velay, to do the ancient pilgrimage route. St. James Way to Santiago de Compostela. They come to this area to visit the old churches and to see the production of lace. Renaissance groupies, come during the *Roi de l'Oiseau* festival. But that is fairly recent. Not much interest in other countries for shooting the bird and becoming king." He grinned.

"Excuse me?"

He sighed but the grin remained, so I knew he was happy to go on. "It is saying." He pulled his arm free and pretended to put on his thinking cap. Then he clasped his hands together in the way children are taught to do across the globe when presenting material to their classmates. "In 1594, whomever shot the Papagai..." At my puzzled look he substituted, "Parrot." At my dismayed look, he laughed. "Not a real parrot, but handmade of material. Shooting this 'bird' and winning the archery competition carried great honor. The winner gained high esteem for the following year, since being a great archer meant you were the best at defending the town from enemies. The winner became good friends with the mayor, and held keys to the city. Best of all, he had no tax to pay."

Rollie's look changed to a downcast one as he continued to play the part of presenter and entertainer. "However, after the French revolution the festival was banned as barbaric and backward." He dramatically paused. "But in the 1940s the celebration was revived and by 1986, a very important year because it was the year I was born, the fête was revived." He grinned again. "It started today's grand festival, allowing everyone to celebrate the past in the present—or have a reason to party, as you say in the States."

"You've been to the States?"

"*Oui*. After graduation, I traveled there for a year. Where are you from, Laurel?"

Touchy. Didn't want to give away too much until I knew more about him. "Originally, I'm from upstate New York. I've also traveled quite a bit."

"I too have traveled over the years, to the complaints of my grandfather who wants me to take over his business in the next year. So he can retire to his vineyard and spend every day in the sun."

"What kind of business do you have?"

"My grandfather is head of the family's businesses—the main one being an architectural firm that has grown into a..." He paused and fought for the right word. "Group...*non*, conglomeration of related businesses."

"You mean a conglomerate?"

"*Oui*, a conglomerate. The headquarters are in Paris, but I have so far resisted moving permanently there."

"You spoke of a shop?"

"*Oui*, we also deal with textiles and construction to name but a few. We are now gearing up to prepare for the holiday celebrations, and groaning for having to return to work after the August holidays. That's why he gets upset, because I'm leaving again so quickly after August, and September is the time when we make a lot of decisions about the holiday preparations for the cities."

"So you have government contracts?"

"*Oui*."

People started shifting toward the front bus and we gathered up our things to move into the boarding line, to be on our way to Le Puy.

EIGHTEEN

Le Puy-en-Velay, the small capital of Haute-Loire, was a beautiful, theatrical-looking town on the right bank of the river Borne. According to my guidebook, the city sat on an undulating plateau on the eastern border of Auvergne, one of the regions in Massif Central. The area was known for geographical oddities called volcanic thrusts that appeared visible aboveground.

As we approached the municipality, two of the hills stood sharply visible amidst the terracotta roofs. I knew one was St. Michel d'Aiguilhe and the other Rocher Corneille. The new parts of Le Puy blended well with the medieval. The buildings boasted little color but were picturesque all the same. Every turn of the head showed booths and vendors setting up their goods. People wandered by dressed in their sixteenth-century clothing, or at least approximations of those types of costumes. Though I'd swear one was an updated version of Madonna's "Like a Virgin" outfit. Traffic packed the streets and lanes and appeared in waves and layers, from bikes and motorcycles to cars, buses, and even horse-drawn wagons.

A local friend, Thierry, opened his home to Rollie every year, so my traveling companion was a festival regular. As he put it, there was a mutual exchange of homes throughout the year. He offered to let me stay with him, no strings attached. I knew I might need a bolt hole soon, so although it felt like I was using him a bit more I agreed to consider the offer, but made no commitment. My plan was to wrap this job up by midnight if at all possible, and I needed to keep my options open. From this point on, I planned to be moving.

First stop on my personal agenda included a visit to the Cathedral of Notre-Dame du Puy, which stood at the foot of the Rocher Corneille, above the old town. According to Jack, the chapel and art there came up in information related to Moran's present whereabouts. Which I hoped would also lead to Simon and the sword.

Ditching Rollie sooner, rather than later, was a priority.

For my cardio workout of the day, accessing the Rocher Corneille meant a step-climb to the statue of the Virgin. I had no idea what to search for, only that I was looking for something to point out a clue to my next move. I also hoped something would tell me how to find Moran's estate. That was my best bet for a lead to Simon and the sword. Moran was too smart, too wealthy and too connected to let his real name be known in the area. I had to count on luck, good critical thinking skills, and damned good eyesight. I was getting antsy on the slow-moving bus.

"We can get off the bus and walk if you would like," Rollie said, turning to me. "It will have an uphill climb, but Thierry's home is only a few kilometers away."

"I'm game," I replied. Before we could stand, several people at the front of the bus called to the bus driver and gestured toward the exit.

Like cake icing squeezed out of a tube with a tip too small, the majority of people on the bus jostled their way out onto the street. Rollie and I joined them. I kept watch, but no one appeared to follow me. Just people in groups having a good time.

By the time we turned down another road, everyone else had pretty much disappeared, and we were alone. Rollie appeared to be what he claimed, a charming, well-traveled, educated, much loved grandson of a wealthy man. I planned to stay on alert nonetheless.

His friend's house was a little jewel. Tucked away on a quiet back street, on a cul de sac out of the main drag, the cream colored stone dwelling rose several stories, crowned by a bright terracotta roof like its neighbors, and boasted an intricately carved wooden door.

Rollie pulled a key from his pocket and swung the door inward, politely waiting for me to enter. I motioned for him to precede me instead and quickly looked around. There was no one behind us that I could see, and as I stepped forward, no one appeared inside.

The leather furnishings cost more than my annual salary, and screamed a wealthy male lived there, but the place had the air of having stood empty for some time. Rollie led me up a narrow staircase to a surprisingly large second story landing. There were at least five closed doors to choose from, and he opened the one nearest the stairs. I silently approved of the location and escape access.

"This is for you. My sister often stays here, and you may find some feminine accoutrements. Please feel free to make use of anything you want. She would not mind. My room is just there," he said and pointed to the door across from mine. "You will not be disturbed and may stay here for the rest of the celebrations if you like." He pushed his pack up higher on his shoulder and smiled. "Or longer if you so desire. It is a nice place to take some time from the rat race."

"Where's your friend?" I had to ask. The name Thierry wasn't familiar, but I wanted to I anticipated any surprises.

Rollie laughed. "Oh, Thierry disappears weeks before and stays away for weeks after the festival. This type of celebration, it is not his choice you see."

He looked around as though forgetting something. "Oh, the bathroom. It is down this way," he said. "As my guest, *passe devant*. I mean, please go first."

Another shower sounded divine, and I knew I really needed to wash and apply disinfectant to my wounds. The one on my arm had not stopped throbbing, and I could feel dampness where my shirt stuck to the blood. I fought the urge to let Rollie shower first so I could search the house. "Thanks, I accept your generous offer."

"I will meet you downstairs in an hour for some refreshment?"

I smiled. "Right. I'll be out of the shower in a jiffy."

He returned my smile. "Take your time, Laurel. After all, this is your vacation."

The shower didn't take long, but I found the warm water coupled with the pain of cleaning my wounds zapped all my strength. A bathroom cabinet held first aid supplies, and I cleansed the wound and used some bandages and gauze to wrap it firmly for protection. I popped a couple more of the British version of Tylenol and laid down on the softest bed known to man. I had to fight to gain consciousness when my cell phone alarm warned a half-hour had passed.

I dressed in a clean pair of jeans and a subdued taupe blouse. I might not look renaissance, but I wouldn't stand out either. I added enough makeup to look human again and grabbed a light pink sweater I found at the bottom of the pack. I wasn't even sure the sweater was mine, but since my jacket was trashed, it became my only warm option.

Rollie waited downstairs with cheese, bread, olives and wine for a light refreshment. I commented on the generosity of the spread and Rollie shrugged. "My friend knew I was coming, and he prepares in advance for me. He has a lady taking care of the needs of the house."

I took a long sip of the wine. I recognized the famous vineyard and the year. "This is delicious."

His dark eyes crinkled as he smiled. He'd freed his rich brown hair from the suede tieback worn earlier, and it brushed his shoulders. He looked very relaxed in a pair of dark jeans and a mulberry button-down shirt to compliment his olive skin. "Do you travel a lot, Laurel?" he asked casually and reached for a piece of cheese.

I contemplated my answer, and how best to get things moving. I didn't have time for an indoor picnic, and I was getting concerned about where Rollie thought this all might lead. I savored the wine on my tongue. Polite chitchat was a requirement, but... "I am often on the road. I've been looking forward to having a vacation. What about you?"

"As I said, I have indulged in various traveling pleasures over the years to the distinct dissatisfaction of my grandfather."

"Forgive my curiosity, but what were you doing in Brioude?"

"Visiting my maternal grandmother. It's one of the ways I persuade the old man to my side. Visiting elderly relatives and showing their deserved respect receives high marks in his books. My grandmother, Suzette, is quite a lady." He grinned. "For further benefit, I can leave my car at her place while I come here."

Well, there was one question answered: if he was as wealthy as I thought, why the hell was he taking the bus?

"You don't want your car in Le Puy?"

He laughed. "What would be the point? There are three main roads into town and you saw for yourself. A mess. The roads are all used up for other things during the festival. Besides, part of the charm of the festival is to relax, let go of the modern day world and let others take charge of the necessary details."

I took my last bite of a sumptuous crumbly farm cheese and topped it with the rest of my wine. He started to pour another glass, but I placed a hand over the rim to stop him. "Any more and I'll be too relaxed to move. And I'm excited about exploring the town."

On the bus, he had obligingly acquainted me with the layout of the town and several of the important places not to be missed. He also mentioned he had plans with old friends for this afternoon and evening's entertainment, which suited me perfectly. I could set out for what I needed to do without fuss.

Rollie stretched back in his chair, his long legs straight and crossed at the ankles, his short boots highly polished. He twirled the wine in his glass and looked over the rim at me, offering a wistful smile. "Are you sure I cannot persuade you to accompany me? Everyone would be most delighted to meet you and even more delighted to kid me about bringing 'a friend.'"

I pushed away from the table. "Now who's kidding, Rollie? I definitely get the impression you are never without friends. You certainly had no trouble making my acquaintance." I stood and took my dishes to the sink. "Ready to clean up?"

Rollie sighed. "Message received loud and clear. You go ahead, *Mademoiselle* Laurel. I will do the dirty work on my own and concentrate on looking forward to seeing you over the breakfast table tomorrow morning. I make delicious coffee by the way."

"I'll look forward to...tasting the coffee," I said, smiling to remove the sting. There was no point in prolonging the discussion by telling him I likely wouldn't be around to enjoy it.

"She kills with words," he mocked, then stood and held out a key.

I reached to take it, but before I could, he held my hand, palm up, and folded my fingers over the key with his.

"*À bientôt, Mademoiselle* Laurel. Be safe, as my

grandmother would say." His face was more serious than I would have imagined.

Minutes later, with my pack, now sans clothes and strapped onto my back, and trusty guidebook in hand, I headed out to see what clues I could discover in the town. I stayed alert to possibly being followed, but a sightseeing venture is a great way to keep a sharp eye on the surroundings without being obvious.

My first objective was to find the car I had asked Nico to arrange when I texted him from the Aston Martin during the trip up with Hawkes. While I hadn't had any idea Jack would abandon me at the hotel, staying self-sufficient was my first instinct, and I'd originally planned to use the car to get out of the area that evening. Slipping Jack's phone from my bra, I made a quick call. I'd left my phone off to avoid anyone's further tracking, so his was the better choice.

"Nico, it's me."

"*Bonjour*, Laurel," Nico said. "*Comment allez-vous? Profiter du beau temps et des sites du Le Puy?*"

"Two words, 'Shut it,'" I replied.

"I figured you would be having a grand time." Teasing aside, he said, "I sent you the coordinates for the car. There's been no chatter, no nothing. It is as if everyone has gone underground and is waiting, for what I cannot be sure. Be careful, Laurel. Something about this feels wrong."

"Careful is my middle name," I breezily replied.

"Laurel..."

"I know, I know. You be careful too."

A non-descript dark blue sedan, which could have belonged to anyone, was parked between a black Mercedes and a red Volvo on a street off the beaten path. Dark tinted windows, nothing illegal I was sure—Nico was too smart for that—made seeing the interior difficult, just as I liked. I was familiar with the make and model, with its powerful engine, ready for any open road. At that point, however, I was more interested in finding the information I knew was buried inside the car. Sensitive data neither of us wanted to exchange via phone.

I slipped a hand under the quarter panel where we always hid the keys. In seconds, the back door stood open, and I saw a familiar courier pack, which contained money, papers and a map. He knew I was more comfortable with a map in my hand than one on a screen, especially with the tendency of some GPS systems to lead drivers into ponds. I wanted to see where I was going before the voice talked to me.

Hanging from the side hook were several items of clothing, including a few formal gowns. Labeled and stacked neatly along the backseat were accessories needed for each costume.

Nico and I had developed a routine over the years. One could almost say we read each other's minds. Fortunately, our relationship had always remained strictly friends and business associates. I couldn't risk losing him.

I put my pack in the rear seat before sitting down in the front seat of the car, package in hand. I pulled the door closed, locked it, and perused the contents.

Disposable phone, maps, money, passport and reports.

Nico had been working to find out who and what Jack represented, but the information was scanty at best. In fact, the scantiness was what made it downright peculiar. I pushed my thoughts aside and read through the report. Still no word from Simon and no information about suspected sightings or theories. Nothing about the Amazon either.

While not having any recent contact with Max had been oddly relaxing, I realized I probably needed to speak with him. Nico contacted him, of course, as we'd discussed. Maybe Max was feeling a bit embarrassed that it was his contact related to the snuffbox now in question. I decided to be the professional and call him, to touch base if nothing else. It was still morning in New York, but my attempt to reach Max with the burner phone got nothing but voicemail—something that rarely happened. It was Jack's phone and a strange number, after all, which could be why the call went unanswered. Just as well. I didn't need anything to steer me off my current course. Something had to break in this case soon. Moran's estate was here. I knew it. *I felt it.*

With the opening ceremonies to the five-day festival tonight, I hoped someone like Moran would avoid mixing with the hoi-polloi by holding his own gathering of wealthy friends and business connections.

I left Jack's phone in the backseat, placed the new one in my bra, and I scooped up my pack. The money, the passport, and the report folded into my money belt, and the map stayed in my hand. I exited the car and locked up.

Time to track down the *Black Virgin* and the *Chapelle des Reliques.*

NINETEEN

I found myself back in the heart of things as I moved on foot toward my destination. The narrow streets were three-deep with people. Crowds spilled out and around the austere old buildings. Except for evidence of modern lighting, it was like being thrust back several centuries. Fortunately, I wasn't the only one wearing modern day clothes, so I didn't stand out too much.

The smells and noises reminded me of a popular amusement park. Preparations of food and revelry were everywhere. Shop doors were propped open between the booths, and the atmosphere remained an anticipatory one. Posted signs announced "this event" or "that contest" to encourage everyone to try their luck. Flyers and brochures provided information, as did all the helpful people setting up. No local police sightings yet, but I assumed the force dressed in costume to not attract attention. Or maybe the presence of the local gendarme was unnecessary until later, when opening celebrations began. Rollie said this was a family-friendly event and revelry could stay to a minimum.

I dodged and smiled as I wound my way through the town heading toward the cathedral, my first stop on a very personal pilgrimage to find what happened to Simon and the sword. He'd been missing a full twenty-four hours by this time. If the sword was an ancient artifact, Moran would want it at all cost. I hoped Simon hadn't already paid the premium.

Cathedral of Notre-Dame du Puy, was a magnificent structure towering above the narrow *Rue des Tables* like a graceful swan. Lying in a valley between two huge volcanic thrusts, the structure looked almost oriental. I couldn't wait to get inside.

I walked up the steps and entered, overwhelmed by the sheer ageless beauty and variety of combined styles. Inside the architecture was its own artistic creation, and I caught my breath as I viewed the marble *Black Virgin* with her son, perched on a baroque high altar.

One of the things I loved about my life was the way it was filled with exquisite art items. This was one of many. Despite knowing from my art history studies this piece was a copy of the original, I couldn't imagine anything more gorgeous and timeless. Tearing my gaze away, I turned to my left to enter the *Chapelle des Reliques* with the large fifteenth-century mural of *The Seven Liberal Arts* spread out before my inviting glance.

At first, I simply admired the majesty of what my eyes saw because it was the only thing I could do. I looked up and around, overwhelmed by the entire building and contents. Even the dim lighting added to the awe-inspiring splendor of everything within the ancient structure.

For a moment, thoughts of my own quest fell aside, and I considered the many men and women who had suffered and even died on their religious pilgrimages here. A journey of such importance they willingly made the necessary sacrifices the completion required.

"Takes your breath away doesn't it?"

The softly spoken words brought me from my contemplation of the past and thrust me back to the present. I kept my gaze forward and calm. "Yes. It's indescribable, Jack."

"What strikes you the most?"

"The building, what else? It has superb architecture, like every other structure in this town. What about you?" I wondered when he would say something about my leaving the hotel. Then I realized he wouldn't. He was playing the same game I played. The only way I was going to learn anything was to remain wary but be ready to take on additional risk.

"I agree with your assessment," he said. "The architecture is unlike anything on earth and only adds to the magnificent contents."

Something in his tone struck me as odd. "Have you been here before?"

"Once, with a group of mates on a bike tour. I promised myself I would return, but life does get in the way. Yet, here I am, with you, despite circumstances beyond my control. Surprise, surprise."

No, I wasn't going there.

"I'm trying to figure out what clues there might be here," I said. "Do you see anything?"

"Other than a spectacular version of architecture built from the fifth to the fifteenth century and priceless artworks? No."

I fought back my disappointment. All this way and...nothing? I hated failure. Still, I had only been in the cathedral a short time. Not really long enough to be sure. I scrutinized the piece once more. Same result. There were so many surfaces on the piece. Since this was a copy I looked for some small etching, a scrap of paper, a mark. Again, nothing.

But I had no idea how long Jack had been here. I wandered back to the *Black Virgin* and Jack stayed at my heels. He might have left the hotel and hotfooted it right over to Le Puy, picked up what we needed and completed the mission already. He had the car. He may have been lying about Geneva or decided not to go.

I looked at him. His gaze left the *Black Virgin* and met mine. The few people in the space disappeared until it was just the two of us staring at one another. I had no idea what he was thinking, but I felt confused. Was it possible he was as genuine as he seemed? Could I trust him?

Probably too risky. He was ready to leave me at the hotel and toss aside the two-day window for the sword he said was part of his mission. Things might have changed since Simon's disappearance, but Max gave me that deadline for a reason. My assignment had simply expanded to recover the man as well as the artifact. I would continue with Jack as long as we made progress, but I planned to disappear from him feeling as guiltlessly as when he left me. So far, these recovery duties had comprised a series of tragic incidents and disappointments. I've never handled disappointment well, but this assignment, including the horrible odd murders, made every experienced emotion feel heightened.

I hadn't truly believed the sword was real, had argued it with myself and Max from the beginning. On a personal level, maybe Simon's strange disappearance was not strange at all, and Jack's bizarre intrusions into my life were nothing more than coincidences in the normal realm of life's occurrences. Regardless, the bottom line—deal with my disappointment the usual way. Alone.

By unspoken mutual consent, we stayed for another hour, wandering the beautiful building and checking anomalies that caught our eyes. The *Black Virgin* and the *Chapelle of Reliques* with its *Seven Liberal Arts* drew me again and again, but I saw nothing to connect with the investigation.

Strangely, Jack's voice was a welcome intrusion from the darkness of my thoughts. "Ready to go up to the statue on the top of the hill? Or has hunger taken over?"

"No food. I'm thirsty, but more curious to see the view from the statue. Let's go."

"If you're sure. You'll really be thirsty when you've ascended all two-hundred-sixty-odd steps to the top."

"No, I won't. I think there are fountains along the way. Don't you remember from when you were here before?"

I let Jack lead the way, and of course he looked great in clothes that looked freshly ironed. My things were less pressed, but at least my London shopping spree meant the clothes I pulled from my pack might be crumpled but attractive. I told myself that was so, anyway. Although, I still didn't remember the pink sweater. My hair, fastened atop my head since my shower at Thierry's, was falling haphazardly down, while Jack's head was perfectly groomed without a hair out of place. How did he do that?

"You should have slept and waited for me at the hotel. Lunch was delicious, and even with the traffic I made great time," he said casually, reading my mind again. I felt like spitting on him. Never mind how I despised people who spit.

"I had wonderful food." I tried not to think about the crushed sandwich and lukewarm water, or what preceded their sampling, focusing instead on the cheese and the wine I'd enjoyed a few hours ago with Rollie. "And I feel great." I wished I had finished off the bottle of wine.

He turned and grasped my chin lightly. "Yeah, I can tell from those big circles under your eyes how much sleep you've gotten." His face changed when pain chased across my face and I couldn't maintain a neutral expression. "What's happened here, Laurel?" His index finger moved lightly over the abraded skin, and he bent to see when he gently lifted my chin. "When? Where? How?" he asked quietly. "That cut wasn't there when I left you this morning."

Thankfully, I could explain quite truthfully what happened. "I'm not sure. I must have scraped it somewhere, but I don't know how. Besides, until you touched it, I had forgotten it was there."

The grimness hadn't left his face as he continued to study the mark. I had no idea why he was making such a federal case out of a little graze. Imagine how he would have reacted if he knew about my arm.

He finally let go of my chin and briefly touched my cheek. "Don't ever lie to me, Laurel. I'm depending on you to tell me the truth. I plan to do the same for you." He held out his hand and his mood changed. "Allow me to assist you, *mademoiselle*, in achieving your desire to reach the top."

I was absolutely *not* ready for this kind of byplay with him. He already lied. Unless he'd had his own personal "Q" to put a rocket app on his James Bond car, he certainly hadn't had time to get to Geneva and back. "I need no help, thank you." I ignored the outstretched hand and brushed past him.

Fortunately, I was right. The area sported plenty of rest areas, fountains, and toilets. The steps weren't even that steep. It was also quiet. I appreciated the solitude. I assumed everyone was down below in the town partying in sixteenth-century style.

When we reached the halfway point, I asked, "Did you know about the festival?"

He picked up a loose stone, looked at it for a minute, then threw it and watched it roll away. It seemed like a deliberate stalling tactic, but I wasn't sure why. Surely, the fact he knew about the festival wasn't a state secret.

"I have heard something about it but I've never attended. It looks like quite a lot of fun if one is interested in that sort of thing."

"Not a renaissance man?"

"Oh, I think I'm a man for all times. I'm just not a fan of a particular period of time in history. I enjoy reading about historical events, but I like living in the present."

"Speaking of the present, have you found out anything more about 'the place' we're wanting to find?"

"Not really," he replied too quickly.

Something in his expression and the speed of his answer told me he was definitely lying. Previously, even when instinct told me not to trust him, I recognized his fairly straightforward actions in our dealings—except of course for Geneva. Yet now I knew he absolutely wasn't being truthful, which struck me as interesting.

I managed to keep my tone neutral. "What does 'not really' mean?"

There was another pause. This time it was obviously significant. Strange, because I would say men like Jack don't make the kinds of mistakes that allow opponents to read them.

It couldn't be climbing the steps, because he was in great shape. Even I wasn't having any trouble breathing, and I hadn't seen the inside of the gym in six months. So I waited.

When he decided to answer, his tone was flat. "Just what it means. I might have heard something, but I'm discounting the story because of the source. The rumor isn't worth giving thought to, much less sharing it with someone."

"The 'someone' being me, I suppose?" I made a disbelieving sound. "Yet, you've thought about what your source said, right? And now you're making a decision to keep the information to yourself, which makes the story important enough to have made a decision about the data."

The argument sounded convoluted, but I knew he knew what I meant.

"There's just one other thing." I stopped suddenly and pivoted on my step. He was one step down, so we stood eyeball to eyeball. From this angle, I could see all the markings in his eyes which made up the brilliant teal, the effect I had really thought was fake, but now recognized couldn't even be duplicated by a master contact designer.

I took a deep breath, then continued speaking, "Moments ago, you were going on about being truthful with each other. But you must have lied about going to Geneva. You'd never be standing here now if you drove your car there and back. You only give me the information you absolutely must, yet expect me to divulge everything I know. Trust doesn't work like that, Jack. Either come clean, or we stop this uneasy alliance."

His expression didn't change, but I knew he was considering my words and weighing whether or not I meant what I said.

"Laurel," he began, his tone suitably regrettable.

I recognized that opening and tuned out the rest, turned and resumed my trek to the top. I couldn't do anything about the proximity of our positions, but I knew better than most how to freeze someone out. Some might say that was passive aggressive. I called it survival of the fittest in a war of attrition. I could handle things on my own, had been doing it all my adult life. Hawkes and his "need to know" philosophy had to go.

We reached the pinnacle. I could only think of the word "amazing" to describe the view of Le Puy, and even that fell short. I was speechless but not on purpose this time. I stared, trying to process each component.

A few other people milled around, but for the most part, it was just the two of us at the top of Massif Central. As he started to speak something caught my eye. Again I didn't hear what he said, but not on purpose this time.

From the vantage point, I looked over a large estate set off far from the main part of town and even other estates in the surrounding countryside. The house appeared to be built directly out of a rock wall, the stone of the building's façade dark, almost black. Some parts even darker than others. In fact, the structure had an exterior façade quite astonishingly different from any other building in this charming locale. My instincts were screaming this was Moran's.

A caravan of delivery vehicles pulled away as I watched. Given the appearance of the trucks, and the festival in place at the moment, I assumed a party was in the works at this mansion in a few hours. It was always easier to search a place when wine flowed and no one knew everyone in attendance. I could pass myself off as the guest of a guest if anyone questioned my presence. Unfortunately, without an actual invitation a front door entrance was out. I had to find alternative entry.

Carefully, I turned and looked the other way to minimize my obvious interest. Jack had finally stopped talking, and I didn't want him to catch on to my revelation. The intuition I had thought deserted me on this case was pinging like crazy. It was too early at this juncture to draw any final conclusions, but I needed to pinpoint the black house's location. Because it was the direction I was headed.

"Laurel, aren't you taking this a little too far?"

I grinned to myself and politely said, "Excuse me?"

"Oh, so you are speaking to me again?"

"I have no idea what you're talking about."

Jack snorted. Somehow, he made even that atrocious noise attractive. "Come off it."

No sense antagonizing him further. I had places to go. "I've seen enough. I'm ready to head back down," I said, my voice soft and serene.

"Laurel..." If he had been the type to go red-faced sweating and apoplectic, now would have been the time.

My answer was to give him a look at my oh-so-straight shoulders and—even if I am the one to say it—the swing of my attractive backside as I headed down the steps.

Of course he followed, and this time we walked in complete silence. I have no idea what he thought, but I knew what occupied my mind. The black estate.

Such an unusual looking house, seemingly carved right out of the side of a mountain. A structure that would appeal only to a certain type of person. An individual who wanted the extraordinary and possessed the money to achieve it.

I had to rid myself of Jack and make plans. Decide how I was going to get to the house and be prepared for any and all eventuality.

Getting to the car became the next hurdle. I didn't want Jack to catch on, and almost everything I needed was inside the vehicle. Except for certain equipment that I hoped to obtain if the necessary stores were still open.

I glanced at my narrow wristwatch. I had plenty of time to find rappelling equipment. Just in case. Surely, there were shops in this town that sold such things. Tourists who tired of the festivities would likely consider a short mountain trekking experience next. I hoped so anyway. I wasn't an expert, but I had engaged in several rock climbing sessions over the years and knew what I needed.

It seemed to take forever to reach the road, but really it was only a few minutes before we arrived back at street level. I could hear the sound of voices around us, but no one was nearby. At this point I would have preferred more of the public around us. My mind processed all the new and old information at a fevered pace, but I worked to control my breathing and make my voice casual as I said, "See you around," and walked away. Only to find myself whirled around to face him.

I couldn't stop the sound of pain that hissed through my lips. Even through the bandage, his grip was tough. Not meant to bruise, just meant to control. But I have a firm rule that no man manhandled me.

The pain had been controlled up until that point by the tight bandaging, but the lightning streaks were released and started a powerful surge of heat through my veins. I barely noticed the look of shock on his face as I reached out my right foot and wrapped it around his leg fast enough to gain the advantage. I was on a slight elevation in the ancient pavement, and I head-butted him once and unbalanced him.

When he fell he took me down with him. Whether the tumble was due to the surprise of my attack or my weight, I wasn't sure, but I scrambled to my feet so he couldn't grab me again. I took a step away and stood victorious. Then I realized Jack Hawkes lay sprawled, unconscious, on the bottom step of the Cathedral of Notre-Dame du Puy.

Breathing heavily I checked his pulse. It was steady, his respiration normal, and pupils were reactive and not dilated. I searched his head for a wound. There was no blood, but a new lump had begun forming on the back of his head near the top. Out for the second time in as many days. He must have caught the lip of the bottom step.

I wished it hadn't happened. Even as I pulled the cell from my bra, he began stirring. For a second I considered what to do. The more I thought about it, the more I knew my original instincts were right and stronger the urge became to flee.

The call connected right then and made my decision for me. After an extended language-barrier hassle, I was done. I even mentioned this was the second bout of unconsciousness in about twenty-four hours. I'd done all I could. The woman at the other end thanked me. I headed back toward the car, but stepped behind a tall flowering bush to watch as Jack started to regain consciousness and sat up. An ambulance siren could be heard closing in on the location. As it pulled to the curb, Hawkes whipped his head back and forth and uttered an oath. I knew then he'd realized I'd again slipped his trap. I smiled, feeling nostalgic. The ambulance would take good care of Bond, James Bond.

TWENTY

It took quite a bit of maneuvering to get through the mass celebrations, but I was finally free of the festival and heading in the direction I hoped led to the estate. Before retrieving the car, I stopped by Thierry's and used the key Rollie gave me to find out where to purchase climbing equipment and change clothing. No one was there, so I checked out the place the way I had wanted to do upon arrival.

It appeared Thierry was a sports nut. Pictures throughout the house showed people skiing, boating, sky diving, and hang gliding. Other than an obsession with sports, he appeared to be a regular guy. I didn't find any firearms, worse luck.

There was one street level door I hadn't tried, and there I found a room lower than the rest of the house. Apparently, it was used as a garage. Various sized water sports equipment sat clustered near snow skis, parachutes, cricket bats, soccer balls, and climbing harnesses and some very sharp associated tools. In the middle of the space, a restored Jaguar XKE almost seemed to growl in superiority.

I folded my arms to keep from touching the highly polished burgundy finish. In college, I drove a similar model, one of the final legacies from my late-grandfather that was ultimately sold to cover living expenses, but this particular Jag looked as though it had just left the showroom floor. The car was insistently calling my name. I didn't really have time to listen and show my admiration, but I did anyway. And it turned out that made all the difference.

On the other side of the sportster, hidden by a large freestanding pegboard I thought held every tool and gadget known to man, I found a cache of everything needed for hanging onto rocks. In one nosy moment, I eliminated my need for the unknown store that may or may not have still been open, along with all associated translation problems I'd envisioned while trying to purchase climbing gear. There in the garage I was in the middle of rock climbing heaven.

Not that I needed much. I hoped to boulder the mountain instead of needing to climb, although that could be dicey since I wasn't exactly sure what the surface would be like, and I knew I'd have to go higher than twenty feet. Both of those factors exponentially increased risk. I also wouldn't have a partner which was another big no-no, but I wasn't going to let that stop me. Heck, the real problem was the dark. No way should I even contemplate bouldering in an unknown place, in the dark, without a partner, higher than twenty feet...and yet...

I quickly picked and discarded climbing apparatus. The only gear that really worried me was finding a pair of rock shoes in my size. I grabbed the chalk and the chalk bag and loaded carabineers, a top rope, a friend and some anchors just in case. I considered the crash pad, but didn't really have room to take it or the desire to carry more weight. Shoes, shoes, shoes. I let out a long breath.

Yeah, he had shoes. For all kinds of sports. On a shelf also hidden by the pegboard.

In Thierry's pictures, he'd almost always been with a female so I was hoping...Yes! Several pairs of sports shoes were tossed behind a box. Please, please let them be something close to my size. I stripped down to bare feet and played Cinderella with the rock shoes. A little tight, but tight would work. Loose would have been a real problem. I changed back to my own shoes and looked for a bag.

A short search revealed a large duffle near the soccer equipment. Too big for the climbing equipment, but large enough to hold it and the rest of my gear. I dumped the contents and stored my treasures. After one last covetous look at the Jag, I headed for the kitchen.

I sat at the table with a large cup of coffee and a sandwich quickly thrown together. Calories and caffeine, the stuff of champions. Darkness would come soon. I didn't have much time. I bit into the food and stared at the map, highlighting a route I believed would head me in the right direction. I picked out some of the street names and thought at least one of the options could get me to the black mansion estate. When I finished my snack, I went to my room and exchanged the jeans I wore for my black jumpsuit, complete with the hoodie I'd brought along.

Soon I was in my car and, fingers crossed, headed toward my goal. I did call the hospital, but unsurprisingly couldn't get any information about Jack.

The last time he and I had tangled, at the *castillo*, I'd been the one to end up on my ass. Sure, I hadn't been knocked out, but I'd been sore and still felt the bruise a couple of days later. Yeah, I was feeling guilty. Another emotion pretty much unfamiliar to me since age eight.

I checked the phone to see if Nico tried to get in touch but had little expectations of his doing so. He had his part of the job to do, and I had mine. I was on my own. Usually I liked it that way.

I wasn't sure why I was suddenly feeling very alone.

Several false turns later, the GPS lady said I needed to turn right. I preferred using maps, but all the ones I found of the region was more recreation than for reconnaissance, so unless she led me astray the GPS brain had to do. Plus, I didn't have an exact address, so had simply plugged in my best guess from what little the maps revealed. Of course, my eyes were telling me the same, nothing different than the last three turns either. The mountain was huge. Several streets seemed to head in the direction of the black estate. Whether or not this mountain was the one I actually needed to be on remained an unanswered question.

The tree cover was too dense to be certain of anything except I was traveling on a winding, narrow road, hopefully leading to some answers. This could also be another wild goose chase. The longer I traveled down the road, the more my returning intuition told me it was the one. In the past, intuition had saved my ass too many times to count. I had learned to trust it.

Seven twisting miles later, I spotted the house. I pulled off onto the narrow verge, parking as close as possible to the trees and my best shot at staying out of camera range.

I didn't dare underestimate security. In fact, I may have been under some type of surveillance since turning into this *Rue des* whatever. The GPS was weirdly silent, but my brain and my eyes busily catalogued how the street dead-ended into my destination.

I hadn't passed one car along this particular stretch of road but counted five possible exits to unknown places. Unknown, since no signs or buildings along the way indicated the reason the other drives existed. This road screamed PRIVATE, but I remembered there had been a street sign, *Rue des Plagues* or *Blagues*, or something like that. No gate barred my entrance. The more I thought about the lack of traffic and buildings, the more worried I became about being monitored or trapped. Should I turn around?

My mind flashed caution-inducing pictures of the creeps and the dead associated with this case. I remembered the destruction of Simon's office and the motorcycle bearing down on me this morning. I felt the bullets zinging around me. My arm still throbbed. I probably should have gotten stitches instead of only wrapping it in the bandage supplies I'd found in Thierry's bathroom cabinet.

Stop it! My mind was wandering, not a familiar event for me, especially during a job. I had to know what I was up against before committing to any decision about trespassing. I sat in the car, half-hidden by the trees, and contemplated my options. There likely wouldn't be any second chances.

The house, massive on its own, butted up against the bulky mountain, and heavy tree cover bordered its property lines. A roughly seven- or eight-foot stone wall, topped with what looked like razor wire, completed the feel of isolation. Forbidding and completely off-limits. A place designed as a fortress. The approaching dusk added to the illusion of danger.

I took a shaky breath and told myself to slow it down, check the place out up close and personal before making decisions about how to proceed. Unlike most jobs—both the legitimate Beacham Foundation ones and the freelance opportunities I periodically took on—I always researched and scouted things far in advance to prepare for any eventuality. However, since the very beginning this case allowed none of those practices.

There was still enough light to see. The immediate land around the wall had been cleared and was kept mowed. I wasn't sure how far back the clearing went, so I pulled out a pair of powerful but petite binoculars from the glove box. Nico was dependable, thorough, and could always be counted upon to anticipate my needs. Jack would never be that conscientious.

Why I thought of Jack at a time like this, I didn't know. I'd always worked alone. I put the binoculars up to my eyes.

The cut lawn perimeter ended at the tree and brush line. The razor wire seemed almost overkill. It could be clipped, but, unfortunately, it sliced and diced before falling apart to allow entry. I didn't see any cameras, but that wasn't unusual. I knew they were there. Zooming the lenses in on the windows, I noticed the lower floors were wired. The higher I went, however, the security wiring disappeared. That suited my purposes. I hoped I was right about the party, too. That would help with a distraction later.

I rolled down the car window to listen for sounds. I love dogs but didn't want to run into any of them tonight, and, right on cue, a dog barked and several answered. I used the binoculars to scan as much of the area as I could. When no baying hounds came into view, I concluded they were inside the wall.

I secured the black hoodie over my head, making sure every blonde hair was inside, and pulled on thin black gloves next. The binoculars securely fitted to a special strap on my jumpsuit. I reluctantly glanced over at the duffle in the passenger seat. I added a couple of metal loops onto the bag's handle, ones I could use to connect to the shoulder harness I wore. Free hands were a necessity in rock, and I needed what was in that bag—extra weight or not.

Did I want to leave the bag in the car for this first sighting, knowing it would slow me down? Without a visual survey of the house or the mountain, was I ready to take the chance? Or did I want to bring the duffle now and prepare to leap whenever a possible chance presented itself?

Seconds later, I stepped from the car with the bag hooked to the harness, then eased the door shut and locked it before returning the key to its original location under the fender. If I was caught and searched, I didn't want anyone to have the key to my only chance at getting away quickly.

I shivered as my brain cycled through all possible consequences. I didn't really like guns, but I sure wished I had one right then. Just in case.

TWENTY-ONE

Noiselessly, I slipped away from the car, sticking with the brush line. Shadows cast long deep purple stretches. Trees I knew to be thick, green, and beautiful rapidly became large, black and menacing. I was surrounded by lush, abundant groundcover that cushioned my shoes but could hide a variety of problems. The cooling air was fragrant with pine needles and mold. If I'd been allergic, it might have been a problem. Thank goodness for small mercies.

I put aside the fear of being visually spotted, intending to avoid the lawn and stick with the tree line. I was more worried about falling over a root, running into poison ivy or oak. Did they have either of those in France? Or coming across a sharp-toothed animal that wanted me for dinner.

I suddenly realized I had no idea what the wildlife was like in this area. Pretty vital information if one explored at night in a foreign environment. Jack probably knew the Latin and lay names for each genus roaming Massif Central.

A twig snapped to my right. I whirled and breathed a sign of relief as a small Roe deer moved into my sight. It scampered off. My breath whooshed out. For a few seconds, I regulated my breathing to even out my heart rate. Despite the dropping temperature I felt an uncomfortable film of sweat form on my skin. My suit might "breathe" like me, but I still felt wet.

With each step I expected to hear the dogs barking or whining, but my ears caught nothing. Maybe the beasts were chomping down on someone else, somewhere else. Extreme stress sometimes made my macabre sense of humor get the better of me.

There were no more cracking twigs, other than my own. I walked along the perimeter until the land went vertical. Pretty much where the wall ended as well. I stepped deeper into the trees, following nature's wall to approach the house.

Still no dogs. Hopefully they were busy with dinner elsewhere.

My vantage point sucked but, as I'd suspected, the house was built into or dead-ended in the mountain. For further information I'd have to either head back the way I had come or climb.

The rising mountain, hill, volcanic thrust, or whatever the geographical formation was called, towered over me. From my angle it seemed to be the largest mountain ever known. I took off my gloves and ran my hands over the exposed surface, using my body as cover to retrieve a penlight from one of my pockets and get a better look.

The façade definitely looked like it could be bouldered. There were plenty of holds and jutting crags. The outer layer of the earth didn't appear to be too brittle. I certainly would have rather bouldered with a buddy during the middle of the day in a place I knew well, but I wasn't too worried. I refused to let myself be.

I dropped my bag and stood for a long moment. I turned back the way I had come, and knew I couldn't wait any longer. Throwing caution to the wind, I grabbed the necessary equipment out of the duffle. I kicked off my leather boots and socks and pulled on the rock shoes.

After stretching, I looked up and scouted my way. I would

go about fifteen feet before deciding whether to return to the ground or head up and over. The duffle was tightly fastened, and I gave it a wiggle to make sure it didn't move. My hands were dry from the magnesium carbonate. Too pumped to feel the pinch in the shoes, I scrunched my toes, relaxed, and took off.

I wasn't breathing heavy as I reached fifteen feet. It was getting darker, but as I moved closer to the top of the tree line everything lightened up a bit. The interior lighting of the house also helped, though it was still too far away to make a significant difference. I needed to continue up and work my way over. I'd gotten lucky because the house wasn't that far from the perimeter wall, at least on this side, so I wouldn't have too long a stretch horizontally. Unfortunately, the house was at least three stories, and I needed to go farther up if I wanted to get high enough to look at the property.

I chalked up and started "walking."

Before getting more than ten feet, there was a strange high-pitched whirring, followed by an audible click, and the place lit up like a subway station. I fought the urge to panic and push into the mountain. I practiced mental imagery, repeating again and again, "I am a chameleon. I blend in with the landscape."

For a second, I closed my eyes against the light pollution to re-stabilize my plan. At this point, if I kept to easy movements, no one could likely see me. Of course, if a big chunk of the mountain fell on a light, or a person for that matter, the first place they'd look is up. At me.

I could wish to be higher and closer to the house before the lights came on, but, as with anything in life, in a second's tick my task grew exponentially harder. Yet nothing really changed except there was light. And in most circumstances, light equaled a good thing. Unless it interfered with the process of breaking and entering.

The first step was always the hardest. I allowed a few

seconds for my eyes to become accustomed to the new environment, then I planned my next three moves.

I chalked for the last time and looked down. From my vantage point I could see pretty much everything on this side and the front. A gabled room split the terrace almost completely in two, with just a wide connecting hallway.

Even if I couldn't make out what was on the other side, I didn't want to climb higher; I wanted to traverse and jump. I was ready to get off the side of the mountain.

A welcoming drive circled the formally landscaped property, but I was more concerned with the not so friendly elements of the estate. The razor wire wasn't visible from the house. Instead it appeared to be an extension placed atop the stone that created the illusion of being surrounded by fence rather than an ugly security feature.

My gaze was drawn to some kind of well-lit water feature set in the middle of the main yard. It looked slightly oriental, with a short bridge leading to a Romanesque structure that appeared to be surrounded by water on all sides. The building was open on three sides. It did not resemble the estate at all. In fact, it reminded me of something I had seen before but couldn't recall. I barely made out a large sculpture within the building. The idea of *Shades of Rodin* filled my head. I wanted to get a closer look.

I adjusted my position and raised the binoculars to my eyes. Shocked at what I saw, I almost fell before steadying myself. In very miniature form, the building resembled certain aspects of the cathedral Jack and I had just visited. I refocused on the Rodin, which of course wasn't a Rodin at all, but a large and vaguely vulgar representation of *The Seven Liberal Arts*. I had no idea who the artist was, but from there it looked like...a big joke?

Could I count this discovery as partial confirmation Moran

lived there? Art was his life, but from what I could see the rendering offered little artistic beauty of such a philosophical topic.

My arms and my legs were growing tired from the unaccustomed activity, but cramping hadn't started, so I knew I needed to get off the mountain. I'd been surprised and happy to see a roof terrace, something I had not counted on since the front looked gabled. I hadn't seen any movement in any of the lighted rooms yet, but I checked again to make sure no one moved onto the terrace before I climbed down.

I concentrated on my movements. Mistakes were easy to make at this point, especially in a climb where I had come so far. When close enough to safely land, I braced myself, unhooked the duffle, and let it fall. I was about to take a leap when I saw lights on the road leading to the estate. I reached for the binoculars again. Another pair of headlights flashed. Then another. All coming this way.

I hadn't seen any vehicles, and now within minutes there was a caravan of cars on the road less traveled. Cars meant visitors, and visitors meant an occasion. A party. Maybe, just maybe, I'd caught a break.

Securing the binoculars, I relaxed, pushed off the wall, and tucked my head into a crash position. I rolled along the paved terrace. I retrieved the bag and made my way to the house. The quicker I got out of sight the better. For a second I hesitated and thought about checking out the rest of the space to see what was on the other side of the house. I might be missing something vital. All the security seemed to be at the door. No one expected an entrance from the top of the house.

Suddenly there was a loud noise, as though someone had dropped a heavy ceramic pot. I darted over to the side of a door, hoping I didn't trigger an alarm system. I had a Swiss-made gizmo that would turn off practically any on the market. I grabbed it from the bag to have it ready, then paused to listen. Nothing. Nothing was a good thing, but I still had to force myself to take a few calming breaths. While I had the chance I grabbed a handful of miniature motion detectors from my freelance stash and slipped their receiver in my ear. By systematically sprinkling these as I went, I'd know if someone slipped up behind me.

I pulled on my gloves, and tried the knob. It turned easily. I entered the dark room and silently pulled the door closed behind me, waiting for my eyes to adjust.

The lavish over-decorated bedroom sat empty, as did the drawers and closet. I moved to the bathroom and turned on the light. An overabundance of expensive bath and hygiene products littered the counter; all the brands any woman could possible want decorated the wall shelves, the deep tub, and the counter. But there was nothing personal about any of it. This had to be a guest room.

I stuck my head back into the bedroom. Through the door, the terrace looked fantastic. But the room? No art, no beauty, no taste in any of the furnishings. Something was off. I left a detector on the doorframe.

I stripped quickly and retrieved the extra items I'd hidden with the climbing equipment. I couldn't be sure if this occasion was formal or casual, but I assumed there would be a variety of dress in a place like this. Most anything should work.

Since I hadn't done my usual research on the property, I wasn't too sure about turning on the plumbing. My hand wrapped around the glasses Nico had given me, and I remembered his remark about their heat sensitivity. I pulled them on and looked toward the faucet to see if the hot water spigot registered on the glasses. No heat showed, but a wealth of other information came up as I accessed the "for my eyes only" menus. The address of the site, the architectural firm that recorded the blueprints—PA Designs. I'd have to check that name out later.

I shoved the glasses back into their case. There wasn't time for this kind of experimenting, no matter how intriguing. But the glasses had given me what I needed and then some. I'd have to remember to credit Nico if the design information led to catching Moran.

After using wet wipes to clean my face, hands and feet, I applied party makeup to match my outfit. I exchanged my jumpsuit for the little black uncrushable dress that could go from office to eveningwear with the right accessories.

I pulled out the wig I'd brought, but I changed my mind about using it and stuffed it back into the bag. Quickly, I undid the pins holding my hair in place, shook it out, and applied a quick brush. For the first time in a long time I thanked my dad for something—the family hair gene. As my blonde curls settled into place around my shoulders and down my back, Laurel Beacham of the Beacham Foundation emerged.

I dove once more into my magic bag and removed a pair of cherry red Manolo Blahnik heels and a matching red clutch that held lipstick, a tiny hairbrush, wet wipes, bling, lock picks, a knife—a woman couldn't be too careful—cash, gloves, some audio bugs, fake nails to match my pedicure, and my phone. The lock picks and knife were bejeweled and disguised to look like hair accessories.

The bugs went into the carefully designed pocket in my bodice, in case my purse was searched. I pierced, clipped, and buckled the tasteful diamond earrings, necklace, and bracelet and donned the shoes.

With the ease of years of practice, I rolled up everything no longer needed and returned the items to the duffle. I stuffed the bag under the bed and sat down. The fake nails went on first, then I pulled on a thin cherry red cloak in a synthetic material that looked like expensive silk but didn't wrinkle. I scooped up my clutch.

I wasn't quite ready to join the party but getting close. First, I wanted my own special tour. I cracked open the door and listened for any sounds. I heard none. I moved out into the hallway, closing the door softly behind me.

A quick search revealed twelve bedrooms on this level, each with their own en suite. None of the exterior doors I opened led to a bathroom. Three suites revealed recent occupation but all remained empty of people. There was a large lounge with windows looking onto the terrace and, again, the space sported an overabundance of everything a guest could want: books, pool table, video games, televisions, etc. A staircase and an elevator completed the floor plan. Motion detectors stood guard as I entered a room, and they stayed when I departed. So many spaces, so little information gained.

I still couldn't believe the absolute lack of taste in all the furnishings. As if this unique and beautiful house had been designed and built at great cost to enshrine—vulgarity?

The stairs were a clever play on a spiral staircase. Not quite as tight in the turns but winding all the same. Not a staircase for running up or down. No quick getaway here but architecturally interesting.

The second floor wasn't quite so deserted. I watched a couple and a single gentleman enter the elevator. The party must be starting. More bedrooms but still nothing personal; no sign of the owner, and not a modicum of taste in the luxurious furnishings. The tackiness might not be obvious to a lay person, but to anyone like Moran this interior design would have been an affront to the senses. Time to head to the first floor.

I left the spiral stairs and hit the doors. Most were locked. I tried eight before a door finally swung open. Books lined the shelves, overstuffed chairs and gaudy lamps filled the room, but once more there wasn't a personal feel to any of it. There was also no smell of cigars, no decanters of special liquors—nothing. Like a showcase for people to see what they expected to see.

I pulled a book from one shelf and thumbed through. It had never been opened. I picked another, and another, all from different shelves. They, too, had never been opened. A room full of books no one read.

I needed to check the rest of the rooms. I pulled the pick from my clutch and headed out to the hallway. I'd been lucky so far. Now I needed to be very careful.

Six rooms later I remained disappointed. I could discern no reason for these rooms to be locked. More bedrooms. More adult playrooms. More *everything*.

I fumbled with the next lock. The pick didn't seem to want to work. Was I getting sloppy in my technique? Redoubling my efforts, I tried again. I concentrated, heard the click and turned the knob, but again the door didn't open. Not ready to give up, I reversed the order I used. The door opened. Weirdly backward.

This space looked promising, definitely used, and I attached my last motion detector to the doorframe. It was a room lived in by someone who made a mess and didn't care. Definitely not Moran. From all I knew of him, he was fanatic about his personal environment and possessions.

Empty bottles, glasses, debris, an overflowing bin, clothes left on the floor. I picked through the room searching for some clue to the owner's identity. A man's patterned sweater lay on a chair. Women's clothing and possessions were tossed as though someone had gotten ready in a hurry and left without bothering to straighten.

I opened the closet door. Both men's and women's clothes inside. As I shut it, I looked back at the sweater. My breath came faster. Something about the collar was familiar. I looked through the men's clothing in the closet more carefully and recognized two of the shirts.

Leaving the door wide open I walked over to the sweater and inhaled a familiar masculine scent. It was Simon's. He was here. With a woman. One mystery semi-solved. He was still alive. Or had been when he'd occupied this room.

I scrutinized the room more closely. Nothing in it screamed "held against their will." Apparently not kidnapped, not tortured, and not dead. All the worry, speculation, the calls, the texts, the emails, yet Simon hadn't responded or attempted to contact me. And here he was, at this possible estate of Moran's, living with a woman. What was I missing? Simon and Moran? Working together?

The sweater still clutched in my hand, I moved to the bathroom and looked for a hairbrush. Hadn't I been told he was dating a woman with hair like mine? Strange, but I couldn't find any kind of comb or brush anywhere. Had they left only some of their things behind?

I turned back toward the bedroom and smelled the sweater again as though the essence of Simon would reveal the answers. Instead memories of us working, laughing and being together bombarded my brain as though a switch had been flipped. I opened my hand and let the sweater fall from my fingers. It couldn't talk, and there was nothing more to be gained from this room. Sick of speculation and sick at heart, I had to locate Simon and find out what was going on. There was no way he'd teamed up with Moran. Not the Simon I knew. Without thinking, I ran into the hallway and plowed right into an older couple.

"*Excusez-moi, mademoiselle. Êtes-vous bien?*" Not much taller than I and a bit stout, the gentleman and his wife were both dressed in formal attire.

"Excuse me," I replied in English. "I wasn't watching where I was going."

He smiled. "You are American. At first I thought you were *Mademoiselle* Jane. But she is English and not quite as," he looked sheepish, "put together as you."

He knew Simon's girlfriend.

"No, I'm her younger sister, Laurel."

"Allow me to introduce myself and my wife. I am René Barnard and this is my wife, Monique."

I used one of the few phrases I remembered from French class. *"Comment allez-vous?"*

Monique took my butchered French at face value. Her face lit up and she began firing off sentences in a way I couldn't possibly understand. Her husband noticed my dismay and said something that made her stop.

"I wish I could speak French," I admitted.

"No worries, *Mademoiselle* Laurel." He offered an arm to his wife and an arm to me. "May I escort the two most beautiful women to the ball?" He quickly repeated his words to his wife in French.

With a sweet smile, she placed her hand on his arm. I needed to search the other rooms, but I also wanted to check out the ground floor in case Simon and Jane were at the party. This couple's presence would help normalize mine.

"Thank you very much," I replied and together we waited for the elevator.

TWENTY-TWO

Monsieur Barnard was a banker and Monique a housewife. They happily gave me details about their family and visits to America. A daughter who lived in Massachusetts with her professor husband and two children. A trip they once took to Florida. They described their plans to visit their grandchildren and peppered me with questions. The elevator was indescribably slow.

By the time we reached the first floor, we were firm friends, and I knew without a doubt they were not friends of Moran. He would have been bored by these solid citizens of Le Puy.

We entered the overly-decorated lobby and followed the music and noise into the main party room. Across one wall stretched endless amounts of food, another table held liquor of every kind, a last wall was taken by a band playing music. Everywhere people talked, danced, laughed, and, unlike their American counterparts, smoked.

Again no art, no taste, just excess. As though the house was playing a role.

Some people wore costumes, but they were much different costumes than the ones I'd observed earlier. These were 'fancy' dress. Not necessarily unique to the sixteenth century, more to the eighteen century, I'd say, with the décolletage and jewels on display. Many older guests, like the Barnards, dressed in formal attire. My little black dress blended well with the twenty- and thirty-somethings like me, and as I'd expected many of the younger people dressed more casually.

The characteristic in common was their wealth and obvious social status. And none of them were Simon. I also did not see anyone who resembled me. The criteria for Jane.

I excused myself, murmuring something about food. The Barnards and I parted company, and I slowly explored the room.

The glass doors to the veranda were closed, probably due to the temperature. As I approached, an overdressed uniformed man opened it for me. Quite a few people talked and circulated around the space, but I didn't recognize any of them.

I returned to the main salon, waved at the Barnards and smiled at other guests as I strolled casually back to the lobby. The area was packed with small animated groups of people talking, probably not wanting to scream over the music in the other room. I made my way to the right, and within minutes the banging pots and shrill voices were a dead giveaway that I was in the kitchen area. I retraced my steps and found myself in a deserted winding hallway of even more rooms. This place was like a maze

Systematically, I searched five rooms, but located nothing resembling a clue to where Simon was, or if this place had anything at all to do with Moran. I also never got away from the excesses in decoration, and the fact that no art could be seen.

Wait. Perhaps that was the clue.

I hadn't seen any of the people I see on the usual circuit, and the only major artwork I'd noticed so far sat in the middle of a pond. And calling the sculpture art was a bit negligible.

I ended my search at the last door on the left, at the back of the hall and away from the partying crowd. The door was locked. I quickly took care of that little problem and walked into the dark room with the only illumination coming from the open door behind me. My mind still working to figure out what was going on. I stepped farther into the room.

Only to be grabbed from behind.

Using my best self-defense moves, I attacked the attacker, not the hold. But the person controlling our tango didn't budge. I kicked hard, and he grunted but didn't let go.

In a guttural voice, he asked, "*Qui êtes-vous?*"

I think he asked who I was. Or something to that effect. Why he asked me a question when it was obvious with his arm around my throat I clearly wasn't going to be able to answer, would have been laughable if it wasn't getting harder and harder to breathe. I tried every defensive move I knew. Nothing worked. I struggled to speak, but gurgled instead.

He pushed me forward and angled me around the other side of a couch. I kicked him. He grunted again but still didn't release me.

So not fair to die in this awful house.

"*Connaissez-vous cette femme? Pourquoi l'avait vous tuée?*"

I knew that voice, but my own voice was still too constricted to reply. Instead, I tried to translate his words. I knew *femme* meant woman, but *tuée* I couldn't quite get. He shook me and repeated the questions, his tone still quiet but even angrier than before and his voice...

I guess he finally recognized the problem, and I found my feet lifting from the ground, my face inclining downward, until I was staring at an unmoving woman stretched out on the floor.

Long blond hair lay in disarray across her back, and blood soaked through her white blouse and onto the baby blue carpet. Her face was to the floor so there really was very little difference between the two of us at the moment. It had to be Jane.

He pulled me upright and repeated what sounded like the

same thing. I had no ear for languages on a good day, and this was far from one of those.

"*Connaissez-vous cette femme? Pourquoi l'avait vous tuée?*"

Did *tuée* mean murder? Did he think I was responsible for this?

"*Repondez-moi salope!*" He insisted harshly.

I knew the word bitch, I'd heard that plenty of times. Hearing it in French was the final straw. I hated name-calling with a passion.

I lifted my feet and slammed down with the Blahnik heels and landed in the middle of a foot. While his arm didn't leave my throat—had to give him credit for that—it did loosen enough for me to croak out his name amid all the names he was now calling me. And this time not one of them was as nice as bitch.

"Jack! It's me!" French language zero; voice recognition ten.

His arms tightened convulsively around me, and I started stomping again.

He let go and helped me turn around, holding me as I swayed. He might have had tears in his eyes, but it was too dark for me to see. Besides, I might have had some in mine.

"Stop, woman, you'll cripple me for life. First you leave me for dead at the foot of a cathedral, and now you're trying to amputate my toes with stilettos."

My laughter was a great emotional release, even if it did sound like a sick cow with a sore throat.

"I did not leave you for dead," I began whispering until he smiled. A beautiful smile, even in that meager light.

"I thought she was you." As if that explained everything. Which it kinda did.

"I know." Well, I figured it out anyway.

"I didn't like the feeling."

"I could tell."

"What are you doing here?"

I wasn't ready to go there. I massaged my throat. "What are you doing here? And how did you know about Jane being here?"

"Who?"

"The dead woman. You know. Jane. Simon's English girlfriend. You introduced them, remember?"

"Simon?"

"Yeah. He's here. Living with a girlfriend. Or at least he was." At his puzzled look, I grimaced. "Don't bother asking me. I'm as confused as you are. But why didn't you recognize her?"

He had the grace to look sheepish. "I kind of lied about knowing her. She was described to me, and I was trying to..."

"Push my buttons?" I raised an eyebrow.

He smiled again. "Have you seen Simon?"

"No. I just recognized his sweater. The evidence supports that he was not held here against his will."

"His sweater." His bewildered expression gave way to determination, a face I knew well. "Never mind. I think we'd better get out of here before someone else comes along."

"Good idea. I don't want to explain a dead body." Another dead body.

By mutual accord, we left, and he locked the door.

"Now what?" I asked as we moved down the hall toward the lobby.

"We find Simon and ask for an explanation," Jack replied grimly. "After I've had a drink. Maybe three."

"I always figured you for a drinker. After all there has to be something wrong with you."

He grunted, but I could tell he was pleased by my remark. Dressed in a beautifully tailored suit, he looked more than good.

"Have you seen Moran?" I asked after he had hit the bar.

"Is this his place?"

"Don't you know?"

He shrugged and asked for another drink. I got one, too.

We finished searching the ground floor. Still no sign of an owner in residence.

"How long have you been here?" I asked Jack.

"I barely arrived when I found the body." He finished off his scotch. He rubbed his head.

I told him about the locked doors upstairs and we headed there. Cutting through the lobby on our way to the elevator, someone called my name.

"Laurel! I thought you said you didn't want to come? Yet, here you are."

Once more I was twirled around. Fortunately, before starting out that evening, and in anticipation of the bouldering exercise, I had taped a thick bandage around my arm.

"Rollie," I said weakly. "How nice to see you."

He, too, cleaned up well. His suit was as nice as Jack's, but with that certain French suavity other men simply can't imitate.

"You must come dance with me, Laurel, I insist. In fact, I think they are just now playing our song."

Jack stood by my side, patient to the last. "Yes, why don't you go and dance with your little friend, Laurel? I'll take care of things." He held out his hand. "I'm Jack, by the way."

Rollie smiled, clearly not having caught the condescension in the phrase "your little friend." "Nice to meet you, Jack. I'm Rollie. I see you know Laurel."

"Who doesn't?" Jack replied carelessly. "She gets around."

My feet were itching again, ready to stomp toes. Jack backed away. Smart man.

"Rollie, I'm afraid I can't go with you. Jack and I have some business we have to take care of. I'm very sorry."

"But, Laurel, you are on vacation. You said so yourself."

We really needed to move along. "Later, Rollie, I'll try. But no promises." I reached up and lightly pressed my lips to his cheeks in continental fashion. Then I waved my hand toward the dance floor. "Have a great time partying."

"I will hold you to your non-promise." Rollie graciously returned my salutation, nodded at Jack, and disappeared into the ballroom.

"That went well," Jack said sarcastically.

"Shut up," I said. "And get your you-know-what upstairs."

Several locked doors and ugly rooms later I couldn't help complaining. "This is the weirdest place. The building is beautiful, but everything in it is ugly and overdone. There's hardly anyone here. I find no evidence of anything personal except in Simon's room. I don't understand building something like this and disappearing."

"We don't know that anyone has disappeared," Jack replied. "Besides, could you live here?"

"From the outside, yes. On the inside, no way."

He closed the door on the last room to search. "Is there anywhere else we haven't looked?"

I thought for a moment.

"I was interrupted when searching the roof. Let's go there." I headed for the stairs.

Jack followed. "The roof?"

"This place has a roof terrace. I guess you haven't been here that long, huh?"

"I told you I'd barely arrived when I found Jane. And then you." His limp increased.

"Just checking," I answered breezily, and wiggled a finger at his foot. "But hey, if we're going to compare injuries, I could cough and choke and hold my throat. Stop being such a ham. I'm going to be bruised for weeks. I'll have to wear turtlenecks."

"You should know better than to be off-guard when walking into a dark room in a strange place. I thought you were trained in combat. Evidently, you're not safe to be let out on your own."

"I beg your pardon. I brought motion detectors to warn about creeps behind me, but the sheer number of rooms depleted the supply. Yours was the last room I was going to check." I was breathing heavily as he opened the door to the lounge. Of course he wasn't the least bit affected. "Besides, I've done just fine on my own, thank you. Want another demonstration on your other foot?"

He shuddered. "Thanks, but no thanks." He looked around. "The room's empty." He stared at the wall of windows. "I've never seen anything like that."

I hadn't noticed before, but from this angle the mountain was strategically and tastefully lighted, emphasizing its geographical features in a way that made the entire structure its own natural art. No light pollution here, but I must have been lit up like a Christmas ornament hanging out there. Thank goodness I hadn't known it at the time.

"The art of the mountain. The art of the building. Nature's own beauty," Jack said softly. "If I'm not mistaken the outside construction is mostly basalt, which is not typically used in building because it's porous. But it is beautiful."

"And the interior decorations of the house, the unnatural part so to speak, is gaudy and overdone, representing man's avarice and envy. Is that where this is heading?"

"It would seem so."

"Like one big joke...which is something I was thinking earlier," I mused.

"Time to check out the roof, Laurel."

"You're not the boss of me."

"Not yet, but I'm working on it."

We passed through the double French doors and were promptly fired upon.

TWENTY-THREE

I grabbed Jack. We ran around the corner of the lounge to gain cover.

"Do you have a gun?" I whispered.

"Of course," he replied in kind. And then I saw he had it in his hand. A nine-millimeter Glock.

We waited, but nothing more happened.

"You stay here while I—"

"No way. We're in this together. Where you go, I go." I wasn't getting left behind again.

"Be reasonable..." he began, only to say, "Oh, yeah. I forgot."

"Forgot what?"

"There's not a reasonable gene in your body."

"Why you—"

"C'mon then. I'm not simply standing here waiting to be shot. Let's find out who's doing the shooting."

He motioned for me to stay behind him, and at that point I was more than happy to do so. I pulled my knife from my clutch and followed closely.

Before we'd gone far, another shot was fired, and another. Someone meant business, but they didn't appear to be trying to kill us. Simply keep us where we were.

I became aware of a distant droning like the buzz of a bee. "Do you hear that?"

"It's a helicopter," Jack said, his mouth grim. "Sounds like it's coming to pick up something."

"Or someone." Was it Simon? The sword? "We need to see what it is."

"I know."

Jack fired off enough rounds to get us near a solid, long lounger. There were a couple of answering reports then nothing. We crouched behind the lounger.

"Maybe's he's run out of ammo," I said.

"We don't know that, and we must proceed with caution."

"But the bee's become louder," I said desperately.

Again the puzzled look, but his expression cleared. "Yeah, a couple more minutes, maybe. Not far now."

He pointed to another lounger, a match to the one we sat behind. "I'm going to fire, and we're going there. Got it?"

I sniffed. "I'm not two, Jack."

"Sometimes I'm not sure."

My ears rang by the time we made it to the next one. There were no other shots, but the helipad was definitely close. It would be a tight fit, but a good pilot could manage.

I couldn't wait. I yelled, "Simon, is that you?"

Silence.

"Simon? It's me, Laurel. What's going on?"

"Why, Laurel, you've made it after all." Simon's voice rose loud enough to be heard over the approaching noise.

Relief at finding him alive was quickly replaced by something else. His voice. The tone wasn't right. Had he been kept prisoner here?

Jack stood and approached. I stayed close behind him.

"Simon?" I called, the question in my voice apparent to even my own ears.

Suddenly, there he was. Still as coolly polished as ever. A man I had shared my feelings and my body with. A man I had thought a friend. Next to his feet was a large bag. Large enough to carry a sword.

There was also a huge shattered ceramic pot. A royal blue pot with the plant lying on its side, roots exposed.

"He's holding a remote to a bomb," Jack said casually, as if discussing the weather.

"Very astute," Simon answered. "As you've surmised I've run out of bullets, but I am holding something else in my hand that might cause a bit of a kerfuffle. You two will stay right where you are until I'm gone. The location and description of the bomb are over there." He pointed to the corner of the terrace and an envelope held down by a rock. "I certainly don't want to be responsible for hurting all these good citizens of Le Puy." He laughed. "Or destroying such a monument to man's excesses."

There were so many questions and so little time. While I'd already made my own deductions after seeing the bedroom, seeing the remote in his hand made it seem more surreal. I couldn't quite believe what was happening, but knew I had to try to play dumb. "Have you been held captive, Simon? Is that why you didn't respond to any of my communications? Is Moran threatening you?"

Simon laughed. "Captive? No. Jane and I discovered life was heating up a bit too much in London, and Moran happily provided an out for both of us. I warned him how good you are, not that he needed my advice. You've always been one to stick your nose into other people's business. I think when you kept outmaneuvering those dimwits he sent to keep tabs on your movements, a soft spot was created for you in his heart—or his head. Or maybe he already liked you since he hadn't taken care of you earlier in your career. But no such luck where I'm concerned. I suggest you remain where you are. I plan on boarding that helicopter."

"Is there a sword, Simon?" I had to know.

"Oh, yes, the sword. If you must know, the item you expected to carry away is with poor Jane. I didn't have the heart to dig it out from under her. She'd gone to so much trouble to steal it from me." He held up his bag. "But this—this treasure is mine and will be the basis for my future."

"You murdered Jane?" I gasped, horrified I'd ever let this foul man touch me. The idea of the poor woman dying over a piece of historic art—even though that same item had been driving me crazy for days—was terrible and needless.

"It was unavoidable, I'm afraid," he said, polite to the last.

"You said Moran provided an out. Are you working with him?" I still couldn't quite believe it even though the evidence was clear.

He stared at me, and I realized irrevocably this was a man I had never known. "Oh, Laurel, so naïve in so many ways. Of course I'm working with Moran. Art is like delicious wine, but money represents blood, life, power. When it became clear there was a cash limit to Beacham, Ltd., I realized it was time to move on. Moran has so much, and everyone else has so little. I saw a chance to grab some for myself and took it."

I thought about the way I seemed to be less effective than Moran in the past couple of years. And how the timing coincided with Simon and I being together and apart. Interesting.

"Where's Moran? And why does he want Laurel dead, Babbage?" Jack's words were clipped.

Simon looked startled. "Moran doesn't want Laurel dead. In fact, just the opposite." Simon glanced over at me. "A new boy toy to play with, darling?"

"Jack's a—"

"He's tried to kill her several times," Jack interrupted.

"You've got the wrong end of the stick there," Simon replied, his gaze moving skyward. "Oops, my ride's here. I'm afraid our tedious little question and answer session is at an end. Not soon enough for me I'm afraid." He picked up the bag. "I suppose it was nice to see you again, Laurel, and officially say good-bye." He looked me over. "Jane really couldn't hold a candle to you, but she was so willing to play along. Still, people do put so much stock in closure these days. Don't know if I believe in such a thing myself."

Something he'd said made me wonder. "In your bag. Is it another sword? Or is it the snuffbox?"

The grin he shot my way was pure evil, but he offered no other answer.

The helicopter was fast approaching.

"Give me the remote," Jack yelled, being a Good Samaritan to the end. "How can we trust you? You might set off the bomb as you fly away. After all, you are a self-confessed murderer."

Hell. I'd barely given a thought to the bomb. I'd been too worried about the whys and wherefores of Simon and the sword. That also meant I must not be too concerned about my own safety. What did that say about my values? For that matter, what did having a man like Simon as an ex-boyfriend say about my ability to read character?

"Jane stole from me. The people of Le Puy haven't hurt me. In fact, they've done nothing but make my stay in this backward place an almost enjoyable one. Lucky for me, the preserved architecture of the town is much nicer than this one, if a little less interesting."

The wind and the noise were incredible as the helicopter touched down, and I realized just how protected we'd been by the mountain as Simon jumped aboard and the big bird rose once again. Another aspect of nature often taken for granted—the art of silence.

We both watched as the helicopter lifted. Jack retrieved the envelope and called someone before walking back to me.

"Time to go, Laurel."

"No way. I've got to get the sword before the local authorities arrive, and you're not stopping me."

Now it was Jack's turn to roll his eyes. I could understand why my grandfather hadn't liked it.

"I wouldn't dream of stopping you from interfering in a murder investigation. Be my guest. I'm going to enjoy watching you fetch it." He headed toward the big entrance we'd come through.

"Hang on a minute." I ran to the other side of the terrace, to the door I'd entered earlier.

I was back at his side in a minute carrying the duffle. He looked at it, but didn't say anything. Which was a bit odd for him. I could only be grateful. We moved downstairs doing another quick search as we made our way toward the body. Still no sign of Moran.

After a grueling, and all-around horrible experience, I finally had the sword in my possession. I hadn't yet examined it. There hadn't been time. From the fleeting glance I'd gotten shoving it into my bag, it might be authentic, or it might be a really great copy.

Jack had left my side after watching me retrieve the sword muttering about finishing some business and meeting up with me later. I figured he had people to bring up to date, maybe an MI equivalent to the Marines. I needed to connect with Max and Nico, but I'd wait until my throat had a little more time to rest and recoup from my most recent almost throttling.

Feeling a bit droopy, I walked through the lobby, briefly wondering about Rollie as I heard the loud music. It was weird to think with so much happening the party and its inhabitants were going on pretty much oblivious to the events we just saw unfold.

A uniformed man smiled and wished me a good evening as he held the door. If he only knew.

I headed toward my car, changed my mind and walked over to the water feature instead. The bridge was delightful, as was the building. But as I approached I could see the seating was, to put it kindly, ostentatious. Though I should have been exhilarated by the job completion, I was exhausted. Another dead woman and the negative vibes from this place left me feeling a little empty. But there was always missing art, and I had no doubt I'd be in the middle of Moran's future plans once more. I needed to regroup and prepare for the next round.

I stopped a moment and stared at the bronze. What a waste of a beautiful metal. The sculpture—I hesitated to even call it that—was of overblown and grossly voluptuous nude women in various odious positions. They were holding items representing grammar, rhetoric, dialectic, arithmetic, geometry, astronomy and music, and it was the crowning glory of the emptiness of the house inside. Quite a contrast to the architecture which honored the natural environment. I wondered how many people understood the message of the black estate that I took away with me. Outward appearance didn't matter if not matched by the same inward integrity.

I sighed. I loved art, and I believed in a certain kind of justice. That was enough. I wasn't, nor would I ever be, a philosopher, a theologian, or an educator.

"What are you doing out here?" Jack called from the other side of the bridge as he continued to approach.

"No, wait, don't bother. I'm coming." I grabbed the duffle at my feet and hurried to meet him before he'd gone more than a few steps.

He glanced over at the bronze. "Is that really what I think it is?"

"No." I replied flatly. "Unless you think it's a terrible waste of a valuable metal and an unspeakable outrage to certain basic philosophical ideals."

His gaze transferred to me. "That's exactly what I thought."

For the third or fourth time, I'd lost count, by mutual accord we moved toward the drive. The gate stood wide open and empty, as we left the estate. I could smell the pine and the mold, and the air was a little cold. I shivered.

"Don't forget to notify MI-6. They might need to coordinate this crime scene with the local gendarmerie. Unless Moran covers it all up, of course," I said, fishing a little.

"Everything's been arranged."

Jack turned toward the cars parked in perfect rows by a six-car garage. So that was what was on the other side. Briefly I wondered what had happened to the dogs.

I turned the other way.

"Where are you going?" he asked. "Isn't it a little late to go for a stroll?"

"My car's parked this way."

He paused a bit too long. "I'll give you a lift."

His hesitation spoke volumes. I glanced back at him and wondered if it was the last time I'd see him. "No, thanks, I'd rather walk. I've got a lot of thinking to do."

I headed toward the gate. I could feel his burning gaze shoot holes through my backside with every step I took.

"What's in the duffle?" His voice sounded irritated.

"Bouldering gear," I answered, without bothering to stop or turn around.

The expletives came fast and heavy. His anger music to my ears.

"And the problem with your arm?" His normally smooth, melodious tones were jerky and gravelly with frustration. Mr. Cool overdosing on steroids.

"I was shot," I truthfully responded as I walked through the gate, leaving him and the recovery site of the missing sword behind.

TWENTY-FOUR

A week had passed since the incident in Le Puy-en-Velay. I kept the sword wrapped and padded in a blanket I'd found in the trunk of the car, then transferred it to my Louis Vuitton duffle when I'd collected my things at the hotel in the Auvergne on my way back to Paris. I'd bought the biggest bag primarily because Max was paying, but since I now needed the length I was glad my intuition was a step ahead of me.

It took some string pulling from Max's end, but both the sword and I hit the English shore in one piece. He personally arrived on my doorstep the next morning to take possession of the sword, the British authentication expert standing beside my boss, twitching a little. I understood. Between the prospect of the sword's history and having to stand so close to Max, I would do some serious wriggling, too.

"The board unanimously voted you in charge of the London office, Laurel, effective immediately." Max tried to smile, but I felt his desire to cut and run, to give all his attention to the sword. I hoped the piece was worth his anticipation, but every time I held it my doubts increased.

The color and patina were right, but would be in the case of a fake. The rubies and sapphires met the criteria of cut in the day for a broadsword, the earliest of the medieval swords, with a two-edged blade. The hilt showed its gold base, and the handle design was that of an Anglo-Saxon ring sword. Definitely special, likely a royal sword, and according to my archaeological contacts a real one was a true find since the ring sword design was not used past the seventh century. The handle was fashioned for grip, and the blade had trace designs near the hilt, but the pattern faded as it made its way toward the killing point. It appeared to be iron. Even the parchment that had been partially rolled around the hilt looked authentic and went a long way to shore up everyone's hopes. Still...

There was something. Simon left this under Jane's dead body, and I had to believe it was for more than to simply make a statement or being creeped out by her blood. Yet we knew Moran was a master at attaining fakes to swap for the real thing. These last two reservations alone were the true reason I kept my expectations low until the final analysis was completed.

The authentication expert burned the midnight oil, usually with Max at his heels, trying to conclusively say whether the sword was true or not. Even her majesty sent a representative to shadow the pair, but this didn't surprise me if I believed Jack's story about how he got involved. The expert didn't say as much, from the outset I think he had the same misgivings I experienced. It had all the pieces that should have made authentication a no-brainer, but something kept everyone from sharing high-fives. I imagined it was for the same reason I held my opinions in reserve—because Simon left it behind when he could have easily taken the sword away forever.

So, it wasn't earth-shattering to me when, before the week was out, the verdict came back as "excellent fake, but counterfeit."

No matter, I had my own crosses to bear as I mopped up the mess Simon and Moran had left. A cleaning crew had already been in to gut the office, of course, as well as a crime scene crew to document fingerprints and DNA evidence. However, there were literal and figurative ends hanging everywhere. I should have been too busy to think, except nagging thoughts kept pressing in my mind. Each answer initiated new questions. And each question led to more thinking. Like the laptop and USB drive Simon left at the office. If he'd known he wasn't returning, I would expect him to take those with him. But he didn't. Did he run because the Amazon hit the office? Or because he'd found out I'd taken the items ahead of her? Simon was enemy number one on my must-find list, and those would be two questions I would ask if I got the chance.

Interpol flagged Simon's passport right away, and his picture was circulated for everyone's facial recognition software, but no sign of him yet hit the radar. They kept us posted, since he was as much a risk to the foundation as he was the world. When it was learned Simon and I had spent months in a more personal relationship, a dapper inspector leading the search paid me regular visits until he finally realized, as I'd sadly concluded, I truly didn't know Simon at all. I was probably a suspect for a time but was never really treated as one. The inspector left his card and asked me to call him anytime, that no memory or idea was too insignificant. I promised and put the card in my Prada. It's still there.

Max was ready to spit nails at the results of the sword's authenticity—or, rather, lack thereof. He believed Simon took the real icon on the helicopter in the large duffle. If such was the case, he truly was using the one under the late Jane Leland's dead body to have a last macabre joke at my expense. Max was never the optimist unless it meant a coup for him, but he couldn't let go of the idea of Arthur's sword, so continued believing it was out there somewhere with Simon. He could be right. Or, like the black mansion, the entire escapade likely was constructed as a joke, with Moran the chief architect behind what shaped up as a perpetual hoax in the art world.

Disappointment reigned, and after a week in that kind of atmosphere the time came when I realized I needed to get away for a moment, to reconnect with the world I bought into a decade ago. I chose art history as a major for one reason—I loved art. I didn't pick the discipline because I wanted a job in my grandfather's business; that was just luck. No, I wanted to make some kind of difference in making sure art stayed available and true for the masses.

It was a gray day for a gray mood, and I headed for the National Gallery. I surfaced from the underground, and offered a nod to the monument of Lord Nelson and the stone lions, picking up speed as I hit the middle of Trafalgar Square. Despite the chill in the air, tourists and pigeons were out in force, and I pulled my new trench coat tighter around my body as I wove through the masses. It was probably a football field away. But that was American talk. I needed to start thinking meters instead of yards. I was in charge of the London office, and I had to start thinking Brit.

I passed through the National Gallery's revolving door and crossed the marble floor, moving automatically toward room twenty-nine, the area holding the Peter Paul Rubens collection. I stood before Rubens's first rendering of *The Judgment of Paris,* still in awe, no matter how many times I viewed the glorious work.

Painted long before the artist had become a world diplomat and established his studio of artists, the work was acquired by the gallery in the mid-1960s. I liked this version for the fact I truly felt Rubens did all the work himself. In later years, the artist too often took more of an overseer position in the works that bore his name. The result wasn't a fake or counterfeit; Rubens always played some role in the final creation. Still, I felt there was something a little off about saying later paintings were "a Rubens," which was why most collections instead noted "from the studio of Rubens."

Coming this day to view his work was not to debate the

issue but to revel in the truth he painted on the canvas. I needed this. I stared at the scene, our hero Paris with the golden apple prize, judging Venus the most beautiful woman there, with Juno and Minerva suddenly also-rans. I felt Juno's palpable anger. I wanted to be the nymph who reclined there on the ground, watching the proceedings and absorbing the moment.

"Does the picture give you a sense of satisfaction? Or rile your feminist tendencies?"

He hadn't really left my thoughts since we parted in France, and now here he was, mysteriously popping up beside me. Again. Looking as good as ever in jeans, a wool jacket and an open-necked blue shirt that lit up his eyes.

"Hello, Jack. No one has wanted to tell me anything about the cleanup in Le Puy. And everyone changed the subject when I brought up your name."

"I like to keep a low profile." He smiled, and I couldn't keep from smiling back.

"Who told you I was here? Or are you tracking me with CCTV again?" I moved over to the second version of *The Judgment of Paris*, the one Rubens finished three decades or so after the first, a work where the mentees in his studio likely played a role in the creation. Jack kept pace with me, stopping to look once or twice across the room at other Rubens paintings.

"No, nothing high tech," he finally said. "I heard you'd been installed in the London office. I stopped in to see you. Your cohort from the V and A was there and pointed me in this direction. Promotion for you, I hope?"

I shrugged. I was still trying to decide exactly what anything meant at this point. Betrayed by Simon. Hoodwinked again by Moran. And now responsible for a physical office, instead of skipping blithely from one art recovery to the next. I felt like a bird with clipped wings, though Max did promise me all of Europe as my gilded cage.

"Cassie and I have had long talks about it. She'd been disappointed about her tenure at the Victoria and Albert Museum ending with no permanent hire, and I had an opening to fill since Martha chose to retire and live with her ailing sister. Being able to stay here and work for the Beacham Foundation helped assuage Cassie's disappointment, and I need someone I can truly trust."

"She seemed happy. Seemed to be reconstructing the office wainscoting."

I rolled my eyes. "I'm never going to break her from being a restorer. I told her I didn't even like wainscoting, and she still persists in trying to put Humpty Dumpty back together."

Jack laughed, steering me toward an empty bench. "Would it be so bad to let her put as much as she can back the way it was?"

"Nothing can go back the way it was, Jack. You know that."

"Ah..." He took my hand in both of his. "What are you fighting? The ghost of Simon, or the specter of four walls keeping you trapped every day?"

I looked down at his hands, so warm, so comforting. His being there wasn't an accident, I was sure of that, but I didn't know what it meant either. "They promised I could just base in London. Leave the day-to-day to Cassie and shoot off with the next assignment. I can live with those terms, even if I will miss the jaunts to Mexico, South America, and Asia."

"So, you'll be primarily Europe?"

"Yes, there's always been enough here and on the Continent to keep one person busy full-time, hence the London location."

"I've heard of worse posts to be left in."

Jack could always make me laugh. "I do sound pretty spoiled, don't I? It's just change. But not enough change to feel like I've had closure from the last case. As mad as I am at Simon, he was right. We humans do appreciate our closure."

He sighed and slipped an arm around me, making it look to all the world like we were enjoying a midday assignation. In reality, the sweet nothings he whispered in my ear were probably state secrets.

"I presume your office grapevine has already informed you Simon is still loose."

I nodded.

"A bomb squad swept the Moran mansion, and the place is still sealed as a crime scene and will likely stay that way. The estate is under constant surveillance in case he returns. And, because the villagers know they had a monster in their midst, they're ready to storm the castle if he shows his face again."

"He should be hung just for creating that monstrosity to art. But why wasn't he there the night of the party?"

Jack stood and pulled me to my feet, then steered me to Rubens's rich vision of *Samson and Delilah*. "Moran sent a representative to act as host for the evening."

I felt the frown in my forehead. "What are you trying to tell me, Jack?"

"His young grandson." Jack avoided looking at me, staring instead at the fallen Samson. "A young man with long hair and an easy smile. Someone who likes to dance with beautiful blondes."

My mouth dropped open. "Rollie! Rollie is Moran's grandson?"

"And the heir apparent."

For a second I couldn't breathe. I thought about Rollie and my conversations before and during the bus ride. His talk about disappointing his grandfather for not yet taking over the business. "No, not Rollie."

Jack nodded.

This put a whole new slant on my ability to be conned and be confident. All the talk about his grandfather being an architect and having a manufacturing facility. Sure, the architect of the greatest art thefts in our century and the perpetrator of manufactured counterfeits and fakes. How could I be in charge of the London office if I couldn't even see when I was being played on the way to a renaissance festival? Worse, how long had he followed me to be sure he was where he needed to be when I arrived? He said he bought his ticket weeks before. Had he done so in preparation, or...I thought back to the old man who chased off the motorcyclist. The one who gave me directions which ultimately led to the bus ride. Suddenly, the name of the architectural firm that designed the house hit my memory. PA Designs. Philippe Aubertine, my ass. The sudden revelation made me dizzy. Rollie's saying the family business was architecture and that his grandfather wanted to retire to his vineyards. My mind again saw the old man's eyes under that funny Greek fisherman-type hat, and I knew.

"You need to tell Interpol I can give them an updated description on Moran, and an alias he employs when in France."

He cocked his head and stared hard at my face. "You got that close to him?"

"I was in the same car, and I had no idea."

"When you got shot—"

"He picked me up after running off the shooter. A shooter on a motorcycle with a full helmet. I can't be certain, but I think the motorcyclist was the Amazon."

Suddenly, I was caught up in an embrace so tight I could barely breathe. I think I cried a little, glad I could hide my tears in one of Jack's shoulders. When he spoke again, his voice was thick.

"She hasn't cropped up anywhere, but Interpol dusted Simon's—I mean, your office, before the cleanup and have a pretty good idea which fingerprints are hers."

I pulled back to see his face. "Is she in the system?"

"Her prints are, but we've had no person to attribute them to until now. We think the Amazon is muscle for hire."

"Moran's."

Jack frowned. "I don't think so. There's another player out there. Someone or some new group causing ripples in the power structure. Currently, it's nothing but chatter. If you're right that the old man was Moran, and if it was the Amazon on the cycle, it could mean she recognized him and that's why she ran."

I thought about all the bogus text messages, especially the one that led me away from my meeting in Italy. "Could the Amazon be the one who killed the Greek and the Welshman?"

We pulled out of the embrace, and he shook his head. "They caught a guy who's taking credit for the Greek."

"You don't think he did it?"

Jack shrugged. "Again, hired muscle, and he won't tell who hired him, but admits it wasn't Moran."

"But the Greek was killed around the same time I was following the bogus text message," I said. "Does that mean we can assume he works for this new underground group?"

"That's what I told my boss. I like your thinking." He smiled, and I felt a little warm.

"And the Welshman?" We walked toward the exit.

"He made it, believe it or not. Then disappeared from the hospital before he could be questioned, despite a guard posted at his door." Jack slipped a hand down to the small of my back. It felt comfortable there.

I remembered the lights and sirens when the ambulance raced away from the docks with the Welshman inside. They only did that when the patient was still alive. I'd noticed at the time, but the evidence didn't register. I wondered whether he was a good guy or bad. I also wondered whether Simon was responsible for his disappearance.

"Which means we all continue looking over our shoulders?"

I asked. "See if we get lucky?"

He shook his head and grinned. "I don't know that you should keep counting on luck. You have some good self-defense moves, but they're almost as rusty as your French. I think you need some private lessons before anything else happens."

"I'm heading for America tomorrow," I said, shaking my head. "A quick trip, I hope, but I can't take you up on the offer of lessons. I'm booked on a morning flight to Orlando to follow a lead we received on one of Simon's safe deposit boxes and bank accounts. I have to follow up on this, no matter how sketchy the possibility."

Jack stopped just short of the door, pulling a phone from his pocket. "I had to get a new mobile. Don't know what happened to the last one, but I'm finding I like this little jewel." He swiped the screen a couple of times, and held it up to show me a flight number and seat assignment. "For instance, I get unbelievable clarity when I need to store e-ticket information."

Everything was suddenly absurd, and I walked and laughed, and generally made a fool out of myself on that somber afternoon. Jack plodded patiently beside me, waiting for my lead on what happened next. We finally stopped at *Aurora abducting Cephalus*, which was appropriate since I felt like my life had been pretty much taken away from me.

"Is this how it's always going to be? Do I not have free will anymore?" I asked, finding I actually wasn't bothered by the feeling. Had I truly given up? Which only proved I really did need the vacation Max had once again swindled away from me.

"Laurel, as important as you are in so many ways this isn't about you at all." Jack put his hands on my shoulders. I thought back to how many times he held me semi-captive in the three days we were together. Three days that packed a magnitude of events and emotions one would normally associate with decades. The thought left me staggered to consider it.

Jack continued, "We still have to determine if the micro drive was truth or fiction. We may still have a major heist on the horizon, and making that determination was my job from the beginning. The sword was a slight detour, but the timing indicates it could be connected. Like you, I've been pulled in to finish the job I started. And, quite frankly, having you by my side raises the stakes in both good and bad ways. I'm as confused about whether or not we should work as a team as you are."

That wasn't exactly what I was confused about, and looking in those lovely teal eyes, I felt Jack wasn't being entirely forthcoming either.

So what was new? I wouldn't know how to act if he actually told me the whole truth.

I reached up and took his left hand away from my shoulder. "Come on, Jack. I haven't had lunch. And I do like a good fish, don't you? Maybe I'll even try vinegar this time."

RITTER AMES

Ritter Ames lives atop a high green hill in the country with her husband and Labrador retriever, and spends each day globe-trotting the art world from her laptop with Pandora blasting into her earbuds. Often with the dog snoring at her feet. Much like her Bodies of Art Mysteries, Ritter's favorite vacations start in London, then spiral out in every direction. She's been known to plan trips after researching new books, and keeps a list of "can't miss" foods to taste along the way. Visit her at www.ritterames.com where she blogs about all the crazy things that interest her.

Henery Press Mystery Books

And finally, before you go...
Here are a few other mysteries
you might enjoy:

ARTIFACT

Gigi Pandian

A Jaya Jones Treasure Hunt Mystery (#1)

Historian Jaya Jones discovers the secrets of a lost Indian treasure may be hidden in a Scottish legend from the days of the British Raj. But she's not the only one on the trail...

From San Francisco to London to the Highlands of Scotland, Jaya must evade a shadowy stalker as she follows hints from the hastily scrawled note of her dead lover to a remote archaeological dig. Helping her decipher the cryptic clues are her magician best friend, a devastatingly handsome art historian with something to hide, and a charming archaeologist running for his life.

Available at booksellers nationwide and online

Visit www.henerypress.com for details

LOWCOUNTRY BOIL

Susan M. Boyer

A Liz Talbot Mystery (#1)

Private Investigator Liz Talbot is a modern Southern belle: she
blesses hearts and takes names. She carries her Sig 9 in her Kate
Spade handbag, and her golden retriever, Rhett, rides shotgun in
her hybrid Escape. When her grandmother is murdered, Liz high-
tails it back to her South Carolina island home to find the killer.

She's fit to be tied when her police-chief brother shuts her out of
the investigation, so she opens her own. Then her long-dead best
friend pops in and things really get complicated. When more folks
start turning up dead in this small seaside town, Liz must use more
than just her wits and charm to keep her family safe, chase down
clues from the hereafter, and catch a psychopath before he catches
her.

Available at booksellers nationwide and online

Visit www.henerypress.com for details

MURDER ON A SILVER PLATTER

Shawn Reilly Simmons

A Red Carpet Catering Mystery (#1)

Penelope Sutherland and her Red Carpet Catering company just got their big break as the on-set caterer for an upcoming blockbuster. But when she discovers a dead body outside her house, Penelope finds herself in hot water. Things start to boil over when serious accidents threaten the lives of the cast and crew. And when the film's star, who happens to be Penelope's best friend, is poisoned, the entire production is nearly shut down.

Threats and accusations send Penelope out of the frying pan and into the fire as she struggles to keep her company afloat. Before Penelope can dish up dessert, she must find the killer or she'll be the one served up on a silver platter.

Available at booksellers nationwide and online

Visit www.henerypress.com for details

Lightning Source UK Ltd.
Milton Keynes UK
UKOW05f1016150517
301151UK00014B/176/P